FIGHT FOR MRIYA

ANTONOV-225

JOE W. BOYOU SR.

978-1-965552-59-9 (Paperback)
978-1-965552-60-5 (Hardback)

Library of Congress Control Number: 2025925027

BOOKWRIGHTS HOUSE

admin@bookwrightshouse.com
☎ (213) 286 6700

DEDICATION

To the children of war, who fall victim
to the whims of evil men.

FOREWORD

To the reader: this is the story of the ANTONOV-225, told as the people of Ukraine might have wished to share it. It honors a true wonder of the world and the forces that sought to destroy her beauty. While the aircraft itself is real, what follows is a work of historical fiction an imagined story inspired by the heartbeat of the skies.

This book is my way of paying tribute, a form of flattery and the highest compliment I can offer to the men who fought the good fight. My hope is that every reader comes away with a sense of admiration for the ancient giant known as the Antonov-225 or (MRIYA).

My deep fascination with what became of this aircraft reflects my lifelong affection for military aviation. The interpretation, however, is my own.

PROLOGUE

LOCATION: SNAKE ISLAND, ALSO known as Serpent Island, Black Sea approximately 35 km west of Crimea Time: 18:36

"Don't stare too hard, kid. Someone might stare back."

A cocky seaman with a thick Ukrainian accent clapped a hand on the young sailor's shoulder, making him jump as he leaned over the edge of the Viatger.

"Give him a rest," another seaman said, dragging on the tail end of a cigarette. A grin spread across his salt-weathered face. "They don't call it the Dead Sea for nothing. What do they call it in your country?"

"I thought it was called the Black Sea," the young German sailor replied, stepping back from the railing and wiping his sweaty palms on his trousers.

"Black, dead makes no difference," the cocky one shot back, his eyes hard. The older crewmen were always screwing with the German, and he was getting sick of it. Still, he was the youngest aboard, and that meant he was at their mercy.

The second seaman pulled out another cigarette and lighter. Shielding the flame with his hand against the gust, he managed to light it on the second try. He took a long drag, smoke sinking deep into the catacombs of his blackened lungs, before gripping the railing again and peering into the dark water.

"He's right. Black Sea, Dead Sea it's all the same, kid. They say Noah's Ark crashed somewhere out here. A wholesome thought, considering nothing survives in certain parts of this water."

The German squinted into the gloom, frowning.

"There's no fish?"

The seaman exhaled a gray cloud and shook his head. "Too thick with salt in some spots."

"Like tar."

The first seaman leaned over the German's shoulder, his breath reeking of tobacco and rotting teeth.

"Thick with death."

"It's deep too. Real deep."

The second seaman puffed like a train, smoke spilling from his lips.

"So why would something be starin' back?" the young sailor asked. "If nothing can survive. Is it haunted?"

"Things don't decay as fast in water like this," the smoker went on. "Bodies can drift for months after the souls are gone. Bloated. Pale like fish. But the faces stay."

The German wanted nothing to do with these old wives' tales. He didn't care for any of it. A sea with a name like this had to be cursed. Bad luck. A one-way ticket.

Warnings said to keep away from these waters tensions in Eastern Europe made them dangerous but the sailors refused to be deterred. Fishing was in their blood, and this time of year the catch all but surrendered itself. The *Viatger* pressed on despite the warnings, her hull shuddering as the churning sea struck again and again, driving her into a wild, stumbling rhythm. She pitched and rolled under the assault of salt-stung winds, battering the port side mercilessly.

The Viatger ignored the warnings as the rippling sea slammed against her hull, forcing her into a rough, staggering dance. The boat rocked from side to side as damp winds battered the port side, sending the fishermen clutching at railings and coats.

The night sky hung heavy with clouds, a single star piercing the gloom from a distant galaxy. Seaport lights flickered faintly on the horizon, while the moon lay smothered behind thick cover.

The young sailor lowered his head toward the black water. He listened to the slosh of currents and churning of the sea against the hull, the bow waves breaking into ripples below, steady beneath the wind. Then he looked up again at the blinking lights.

Inside the vessel, other men stayed warm in their bunks, lulled by the constant sway. They were used to this constant motion and utter bravery by now. One more night of rough weather, and they would be in the clear for deep-sea fishing.

As the vessel plowed across relentless swells, a sudden commotion in the captain's quarters drew the attention of all three men.

"Something's going on," the young sailor muttered, pulling the eyes of his two Ukrainian counterparts.

"Come in, Viatger," a voice boomed through the comm system. It was clear. Unwavering. Commanding. The Russians.

"Who is this?" Roman Hrybov, captain of the Viatger, demanded. "State your position and your business with this vessel."

"Are you sitting down, Captain? If so look to your right."

The Russian's voice echoed, smug and unhurried. Hrybov turned his gaze as instructed. Out on the dark horizon, a massive silhouette emerged, flanked by escorts bearing down on their course. A strange sight indeed. The Viatger had threaded these waters countless times and never once crossed paths with a military carrier. The worst they'd seen were low ceilings, biting rain, and the occasional angry swell.

But this was different. This carrier was barreling forward at sixty knots and closing fast. A geyser erupted from its bow as spotlights cut through the gloom and lit the flattop in stark white. Through his viewfinder, Hrybov could make out the dull gray hull, Russian inscriptions etched along its steel. The infamous Admiral Kuznetsov.

"Bozhe moy…" the captain whispered to no one in particular. He swallowed hard, then sounded the alarm.

Below deck, fishermen scrambled from their bunks and rushed to the bridge. They pressed to the tiny windows, necks craned, as the massive warship knifed through the swells on a direct collision course with the Viatger.

The comm crackled again, the signal ragged but unmistakable.

"This is Russian…warship…weapons down…or we will attack…copy…"

Captain Hrybov uncorked his schnapps, took a long swig, and belched.

"Idiots," he growled. "What weapons?"

His crew glanced at one another, just as baffled as their captain.

Panic flooded the bridge as men spat, swore, and prayed. On deck, though, the German and the two older sailors kept their composure. The German muttered something harsh sounding in his native tongue, no one understood him, but they didn't question it. He looked brave saying it.

The old man stubbed out his cigarette on the sole of his boot and tucked the butt into his pocket. Tossing it overboard might let a draft carry it to the lower deck, where flammables waited. They already had enough problems.

The Russians hadn't been friendly to Ukrainians since the seizure of Crimea. Now, the Viatger was dwarfed beneath the overwhelming bulk of the Admiral Kuznetsov. She towered over the fishing vessel like a steel mountain poised to crush whatever lingered beneath her shadow.

"We're sitting ducks," the old man muttered, motioning for his companions to follow him down to the bridge.

"Continue to ignore them!" one defiant voice shouted at the captain, who was already transmitting a distress call to the mainland. "Their threats are empty! An attack would start a war!" His words carried no certainty, only desperation.

"Are they going to attack?" one crewman asked another. Silence answered him.

The captain lifted the receiver, pressed the talk button, and spoke slowly. "Are you going to attack?"

He lowered the receiver, waiting. Both vessels had come to a halt, holding at roughly ten nautical miles apart.

"They're Russians," one crewman rasped. He coughed, then added, "Russians don't cry wolf."

"So, what do we do?"

The captain's eyes darted between the warship and his men. Some he didn't know well, others he didn't trust. But none of that mattered now. They were standing before Goliath in the middle of a sea named for death itself. These men flawed as they were were all he had.

"We're gonna tell them to fuck off," one crewman said flatly. He drew the half-burned cigarette from his cracked lips, exhaled, and locked eyes with his captain.

Aboard the Admiral Kuznetsov, men in camouflage moved with precision. Colonel Sergei Poroshenko a burly man with a squared jaw and a trimmed goatee climbed the ladder to the bridge. The soldiers on duty snapped to attention, saluting. He returned the gesture with the weight of command.

"What is this?" Colonel Poroshenko asked, his eyes fixed on the viewfinder. The Viatger appeared as nothing more than a speck on the radar.

"This is not us," the major replied.

"Then destroy it." Poroshenko cut the air with a sharp wave of his hand.

Suddenly, a voice crackled through the comm channel.

"This is the captain. We don't have any weapons."

Poroshenko leaned over the console, seized the receiver, and pressed the talk button. "Then you must die."

His steely blue eyes were void of mercy, empty of soul.

He set the receiver back into its cradle and barked another order. "Stand by!"

"Stand by!" the major echoed, the words vibrating across the bridge.

From afar, the fishermen on the Viatger watched as the cannon swiveled, its barrel locking onto their vessel.

Chaos erupted. The crew scrambled, clutching at anything solid, their voices torn between screams, prayers, and curses. They cried out to the sea, to the comm, to anything in those dark waters living or dead that might hear them.

Knowing the end was near, Captain Hrybov snatched the receiver and gave one final transmission. "Hey! Russian warship! Go fuck yourself!"

His defiance echoed through the cramped cabin.

At that moment, the sailor with the cigarette flicked it into the night. The German watched through the window as the ember drifted downward, swallowed by the black water.

And then the cannon roared.

Like the breath of a dragon, fire engulfed the Viatger. In a single, blinding instant, the sea claimed her.

TABLE OF CONTENTS

CHAPTER ONE

(KYIV, UKRAINE)

OF ALL THE PLACES he might have faced death, Kyiv wasn't on the list. He only visited Ukraine once in a blue moon, and his ties to the country were minimal at best. But tonight was different. Harvey Arnott would later wonder whether it was his Air Force training that saved his life or just dumb luck. Go figure.

One thing was certain: his assailant had bitten off more than he could chew. In just a couple of weeks, Harvey would have been back home at Travis Air Force Base in California, worlds away from his Hurricane Hunter days in Biloxi, Mississippi. For now, though, he was on foreign soil, and survival was the only objective.

The night had started innocently enough bar-hopping, some sightseeing, catching up with people he barely knew. "Old friends," they called themselves, but in reality they were employees and former bodyguards of his grandfather. Harvey had come to visit his aging grandfather, now bedridden inside a heavily fortified family ranch.

With his drink order in the works, Harvey sat on a barstool tucked into a corner, his back to the wall. Old habits. Years of intelligence work and officer training had drilled operational awareness into him. He amused himself by playing a game his grandfather had taught him nearly a decade earlier: spot the Russians.

Tonight's arena was Club Heaven a sprawling, multi-level nightclub smack in the middle of Kyiv's Khreshchatyk Street. It was packed with college kids, making Harvey feel like a tourist who'd crashed the wrong party. At thirty-seven, six feet tall, with a movie-star jawline and neatly cut hair, he felt like he'd outgrown the club scene. But he was on vacation, and there wasn't much else to do. That was that.

From his corner, he caught glimpses of wall-mounted TVs flashing silent images, drug paraphernalia changing hands in shadowed corners, and dancers gyrating in cages suspended above the crowd. Most voices around him blended into a steady stream of Eastern Slavic chatter, though every so often he caught fragments of English, spoken with a heavy Ukrainian lilt.

The object of the game was simple: imagine your family is an enemy of the Kremlin which, for Harvey, was true. How do you spot a Russian agent? Look for the eyes. A gaze held too long. A mannerism out of sync with the crowd.

Harvey couldn't afford to take chances. He was an American asset, and falling into Russian hands would send shockwaves across the globe.

He did his best to ignore the muted TV above the bar, where the same reel of Russian aggression in the Black Sea played on repeat. The bartender had cut the sound after one too many grim faces turned her way. Still, Harvey wondered why she didn't just turn it off or at least switch to sports. After all, this was supposed to be a bar, not a war room.

The few patrons who watched the news feed looked sour, their moods soured by the images. Harvey knew the feeling. With his background in counterintelligence, he'd seen worse briefings filled with horrors. The last one in the SCIF had been about Boko Haram abducting schoolgirls in a remote Nigerian village. He'd built armor against images like these.

What he needed now was a distraction. And there she was.

Harvey's gaze drifted across the lounge area, landing on a statuesque woman seated on a leather couch. She was a solid eight, maybe more. Too good to be true? He smirked to himself. Nah. Even if she was a spy, he'd spot her play before she got close enough to do damage.

She sat like she wanted to be noticed, and she was. Long legs his type. A skintight black dress that clung in all the right places. Cleavage like a lure, was the perfect balanced against the nervous curl of her toes inside nude wedges. She sipped a fruity cocktail with deliberate grace.

Trouble had never looked this sweet.

Harvey admitted to himself that no one had caught his eye in six days of being in Ukraine, but there was something about her he couldn't put his finger on. Against his better judgment, he felt his guard slip, just a little. She wasn't the kind of girl he'd take home to his mother but right now, she was exactly the kind of trouble he wanted. She was the kind you didn't just put a finger on, but rather the whole hand, in the right places.

If nothing else, Harvey told himself, he had to get her name. It would be a bonus when his friend arrived later and saw him with something stunning at his side.

He gave her a slight nod. Her small mouth blossomed into a petite smile. His courage rose; he was ready to saunter over. Still, he had to be sure she wasn't already waiting for someone.

Careful, Harvey. She was the type who knew her beauty was a weapon, and she'd wield it without hesitation. But Harvey was an American fighter pilot an easy ten in any country ... except Russia, of course. His grandfather's warning rang in his ears: Stay away from Russian territory while you're in town.

Excitement churned in his gut. He was single, after all.

Before leaving the ranch earlier that day, his grandfather had warned him again: trouble often hid in plain sight. Harvey knew he was blind to the subtleties of Ukrainian and Russian interactions, but the rumors weren't rumors anymore. Russia had seeded Ukraine with spies, preparing for an invasion. It wasn't folk tales it was proven fact.

Even before Harvey arrived, there had been reports of Russian activity. Not enough to be labeled a hostile takeover, but enough to make the air heavy with tension.

His grandfather's warning had been simple: Be very careful.

Matviy Arnott, sixty-seven, had survived two assassination attempts by the Kremlin regime. Most of his later years had been spent running BGK, a counterterrorism outfit dedicated to thwarting Kremlin aggression at every turn. BGK had been successful too, exposing and dismantling Russian provocateurs intent on stirring conflict in Ukraine.

For Matviy "Grandpa Arnott" it was personal. The last serious attempt on his life had come in the form of a poisonous gas, one that left him in a coma for two weeks.

He had been a thorn in Putin's side for decades. Once, long ago, the two had even stood side by side as lieutenants in the KGB. But when the Soviet Union collapsed, Matviy defected, building a new life in Ukraine. He rose through the military ranks, eventually becoming a general.

With his insider knowledge of the Kremlin's machinery, Matviy had become an influential advisor to President Zelensky after retirement and an even sharper thorn in the dictator's side.

Be very careful. Watch your six.

His grandfather's warning echoed in Harvey's mind as he took a sip from his glass. He rarely drank only when social decorum demanded it. Normally, he was a protein shake-and-water kind of man, bound to a strict fitness regimen. That morning, he had logged three miles on the treadmill, followed by pushups and an obscene number of bicep curls.

Now, he scanned the room again and again, watching hands, watching feet. Those could do the most damage. Military training ran deep in his blood. Yet nothing set off his instincts and that unsettled him.

Why are you still here? he asked himself.

The music was deafening, a mix of hip-hop and techno pounding through cheap walls, drowning out the rain hammering the roof. The wall-to-wall carpet was a dirty brown, long past its original gray.

A soft hand brushed his shoulder. Harvey turned.

A petite waitress in her twenties stood over him, her bold, voluminous hair offset by silver-rimmed glasses that gave her a bookish, schoolgirl edge. She spoke in English, tinged with a Ukrainian accent.

"Another round?" she asked, her gaze steady, almost flirtatious.

Harvey looked down at his nearly empty glass. He pulled the toothpick from his mouth and set it aside.

"No thanks."

He handed her a crisp bill. "Close the tab. Keep the change."

Her perfectly arched brows shot up, then she flashed a smile before slipping the bill into her gothic-style bralette.

Harvey checked his watch. A few minutes past nine.

As if on cue, a man with long, wavy brown hair appeared over the waitress's shoulder, pushing through the crowd. His head was on a swivel, scanning the room.

"Here he is!" Harvey waved the waitress off. "Give us a minute."

"Of course," she said, leaving a folded napkin by his glass before moving on.

The stool crashed to the floor as Harvey stood and embraced the man.

"Sorry I'm late," the newcomer said. "Ran into an old friend Mika." He gestured across the room to a striking woman. "You remember her?"

Harvey didn't. The face was unfamiliar, though the name rang a faint bell.

It had been years since he'd last seen Fedir. But one thing hadn't changed: Fedir was a magnet for women. Harvey couldn't remember a time his old friend didn't have one or two on his arm.

Harvey wasn't exactly innocent in that department himself. It was one of the things they had in common.

"How's this place?" Fedir asked, scanning the club, his eyes sweeping over the nightlife.

"Not my cup of tea," Harvey admitted. Then mirked. "Except for that."

Harvey glanced back toward the leather couch in the lounge. The woman with no name had vanished. Restroom? Gone for good? He couldn't be sure.

"What?" Fedir asked, catching the look.

"Never mind."

"So good to see you, Harv. How long has it been? Ten, twelve years?" Fedir's accent was heavy, his English rough around the edges but passable. "I no longer work for your grandfather."

"Moving on up, so I heard," Harvey quipped.

Fedir grinned. "You found me an American woman yet, Harv?" The joke was delivered lightly, just enough of a grin so Harvey knew not to take it too seriously.

The two men chatted for a few minutes before Fedir lifted his chin toward the crowd. "There she comes."

A young woman swayed through the club, sashaying straight toward them.

"You don't need my help," Harvey said dryly. You're doing fine on your own."

Fedir introduced them. "Harvey, this is Mika."

Small talk followed, easy enough, until the waitress returned with menus. They ordered finger foods.

"And a large pitcher," Fedir added.

The waitress collected the menus and slipped back into the crowd.

"I was surprised to hear you were in town, Harv."

Harvey shrugged. "Just glad for a break. Finally get to eat some authentic Ukrainian food."

"What burgers and fries not cutting it?" Fedir teased. "You Americans and your burgers."

Mika chuckled. Fedir and Harvey grinned from ear to ear.

"Harvey here is an American pilot, and he"

"Hey." Harvey cut him off. "We don't discuss work, remember?"

"Oh, right. Sorry. Forgot." Fedir raised his hands in mock surrender. "I called the house yesterday, and they said you were out."

"Yeah. We went to the museum."

Harvey leaned back in his chair. "Which one?"

"The Oleg Aviation Museum, right outside ulyany."

"Oh yeah. The graveyard."

Fedir had always been a cynic, so Harvey wasn't surprised to hear him dismiss Ukraine's rich aviation history as nothing more than a graveyard.

"It's home to the Antonov-225," Harvey said. "Now that's a bird worth seeing."

"Too bad they only had the replica," Harvey added. "I can only imagine what the real thing looks like up close."

Even as he spoke, his eyes kept searching for the woman in the black dress. She hadn't returned.

Of all his grandfather's bodyguards past and present Harvey had always liked Fedir the most. His exuberance, his frenetic energy, the way he watched over Harvey whenever he came to Ukraine. Fedir had protected him like he was the son of President Zelensky himself.

His grandfather's influence explained that. Matviy Arnott had long been one of the most powerful men in the country, rubbing shoulders with every heavyweight in Kyiv. Even in retirement, nearly a decade out of uniform, he still served as a trusted advisor to President Zelensky.

And yet, despite all those connections, Harvey had never met the Ukrainian president in person.

The food arrived. Plates clattered, the scent of fried spices cutting through the haze of smoke and perfume. They dug in while the music thumped through the club walls behind them.

"Come to the ranch tomorrow," Harvey said between bites. "We'll catch up."

Fedir's expression darkened. He shook his head. "I can't come back. Not after what happened last time."

Harvey sat up straighter. "What happened last time?"

Fedir forced a smile and waved it off. "Another day." He quickly changed the subject. "So when are you heading back to the States?"

"Whenever I'm ready," Harvey replied, careful not to give away what he considered sensitive information.

He trusted Fedir mostly. But after more than a decade apart, who could say? In a country swarming with spies, anyone could be compromised.

"I'm glad to see you landed on your feet," Harvey added, "given all the uncertainty here. What about the military? Are you still"

Fedir leaned in close, lowering his voice so Mika couldn't hear. "The Russians are here. We expect an invasion at any moment. Zelensky is preparing to issue a draft. Young men are already lining up."

As a United States Air Force officer, Harvey had known this for months. Still, hearing it from Fedir gave it weight.

"We are fighters," Fedir said firmly. "We're not waiting for Washington to save us. We stand ready to defend this country."

Harvey nodded, acknowledging the sentiment. He kept scanning the room as they spoke, eyes flicking to the upper deck, checking corners, studying exits. Old habits.

So far, nothing. No tells. No shadows. Just a noisy nightclub in a city that felt like it was holding its breath.

As for Russian leader, Harvey knew the truth. President since Yeltsin's resignation in the late nineties, reelected time and again in rigged contests, the man was nothing but a thug to Ukrainians. A thug wrapped in the veneer of power.

"So," Fedir said, shifting gears, "what's this uthentic Ukrainian food you were talking about?"

Harvey named the restaurant.

"Good food," Fedir said with a grin. "Been there a few times."

By now, Mika had pushed her plate aside. She sat back, sipping her drink through a straw, eyes half-lidded.

"Sorry I forgot to ask," Fedir said, trying to lighten the conversation. "How's your dad?"

Harvey's face fell. "He passed away. Colon cancer. A few years back."

Fedir's expression softened. "I didn't know. I'm sorry, Harv. He was a good man."

"Yeah," Harvey said quietly. "His last days were hard. Years of failed chemo. But ... he went peacefully."

Fedir blinked, surprised. He had expected a one-word answer, a quick deflection. Instead, Harvey offered something personal intimate even. Unusual for him.

They chatted for another half hour before Harvey finally glanced at his watch. "Shoot, I gotta go."

He stood, extending his hand. Fedir rose as well, and the two men shook before sharing a final embrace. Pulling away, Harvey bid goodbye to Mika, then turned and slipped out through the wooden archway.

Through the glass window, rain glittered in the parking lot's glow. It had been pouring for an hour, leaving the ground slick with grime. Creek beds along the roadside swelled, water rushing downstream.

His grandfather's words echoed in his head: Always watch your six. Harvey looked left, then right, before crossing the street.

The downpour had emptied the normally busy avenue, leaving only a few stragglers scattered in the mist. Great. Just great, he thought as his foot sank into a filthy puddle. No time to worry about wet shoes it was dark, he was exposed, and he needed to get back to the ranch, a forty-five-minute drive away.

His car a black Renault sport sedan from his grandfather's collection waited at the far end of the nearly deserted lot. He broke into a half-jog, doubling his pace under the night sky. The rain and asphalt shimmered black under the dim streetlights. Water streamed down his face, dripping off his chin into his shirt.

Harvey closed the forty yards to his car quickly, weaving through the almost empty parking lot across from the club.

There it was his car, parked with the headlights facing the exit. Old habits. Be ready to leave quickly.

With just a week left of R & R after his last deployment to Afghanistan, the fieldcraft drilled into him hadn't faded.

As he neared the vehicle, a flash of lightning split the sky.

Suddenly footsteps. Fast. Closing in from behind. He wasn't expecting company.

Shit. For a split second he thought it might be Fedir, but no Fedir would've called out, said something. You didn't sneak up on a man in Ukraine these days. Someone could get killed.

His senses spiked before he even turned. The street was dark and empty, the nearest pedestrian too far to hear. He pivoted sharply, setting himself in a defensive stance, buying space and time to react.

A figure closed the distance with quick, purposeful strides. Tall. Lean. Around six-two, with dark, silky hair plastered wet against his face. He wore a camo jacket, his right hand buried in the front pocket.

Lightning flashed again, illuminating just enough for Harvey to see the truth this was no Fedir. The stranger's expression carried a chilling certainty: this would be easy.

Harvey had to change that. Desperately.

"Hey, man! What do you want?" Harvey shouted.

The mugger kept coming, unfazed. His silence was an answer all its own.

A sudden glare at the mugger's waistband Harvey saw the outline of a handgun.

The man's cold, unblinking stare left no doubt. This wasn't some junkie or petty thief. He was here to kill. And from the way he closed the distance, it felt personal.

Is this what Grandfather warned me about?

Harvey processed the thought in an instant, renaline firing through his veins. Maxwell Air Force Base had drilled him in discipline, but not this. No training exercise had prepared him. What had prepared him were the endless hours of calisthenics and weight training building not just strength but the will to act when others froze.

Is this how it ends? After traveling halfway across the world, do I die here on Khreshchatyk's streets?

The man's right hand moved, rising from his thigh to his waist. The gun was coming up, and his gaze never wavered.

Harvey moved first. He lunged, breaking the man's rhythm, seizing the initiative.

The attacker was caught off guard. He had expected fear, panic, surrender the weapon alone should have done the work. Instead, Harvey closed fast, his left hand snapping onto the barrel just as it leveled at his chest.

He pivoted hard, sidestepping the line of fire. The mugger pulled the trigger crack but the shot went wide.

With his right hand, Harvey clamped down on the attacker's wrist, locking it tight. He recognized the weapon now: a Glock. Using his weight, he pressed down, sliding his grip to the fingers, then wrenched violently.

A muffled scream tore from the man's throat, pain flashing across his face.

They struggled, both straining for the gun. Desperation surged through the attacker as he threw his body forward, slamming into Harvey. Together they crashed into the side of the Renault.

The pistol slipped free, skittering across the pavement, bouncing beneath the car, out of reach.

Rain poured over them as they grappled in the mud.

Harvey shoved hard against the ground and sprang to his feet, using every ounce of strength left. His opponent scrambled but faltered he wasn't trained. A professional would have ended Harvey quickly in this dark, empty street, far from what little nightlife still survived under curfew.

But this wasn't a pro.

Later, Harvey would learn the truth: the man had been a reconnaissance operative, sent to observe and report back. Instead, he'd decided to take matters into his own hands and it had cost him.

The man staggered up slowly, winded. First to a knee, then to his feet, using the sedan's hood for leverage. His right hand dipped inside his jacket and came out with a blade.

He's got a knife.

No more closing the gap. A knife meant you had to get close close enough to puncture a throat, gut, or worse. And this man wasn't here to scare Harvey or rob him. He was here to finish him.

Harvey's chest pounded, his breaths shallow. Back home, he was an NRA-certified concealed-carry holder. But this was

Ukraine. His license meant nothing here. He wasn't armed. No equalizer.

The last time he'd been in a trap like this was Baghdad, clearing a building with his unit when insurgents rushed them. Then, he'd survived with a quick draw of his sidearm. Today was different. There would be no pistol.

Harvey's elbow brushed his hip nothing. The comfort of a holster bump wasn't there.

He patted his trouser pocket. Empty. His car keys might have served as a weapon, but they were zipped inside his jacket. Too far. No time.

The hesitation must have shown. The man surged forward, knife flashing, blade slashing in a zig-zag toward Harvey's face.

Think on your feet, Harv.

He whispered a quick prayer and lunged for the driver-side mirror. Both hands locked around it. With a grunt, he ripped it clean off the sedan, wires dangling loose in the rain.

The attacker slowed, circling, the knife weaving fast in his hand, ready for a chest-high slash.

That's when Harvey realized the man hadn't asked for anything. Not the watch on his wrist, a two-tone silver and gold piece his father had given him when he earned his wings. No threats, no demands.

This wasn't a mugging.

This was an assassination.

And Harvey's heart hammered like it was trying to tear out of his chest.

Think quick.

Harvey hurled the broken mirror with everything he had. It struck the man's chest, clanged off, and skittered across the wet asphalt.

The hit staggered him just for a second. Not enough.

Stay away from the pointy end, Harvey reminded himself.

He edged backward, sidestepping onto a slick patch of grass. The attacker followed, his foot slipping for a moment before he regained balance. Then he came on harder, blade flashing with desperation.

The man slashed high, low, left and right with wild swings, fast and reckless. Harvey slipped out of range each time, retreat in his mind. Live to fight another day. But the man pressed forward, relentless.

The knife cut the air in a final, desperate arc. Harvey timed it perfectly. As the blade passed, he clamped down on the man's wrist, redirecting the strike. Driving the forearm down, he pinned it under his own armpit, trapping the weapon.

With his free hand, he grabbed the man's shoulder and spun him, using momentum against him. Then he hurled him headlong into the sedan's driver-side window.

Glass exploded, shards raining across the asphalt.

The man reeled, half his body sprawled inside the vehicle, the rest in the mud. His face twisted not rage, but hesitation. Doubt.

He yanked himself back out, swinging the blade in wild arcs. One slash caught Harvey across the forearm.

A sting. Blood welled. He glanced down. Superficial.

Not enough to stop him.

Lightning ripped across the sky, illuminating the man's lacerated scalp. Blood streamed down past his ears.

He touched the wound, stared at the crimson on his palm then roared. A savage, warlike cry. He spat blood into the rain, red mixing with black asphalt.

Harvey spotted the broken side-view mirror glinting nearby. He snatched it up.

The two men clashed, weapons flashing. Knife against jagged metal sparks flew with every strike. Lightning flashed again, the storm drenching them in sheets of rain.

Harvey blocked a slash with his left arm, then lunged forward, trapping the man in a crushing bear hug. A brutal head-butt smashed into the attacker's face, snapping his head back.

The man staggered, lost his footing, and toppled into the mud. He hit the ground hard with a sickening thud.

For a moment, the knife slipped free, clattering onto the ground just inches from his outstretched hand.

Pain flickered across the man's face as the night breeze picked up. He wiped the blood from his eyes, refocused on Harvey, and rolled sideways, pushing up to his knees.

His gaze darted across the ground. The blade lay bare between them, eight inches of steel glistening in the rain.

They saw it at the same time. The man was closer.

He lunged. Harvey charged.

Both men crashed together, grappling for the weapon. The man hit the ground first, Harvey on top, hands clawing for control. The struggle turned brutal, mud, rain, fists, steel.

Pinned beneath him, the man flailed, but Harvey finally got a clear look. Mid-thirties. A dog tag dangled around his neck.

Military. Not a street thug. I'm alive by dumb luck, Harvey thought.

"Who are you?" Harvey shouted. "What do you want?"

The man's eyes were blank, uncomprehending, as though Harvey spoke another language.

Switching to the little Ukrainian he knew, Harvey barked: "Shcho ty khochesh?"

Still nothing.

The rain hammered them, streaming down their faces as they wrestled for the blade. Both men locked together, strength against strength, seconds dragging like minutes.

From the street came the low growl of an engine. Headlights cut through the storm, tires hissing on wet pavement. A sheet of water splashed up against concrete barriers.

Then the car was gone, red taillights fading into darkness.

The attacker never looked away. His grip trembled, his strength faltering.

At last, through clenched teeth, he forced out words in Russian: "Ya delayu eto dlya matushki Rossii."

For Mother Russia.

It was all Harvey understood.

Mother Russia.

Harvey didn't need a translator. He was facing a Kremlin operative.

No one else knew what was happening in that moment not his grandfather, not Fedir, not even his base commander back at Travis Air Force Base in California. Harvey Arnott, captain and aviator in the United States Air Force, was fighting for his life in Kyiv while tensions in Europe threatened to boil over.

He pictured the headline: American pilot bested by Russian spy on Ukrainian soil.

Not tonight.

With a final surge, Harvey twisted sideways and drove his heel deep into the man's abdomen. The attacker doubled over, dropping the blade. Harvey seized it.

The man's eyes went wide with fear. He tried to scream, but Harvey clamped a hand over his mouth. Pain shot through Harvey's palm as the man bit down hard.

That was the breaking point. Harvey shoved the knife forward. Steel met flesh with a piercing crunch.

The man gasped, choking on the rain, his cry cut short. His face drained of color. He twitched once, twice, then went still.

Harvey's chest heaved. His hands shook in rhythm with his heartbeat as he scanned the street. No witnesses. Just rain, shadows, silence.

He stared down at the lifeless body. Part of him wanted to feel sorry for the man. But sorry for what? He'd tried to kill him.

Conflict twisted in Harvey's gut. He had promised his grandfather he would stay away from crowds while in Ukraine. He had broken that promise, and guilt gnawed at him. Should he confess what had happened? Or bury it with the body and take the secret to his grave?

If the local cops or worse, federal authorities got involved, the fallout could be explosive. If word reached the United States, it could raise questions Harvey wasn't prepared to answer.

The headline alone could be salacious, given the delicate ties between the United States, Ukraine, and Russia: American officer kills Russian on foreign soil.

He was the victim. But without witnesses, would it matter?

Why had the man come for him? Mistaken identity? No. It can't be.

A sting flared in Harvey's forearm where the attacker's teeth had broken skin.

Club Heaven wasn't the best or worst spot in Kyiv, but it was perched on a busy street. Normally, good for business. Tonight, well past 1:00 a.m., the street lay empty. The cars that had filled the lot earlier were gone.

Harvey's eyes went to the battered sedan, its side mirror torn away, glass shattered. His pulse was still pounding.

What would he tell his grandfather?

An accident, Harvey thought. Yes. That's it. An accident.

Three minutes after the man drew his last breath, Harvey was pulling out of the parking lot.

It wasn't until he reached home that he noticed the cellphone on the driver's floorboard. It must have fallen from the attacker's pocket when he crashed through the sedan's window.

Harvey hadn't escaped unscathed. He'd won but carried wounds of his own. He glanced at his palm. The skin was intact.

"Thank God," he muttered. At least hepatitis-C's off the table ... I think.

This wasn't the first time his life had been pushed to the edge. But tonight felt different.

CHAPTER TWO

(LUFTHANSA)

"Hey, you need to take this seriously. You're in deep shit," the shorter of the two detectives growled at Harvey.

"I am, I swear, man," Harvey replied.

"It doesn't look that way," the heavier man in the cheap suit shot back.

"I'm sorry what did you say your name was again?"

"I'm Detective Andriy Rozniak." He paused. "And this is my partner..."

"Yes, Baron," Harvey interrupted.

"No Barahn," the taller detective corrected sharply, his thick Ukrainian accent cutting through the room.

"Sorry about that," Harvey said, his voice uncertain.

Detective Barahn was a slender man in his mid-forties with thinning black hair. His partner, younger, was broader in build. Both wore black suits over white shirts, shoulder holsters visible beneath their jackets. They sat across from Harvey, a metal table separating them from their suspect. On the table sat a rubber pitcher half full of ice water, a glass beside it.

The detectives took turns grilling Harvey about the incident in Kyiv. Sweat beaded on his forehead, and he wiped it away with the back of his hand. His fingers trembled as he drew in a deep breath, trying to steady his heart, mind racing. How had they tracked him down so quickly? He had already given a statement before arriving at the station, one he thought airtight enough to satisfy any investigator. Now, though, he retraced every word, weighing how much the detectives already knew and how much he should hold back.

He realized with a chill that he had contradicted an earlier statement and hoped they hadn't caught it. Had a witness come forward? Each scenario flashed through his mind. He was thinking like a criminal and he didn't like the feeling.

Be cool, Harvey. They only know what you tell them, he reminded himself.

Rozniak kept firing questions, more repetitive than investigative.

"What are you doing in this country? Are you a spy?"

"No, I'm not. Like I already said, I'm here on vacation, visiting my family."

Barahn rose from his chair, never breaking eye contact with Harvey as he sauntered to the far corner of the interrogation room.

"Tell us about your day from the morning, through the nightclub, and then the attack," Barahn barked. "And don't skip a single detail."

Harvey had known this moment might come, but he had expected more favorable circumstances. circumstances where his grandfather's influence in the community could shield him. He had figured the odds were decent that he'd cross paths with law enforcement eventually, but not this soon, and certainly not without backup from his grandfather or at least a high-power attorney.

After all, he was an American but he had already played that card, and the detectives hadn't budged. With the club's security footage, they thought they had him dead to rights. Cops were always sneaky with these types of cases; if they didn't have the full recording, they'd never lay all their cards on the table.

"I started my day with a workout."

"Fast forward," Rozniak cut in.

You're in it now, Harvey. He hadn't denied being the man on the CCTV leaving the club. He hadn't disputed being a witness to the murder. Whether he mixed lies with truth was yet to be seen. Rozniak's forehead creased, his brows furrowing into a stare that said plainly: I'll know if you're lying.

"I arrived at the club around eight maybe a little after."

"Which one?"

"Heaven … I believe that's what it's called."

"Huh. He believes. Go on," Rozniak quipped.

"I met up with some friends."

"How many?"

"Two."

Sweat streamed down Harvey's face. "Can we open the window?"

"What window?" Barahn asked.

Harvey scanned the room. No window. What's happening to me? I was sure there was one when we first came in. Am I losing it? Going crazy?

His freedom felt like it was slipping away fast. His breathing quickened. He hooked his right index finger inside his shirt beneath the collarbone, stretched his neck side to side, then tilted his chin upward as if the collar was strangling him. It didn't help much, but it was something.

Barahn stepped to the table, lifted the pitcher, and poured ice water into the glass. With two fingers, he slid it across to Harvey.

Harvey wrapped his hand around the glass, condensation slick against his skin. The icy touch pressed against the spot where the mugger had bitten him, sending a flash of pain up his arm. The detectives caught the wince.

"Is everything okay with you?"

"Yes. Yes, it is."

Harvey nodded in appreciation before taking a big gulp.

"It was raining heavily when I left."

"Around what time?"

"Around midnight. I ran to my car."

"Ran?"

"I guess you could say jogged," Harvey added quickly.

"What would you say?"

"Well, as you can see on the video outside the club, it was a light jog to my vehicle."

"And then what?" the shorter detective cut in before Harvey could finish.

"We found items at the scene tying the murder to you," Rozniak warned. "So be very careful how you choose your next words."

A jolt ran through Harvey's body, and he shivered violently. The two detectives exchanged a glance.

Frustrated, the shorter one leaned in. "Look, man, truth be told we don't really care about the dead guy. He was a spy."

"We don't like spies," the taller detective cut in.

"If what you're saying about your visit to Ukraine is true," he continued, "we'll need to speak with your commanding officer before you're allowed to leave the country."

"Standard practice," he added flatly.

My commanding officer? But … how did they know I was Rozniak pulled a leather-bound wallet from a folder and set it on the table. The embossed American flag glared up at Harvey. Rozniak opened it, slid out a Common Access Card, and slapped it down.

The rectangular plastic, the size of a credit card laid in front of him and there was no mistaking the man on the military ID card. Harvey stared at his own face and military rank of O3 printed on the hard white plastic. His shoulders collapsed, and he slumped in his chair.

"Are you a spy?" Rozniak's voice boomed across the room. "Did you know the dead man before …?"

"Self-defense!" Harvey burst out.

"Go on."

"Then what happened?"

"It was dark and pouring rain."

The room seemed to grow darker. Harvey glanced around to see what was happening but the two men did not seem to notice. They kept on hammering him with questions. It felt like he was in a tennis match and he was the luminous green ball bouncing back and forth. One of the men leaned across the table, the glint from his wrist watch catching Harvey's attention. When the man noticed Harvey eyeing his time piece, he stood up straight and slipped his hand into his pocket.

The air in the room was thick with the scent of damp furniture and stale cigarette smoke, a silent testament to the hours that others had spent in that very chair he was sitting in. The interrogators voices, a mix between low and high rumble of accented English, were the only sounds breaking the silence as they meticulously probed for information, each question a deliberate hammer blow against the American's unwavering resolve.

"Go on, the tall man barked."

Harvey swallowed hard and slipped a finger into his collar.

"You want some more water?" The tall man pushed the glass towards Harey.

The American, pale and unshaven, squinted at the glass. "No, thanks. I'm good." His voice was a dry rasp. "Can we just get on with this."

Barahn leaned back against a wall, a small grin playing on his lips. "Impatient. that's a very American trait." He stood straight and approached at an angle. "You know, we could do this the hard way, but he, pointing to his partner, prefers a civilized conversation. We are all professionals after all. Now, please continue."

If he meant to intimidate Harvey, it had worked, but the American betrayed no evidence of that.

"Then I heard ..." Harvey continued.

"What did you hear?" Rozniak shot back.

"Look man, I was in the wrong place at the wrong time."

"What did you hear?" Barahn said, his eyes narrowing slightly. "And stop playing games."

"I told you everything that happened." Harvey insisted, running a hand through his matted hair.

"I came here on vacation and I was in the club minding my own business when I was attacked."

"You were attacked inside or outside the club."

"Outside. My mistake." Harvey replied calmly.

"A very convienient mistake," Barahn countered. His tone calm, but with an edge of steel underneath. "You see, a week before you arrived, there was a ... security incident at one of out military installations. It has foreign intelligence written all over it."

Harvey stared at him, his face ghostly blank. "What are you talking about?" Harvey shook his head, a desparate weariness in his eyes as he went silent.

"Sir." The tall man stared at his partner. The shorter man snapped his finger in Harvey's face.

"Sir. Sir. Sir!"

Harvey opened his eyes to find a gorgeous flight attendant standing before him. He blinked twice, making sure it was real and it was. She was a knockout.

His first thought: Had I been drooling? And if so, did she see it? He casually wiped the corner of his mouth. Dry. Good.

The plane shuddered with light turbulence. Passengers around him snapped their tray tables upright. I'll be damned, it was all a dream, Harvey realized.

"Sir, please stow your tray table and fasten your seatbelt. The captain says we're approaching turbulence."

Nothing new to Harvey. He complied quickly.

The attendant moved down the aisle, exchanged a word with another passenger, then strapped herself into the jump seat at the front. She glanced back once at Harvey.

The boy seated beside him clutched the armrest, fear written all over his freckled face.

"His first time," Harvey observed.

"Yes," the boy's mother said with a playful smile. "He was so excited when we left home, but now … not so much."

The redheaded kid, no older than seven, looked ready to bolt.

"Hey, I'm a pilot," Harvey said gently. "I go through this all the time. It'll be over in no time. We just have to trust the men in the cockpit, okay?"

The boy nodded, though his eyes betrayed more doubt than courage.

"Are you really a pilot?" his mother asked.

"Yes, ma'am."

Harvey pulled out his wallet, slid out a photo of himself in a flight suit. His Common Access Card slipped onto his lap. The sight of it sent a chill through him, reminding him of the dream he'd had just moments earlier.

It had felt so real, detectives, interrogation, the threat of prison. He almost pinched himself again, just to be sure, but stopped. If those detectives had been real, I wouldn't be sitting in first class on a Lufthansa airbus. I'd be in cuffs, locked in a cold cell.

Harvey replayed the day's events when he got home, the would-be assassin's head slamming into the windshield of his grandfather's Renault sedan. The adrenaline still burned in his system, and he barely slept. Three, maybe four hours at most.

Before dawn, a rooster crowed somewhere on the ranch and jolted him awake. He showered again, still feeling unclean from the night before, then dressed and stuffed his bloodied clothes into a black garbage bag. He carried it outside and tossed it into the large bin scheduled for pickup that morning.

Back in the kitchen, he brewed himself a cup of coffee and drifted into the living room. The cleaning lady was already there, sitting in front of the television. She always arrived early, waiting quietly until the household stirred before starting her duties. Today, she was glued to the morning news.

The broadcast covered a highway accident involving a semi-trailer, then pivoted to widespread corruption scandals, fueled by rumors of a looming Russian takeover. But there was nothing, no mention of a dead man in a parking lot near Club Heaven.

"Nothing." Harvey muttered under his breath.

No crime report. No witnesses. That could mean something or nothing. He cut the thought short, forcing his mind not to wander too far, lest he start convincing himself of guilt. For the next half hour, he scanned both the televised news cycle and online chatter, searching for any mention of Khreshchatyk Street. Nothing. He thought about calling Fedir, but loved him too much to drag him in as an accessory.

Instead, Harvey borrowed a Vespa and a tinted helmet from the garage. He gunned through back-road traffic until he reached the Jersey barriers across from the parking lot. The dark helmet kept his face hidden from any potential cameras.

The rain had stopped, and dawn was breaking. Puffy white clouds replaced the storm from the night before. Creek beds drained into the gutters, and the branches of overhanging trees swayed gently in the morning breeze.

It was a little past eight, and the shops along the street were preparing to open. From a distance, Harvey spotted a string of yellow police tape looping around the area where he had parked the night before.

He eased closer but took care not to look too interested, no need to draw attention if officers or detectives were still canvassing. He rolled past the tape at a snail's pace, rode to the dead end of the lot, then made a U-turn for another pass.

His eyes swept the area, searching for anything that might connect the scene to him or to his grandfather. He scanned the embankment beyond the guardrails and Jersey barriers. Nothing. By now the police had already combed the area, and aside from shards of glass scattered in the gravel, the site looked unremarkable.

Beyond the barriers, rush-hour traffic had thickened, the hiss of tires sending up mists that lingered in the air.

Satisfied his recon had turned up nothing, Harvey knew it was time to get out of Dodge before the boys in blue came knocking. He maneuvered the Vespa around the embankment, avoiding a soup of mud and patchy brown grass, then guided it down a slope where branches, heavy with moisture, drooped low overhead.

Minutes later, the ranch was in sight. In his mind, he had already decided: vacation over. Better to leave before things took a darker turn.

A plane streaking high across the morning sky reminded him of what he needed to do next. It was time to get back to work.

The freckled-faced boy and his mother on the flight flickered across his memory enough of a distraction to keep his mind off capture. For now, he had crossed the Black Sea and vowed never to return to this part of the world. No more crossing the Rubicon for this American warrior.

With his neck craned toward the window, Harvey watched the darkened landscape form beneath the plane. After drifting in and out of sleep, he finally opened his eyes to see the twinkling lights of Los Angeles slowly come into view.

He pulled his cell phone from his pocket, tempted to turn it on, but resisted. Instead, he tucked both hands, phone included, into the pouch of his hooded Nike sweatshirt.

The pilot came over the intercom, reminding passengers they were just minutes from descent into LAX. Harvey, familiar with the drill, already had his tray table upright and his seatbelt snug across his lap.

The flight attendant made one last walk down the aisle, checking for compliance and scooping up trash. When their eyes met, Harvey wasn't sure if she found him attractive or if she wanted to silently inform him he was an ugly sleeper. Given his tendency to sleep with his mouth open, he decided it was the latter.

His thoughts drifted to his first order of business once on the ground. Food. No, rental car first, then food. Drive-through on the way home. Welcome back to America: salt, fat, and sugar.

He was exhausted. Nearly fifty-four hours in transit: Kyiv to Frankfurt, Frankfurt to London-Cork, then Paris for a layover before boarding the final leg to Los Angeles. His body ached, but his mind was elsewhere deciphering what had really gone down at the club. The phone he had taken from the would-be assassin burned in his thoughts, heavy with the secrets it might contain.

Greece, two years ago, had passed without incident. Ukraine, by contrast, had been nothing but chaos. Harvey resolved to stay out of Europe for a while if he could help it.

The wing flaps extended with a mechanical hum, adjusting for speed. The plane jolted slightly, then steadied as it bled altitude. Smoky clouds peeled away to reveal a glowing grid below. Rows of lights stretched across the sprawl of the city, rising closer with every second.

Harvey could almost taste freedom. And it felt good. He saw the sign; LAX.

CHAPTER THREE

(KYIV, UKRAINE)

THE OLD MAN HAD been up since five o'clock, as he usually was these days, with little to do but read the newspaper and keep up with current events.

Matviy stood on the back porch, tossing grains of rice to the chickens pecking in the dirt. After a few minutes, he turned and stepped back inside. To his surprise, the morning news carried a strange report about a mysterious dead body.

The reporter spoke in Ukrainian:

"Police say a man was killed on Khreshchatyk Street, not far from a popular nightclub on the strip, about two weeks ago. The victim has yet to be identified, but authorities believe him to be of Russian descent. The incident may have occurred sometime between midnight and three a.m. A curfew has now been reinstated until further notice. Authorities are asking residents to ..."

Matviy muted the television, rose, and poured himself a refill of espresso. He picked up a walkie-talkie and called for Igor to meet him in the living room.

It didn't take long. Igor trotted in, his military haircut neat, his bearing disciplined. Even though the man was years removed from the Ukrainian military, he still maintained the image. An image the comes handy when you're assigned to a detail of a prominent figure like retired General Matviy Arnott.

"Hey, Igor. What did Harvey say happened to the car he borrowed when he was here?"

Igor, caught off guard, thought for a moment before answering.

"An accident, sir."

"And where did he say it happened?"

Igor's eyes flicked toward the muted television, where the Khreshchatyk Street story lingered on the screen.

"Khreshchatyk Street," he said at last. Then, hesitantly, he added "Is that what they're discussing on the news?"

"Perhaps there's a correlation,"

Matviy admitted.

"But I can't be too sure. Besides, the story Harvey gave us had plenty of holes. They haven't identified the body yet, but word is it might be a Russian operative."

Igor shifted uneasily. "Do you think Harvey was …?"

Matviy cut him off. "No. It's probably nothing."

Matviy pulled out his smartphone and opened WhatsApp. He scrolled until he found Harvey's picture, tapped it, and went straight to Messenger.

Hey, we need to talk.

He closed the app and turned to Igor. "Get the boys. We're going for a drive."

The air outside was filled with humidity. Matviy and his men piled into an SUV. The doors were yanked open and slammed shut until Matviy was satisfied he had enough fire power to face any potential threat. In large duffle bags were a jumble of gear. Rifles and shot guns, their black metal glinting menacingly as the men rationed them out. Magazines were checked and re-checked, the click-clack of metal on metal echoing in the confined space.

One man wiped the condensation from the window with the back of his gloved hand, his eyes scanning the streets. The low murmur of their conversation was punctuated by the sharp rattle of bolts being racked home.

The engine rumbled to life, and the SUV lurched forward, pulling away from the parking spot and navigating towards the wrought iron gates.

"Take the express way, we get there quicker," Matviy said to the driver.

The driver turned in the direction as instructed.

"Hey boss, is Harv in some kind of trouble?" The driver asked.

"I don't think so, but we have to go take a look." The old man replied.

They were on the expressway for about twenty minutes before a bilborad advertisement of the nightclub became visible ahead of them. The vehicle took the exit and ease down an off ramp.

The black SUV, its dark windows reflecting sun light, pushed through heavy traffic with congested lanes. Its powerful engine rumbled softly as it edged past a delivery truck, its tires humming on the asphalt. The brake lights of the cars ahead created a river of red, and the driver navigated through vehicles with a steady precision before turning onto Khreshchatyk Street. The driver was moving slowly, less than twenty miles per hour when the opportunity presented itself. They drove the long stretch past shops, dealerships, and nightclubs until they reached the spot where police had discovered the unidentified body.

Yellow tape still hung between posts, though one end had come loose, flapping in the breeze, thanks to curious bystanders. The sky was clear, the sun already climbing. The drizzle from the night before left a sheen of moisture on grass and leaves, the overhanging branches swaying under its weight.

It was half past seven, and the parking lot stood empty.

Then men climbed out of the SUV, leaving their weapons in the vehicle and followed their boss. Matviy was focussed, his cane tapping the pavement. The cane was more of an accessory than necessity, a symbol of authority rather than frailty.

Matviy scanned the area. No police in sight. Satisfied, he and his men crossed beyond the yellow tape, their breaths steaming in the cool morning air.

They stopped to examine the ground. Loose strands of police tape clung to the dirt, along with shards of glass where the sedan had once been parked.

Igor bent down, picked up a fragment, and studied it before holding it in his palm for the boss to see.

Without a word, they all reached the same conclusion: the broken glass resembled the tinted windows of the damaged vehicle back at the ranch.

In his mind's eye, Matviy pictured Harvey locked in a fight with a dangerous man and somehow walking away alive. It was only half true. Harvey had kept his wounds hidden from everyone at the ranch and had returned to the United States far sooner than expected.

Matviy could only hope his grandson hadn't left behind anything the police could trace. An extradition for murder would be disastrous and an embarrassment to the family.

At least, that's what he told himself.

He glanced around. The parking lot was beginning to stir with life. Matviy sauntered over to a nearby guardrail, climbed over, and picked his way down the embankment until he reached the edge. Below stretched a wide patchwork of green and yellow grass. No signs of struggle. Nothing disturbed. Everything looked peaceful, at least to the naked eye.

Beyond, Khreshchatyk Street buzzed with growing traffic. Cars streamed past, sending mist curling over the concrete barriers.

Matviy had nothing. For now he would have to rely on the words of his grandson. He scanned the surrounding buildings for security cameras but there wasn't any visible from where he was standing. He instructed the men to canvas the area while he got on the phone to make a call. The men were careful to not draw too much attention to their presence.

CHAPTER FOUR

(FAIRFIELD, CALIFORNIA)

Harvey woke around noon, though the night had given him little rest. He had stirred several times, staring at the clock as if it mocked his attempts to sleep. Time seemed frozen. He rose for water, used the restroom, then lay back down, tossing and turning until he finally managed ten solid hours.

When he surfaced from REM sleep, his mind replayed the past three days: the mugger dying like a dog in the street, and Harvey walking away almost unscathed. He wanted to feel sorry for the man, but why? It had been combat, and in combat the rule was simple: may the best man win. One thing Harvey knew for certain it had not been a case of mistaken identity. The thought that it could just as easily have been his own head shattering through that windshield twisted a knot in his stomach.

He yawned, stretched, and winced at the stiffness in his neck. After a short while, he sat in the steam room, enduring the heat until the tension drained from his muscles. Back in his suite, he slipped into a T-shirt and sweatpants, then dropped onto the faux-leather couch, his mind racing a hundred miles an hour.

His attacker, Harvey admitted, had been an opportunistic predator. The planning and timing had been impeccable but the end result, disastrous for the mugger.

What was he thinking? That I'd just lie down and take it? Harvey hated being blindsided. The man's distraction tactic had worked sneaky bastard. Why hadn't he simply taken the shot inside the nightclub, where pounding music and drunken revelers would have masked it? No one would have known where it came from, or who had pulled the trigger. Maybe the mugger preferred a quieter setting, where he could finish the job and record his kill on the cellphone he carried as proof.

The phone.

Harvey rose from the couch, stepped into the bedroom closet, and keyed a six-digit code into the wall-locker safe. The bolt released with a metallic thunk, and the door swung open. He pulled out the mugger's cellphone and carried it into the dining room. After pushing his laptop aside, he sat at the table and studied the device.

He powered it on, set it down, and walked into the kitchen. Filling a glass with tap water, he returned to find the home screen waiting for authentication. Three failed attempts later, a warning flashed: one more incorrect entry within the hour would lock the phone permanently.

"Damn it."

Harvey flipped open his laptop and pulled up www. jailbreak.com, a site promising ways to bypass stubborn security systems. He skimmed articles, scanned forums, but found nothing useful.

His gut told him the man hadn't been a random thief. If he were, he would have demanded cash or stripped Harvey of his watch and jewelry. A junkie would have pawned the smartphone at the first twitch of withdrawal. No, this man was something else disciplined, prepared, part of something larger. Harvey was convinced he had been working for the Russians.

Think, Harvey. Think.

He rose and walked to the balcony window, gazing out at the airfield. In the distance, cargo planes rumbled along the flight line, landing and taking off in steady rhythm. A row of fighter jets sat in tight formation at the edge of the tarmac.

Stepping outside, he looked down. Most squadrons were out for afternoon PT, their cadence carrying across the base. From Flight 221 came the call:

"Here we go, here we go All the way, all the way. I signed my name on the dotted line, And all I do is double time.Up the hill, up the hill, Down the hill, down the hill."

No time for a formation run. He decided he'd hit the gym later.

Harvey reached into his pocket, pulled out his phone, and scrolled through his contacts until he found the name he wanted. He pressed dial.

"Highland Electronics," a voice answered.

"Is this Shireef?"

"No, this is Jaylen. Who's calling?"

"This is Captain" Harvey stopped himself. He never introduced himself to strangers by rank. Civilians didn't care, and it wasn't necessary. So why had he started to now? Subconscious, he thought.

"This is Harvey from the Air Force Base. Is Shireef around?"

"Yes, he is."

"Please tell him it's his buddy, Harvey."

"Okay."

A long pause followed before the line came alive again.

"Yoooo, Harv!" The voice rang with excitement.

"Hey, brother," Harvey said.

"Haven't seen you in a while. I ran into Webb on base last week he said you were on R&R but wouldn't tell me where."

"OpSec. You know the drill."

"Yeah, I can't say I miss it. Still as much fun as the day I left?"

"Every bit of it," Harvey replied.

"Okay, man, whatever you say." A chuckle. "So, what's up?"

"Listen, I need a favor. I've got this phone, and I've lost the passcode. Can you help me crack it?"

Shireef Verena owned Highland Electronics, a small repair and cyber-security shop just outside Travis Air Force Base. If it spoke a computer language, Shireef could read it and twist it. Back on active duty, he'd been a master hacker and intelligence officer, serving alongside Harvey and Webb. He might have stayed in, too, had a helicopter crash not left him with a ruined knee and a medical discharge. Still, he and Harvey had stayed close long after.

"Sure thing. Bring it over, let me take a look," Shireef said.

Harvey ended the call. Pulling up his phone's camera, he snapped a few shots of the mugger's device, capturing the markings and serial numbers. He checked his watch. A little after 1 p.m.

Harvey felt a tingling sensation course through his body. He scratched his head, then rubbed his nose. Someone had tried very hard to kill him overseas and that someone had an accomplice: a brunette bombshell, the devil in disguise. They had worked as a team, even if the woman hadn't seen it through to the end. Having someone hunt him down directly wasn't new. The last time, it had been the Taliban, Shiites, or Sunnis fighting back in modern warfare. But this was different. It felt like a lone wolf trying to make a name for himself. Harvey realized that his vacation status had lured him into a dangerous complacency.

He drove past the gate security and headed west down Main Street. If this had been a matter of national security, he would have had help from the rank and file, maybe even the bigwigs on base. But this was something else something covert. For now, Shireef was all he had.

As Harvey pulled up to the store, he saw Shireef hobbling toward his Chevy truck. Harvey's tires screeched to a halt beside him.

"Hey, where you headed?" Harvey called.

"Late lunch. I'm grabbing a sandwich and a drink. Why don't you leave the phone with my assistant, Jaylen?"

"No can do, bud. This is for your eyes only."

"You serious, man?"

"Very."

Shireef could tell from the look on his friend's face that he meant business.

"Fine. Hand it over, and I'll do it myself."

Harvey passed him the cell phone.

Shireef gave the device a quick scan, his eyebrows shooting up. "Sorry, man. I don't have the charger. I assume you can find one that fits. Come back in a few hours."

Harvey left, heading back toward base. But on impulse, he pulled into the CrossFit gym two blocks away. A workout, he decided, was exactly what he needed.

Five minutes after dropping off the cell phone, Harvey was heading east on Main Street, retracing his steps back to the base. He always kept a go-bag both in the field and stateside.

When deployed, his go-bag held tactical gear, energy bars, ammunition, and other essentials needed far from base. At home, however, it contained gym clothes, protein powder, and energy snacks all the regular gym-bro stuff.

He pulled into the parking lot and stepped out of his MK350 Mercedes-Benz SUV. Closing the door, he walked around to the back and popped the trunk. The rear gate lifted, revealing a gym bag and a pair of running shoes. Harvey grabbed both and headed inside.

At the entrance, he scanned his keycard and walked through the double doors. Earbuds in place, he set the treadmill to difficulty level 2 and started a light jog, fumbling with his phone as he searched for the right playlist. Once the Head-Up Display registered a lap, he increased the setting to 4.5 and pushed into a sprint. He held the pace for seven or eight minutes before switching to cool-down mode.

Just then, a chime sounded and four men walked in. They were clearly from the Air Force Base, and Harvey recognized two familiar faces. Snatching his cell phone, he stepped off the treadmill and walked toward them.

"Hey, fellas."

"Fuck you, Harvey. You're a damn rat."

Harvey froze, shock written all over his face. He hadn't seen this coming.

"What? What are you talking about?"

"Don't play dumb with me, man. How else would the Wing Commander find out about the gifts?"

"I swear, it wasn't me. Someone gave you bad intel."

The other two airmen drifted away, leaving Harvey and Webb to settle things. Webb was a year younger, a couple of inches shorter, and had been Harvey's friend for years. That made it harder for him to believe his buddy had ratted him out after their deployment to Afghanistan.

"Look, man, it's common to get gifts from the locals over there. I wouldn't make a big deal out of it. I swear."

Suddenly, Harvey's phone chimed. He glanced at the screen. A message from Shireef read: All done. See you shortly.

The look on Webb's face told Harvey he wasn't buying it. Not wanting to stick around, Harvey grabbed the gym bag he'd dropped at his foot hoping for a handshake, not a fight and bolted out the security door into the parking lot.

He drove straight back to the electronics store, his mind looping between Webb's accusations and the information Shireef might have pulled from the phone.

Inside, Shireef ushered him into a back office where a laptop and the phone sat on a metal desk. He locked the door behind them.

"How's everything?" Harvey asked.

"I cracked the phone. I might have found something."

"Great."

Shireef tried to contain the anxiety bubbling beneath his calm exterior.

"What have you gotten yourself into, Harv?" he said.

"Is it that bad?"

"Well, it's not good that's for sure."

A chill ran down Harvey's spine.

"Before we get into this, I need you to be straight with me. Don't lie."

Shireef locked eyes with him.

"Are you some kind of spy, Harvey?"

"No. What made you say that?"

Shireef studied him. Either his friend and former colleague was auditioning for a lead role in the Bourne franchise, or he was just a damn good liar. Either way, Shireef had to deliver.

They hovered over the table, fixated on the electronic devices, when Shireef said, "The phone was practically wiped, but I managed to restore deleted texts, photos, and PDF files. I almost forgot how good I am at this nothing gets past the Reef."

Harvey chuckled. It had been a long time since he'd heard Shireef call himself that.

"We're in."

With a few clacks of the keyboard, the phone's contents filled the computer monitor.

"I found these."

A folder appeared on-screen. Harvey leaned in, scanning it deeply, but nothing looked familiar. Shireef double-tapped the folder, and the image expanded.

"That's my grandfather," Harvey said reluctantly.

He pointed at the screen. "And that's his ranch."

Shireef scrolled down until the first block of text appeared.

"That's my grandfather's address. That's where I was staying during R&R."

The text was in Ukrainian, but Harvey recognized the sequence.

"Yeah, man, this looks sketchy as hell, Harv. There are code names in here and everything."

Shireef clicked through more tabs. "I ran the Russian parts through Google Translate. That's when I realized this phone belongs to a Russian. Last I checked, you were an American airman."

He minimized the folder and opened another. Harvey's stomach tightened when he saw his own face staring back at him, buried in the mugger's phone.

Shireef pointed to the Russian description beneath the photo. "That says targets … and something about hostages. Did you run into Russians out there?"

"Something like that," Harvey shot back.

"This translates to kill shot. And this one says take no hostages. And here names and numbers in Russian. What do you make of it?"

Harvey finally had an answer to a question that had haunted him since leaving Ukraine: was his mugger a lone wolf, or part of a larger group already in-country, waiting on orders from the Kremlin?

"It's a long story."

"Give me the condensed version, Harv."

"Right. About two weeks ago, I was visiting family in Ukraine when a local fishing boat clashed with a Russian warship. The Ukrainians were outmatched, outgunned but they stood their ground and paid the ultimate price. It was all over the local news. At the time, like everyone else, I thought it was just an isolated incident. I guess I was wrong."

"What's that got to do with you?" Shireef pressed.

"I'm getting to it."

Harvey grabbed the clicker and dragged the cursor across the screen. A photo popped up: a still image of a nightclub.

"There that's Club Heaven. See the timestamp? I was there that night with some friends, having a good time, when I was ambushed."

"You were attacked inside the club?"

"No. He waited until I was alone in the parking lot. That's when he struck. He didn't make it, but I want to know why I was targeted."

"And this is his phone?"

"Yes. It is."

Shireef narrowed his eyes. "Your grandfather he works for the Ukrainian government?"

"No. But he's close friends with Zelensky. Still has some old connections."

"I see."

Shireef absorbed the flood of information. It was a lot to process, but as a former military officer, he was no stranger to debriefs that cut even deeper than this.

"From the breadcrumbs, this guy was a Russian operative special forces, maybe some Kremlin commando. If things happened the way you said, you're lucky to be alive."

He didn't admit it out loud, but Shireef felt proud of his friend. Harvey had always been into CrossFit and hand-to-hand combat. Who knew it would pay off one day?

"So, what do you make of these other images, Harv?"

Harvey leaned in, pointing at the screen.

"July 5th that's the Embassy. Same day, they photographed City Hall."

The next three images showed reconnaissance shots of Harvey inside the club that night. Grainy, distant but unmistakably him.

A knot tightened in his throat. The assailant had been close enough to finish the job right there in the club. The realization hit hard: he wasn't targeted randomly. He was a mark because of the name he carried because he was the grandson of Matviy Arnott, a sworn enemy of the Russian government.

Harvey knew it was only a matter of time before he'd have to face his grandfather and tell him everything even the truth about the shattered windshield of the Renault sedan.

His eyes darted across the monitor. "Over there..." He jabbed a finger toward another image.

"...that's the airport. And in the background that's the Antonov."

Shireef zoomed in for a closer look and there it was. The Antonov-225, basking in all its glory, sat majestically in the far corner of the runway. His jaw dropped at the sight of the world's largest cargo plane.

Still staring, Shireef muttered, "I'm glad you're not a traitor. That would've made one hell of an interview when the FBI came knocking."

Harvey stayed silent.

"Wait... I'm not expecting a visit from the FBI or CIA, am I?"

"No. And thanks for everything you've done today."

"No problem, buddy. Just... stay out of trouble, will ya?"

"Sure thing."

A short while later, Harvey pulled up to the security checkpoint at the Air Force Base. His mind circled back to his grandfather. Whatever had to be done had to be done quickly.

He retrieved his military ID from the visor and handed it to the gate guard. The senior airman scanned it, returned the card, then snapped to attention and saluted, as he did for every commissioned officer entering the base.

"Welcome back, Major."

Harvey returned the salute, lowered his hand, and eased the accelerator, letting the SUV roll through the security barriers. Once clear, he exhaled.

Overhead, a plane descended toward the runway while a flock of birds scattered in the opposite direction.

It all made sense to Harvey now something bigger was at play. His trip to Shireef had answered a few questions, like why the mugger had acted the way he did and how he'd managed to stay hidden until the moment of attack. But one thing didn't add up: if the man was as skilled as he seemed, why hadn't he finished the job? A suppressor would have dropped Harvey before he could even mutter, Hey pretty lady, what's your name?

Then it hit him his own carelessness. He remembered a social media post he'd made right before leaving for vacation. Dammit, Harvey. How could you be so reckless? He had abandoned years of training and instincts for a quick engagement online. He had walked straight into a bear trap and he knew it.

The thought unsettled him, and his mind raced. She had to be in on it. His memory circled back to the woman in the black dress from the club. Where had she disappeared to? Harvey could still picture her curves that had distracted him, weaknesses he hated to admit. He felt a wave of disgust just thinking about it.

His R&R had dulled his edge, caused him to ignore the warning bells. That kind of lapse was deadly. Maybe not back home, but in the deployment AOR, mistakes like that ended with a body bag zipped tight inside a transfer case.

One thing was certain: whoever the mugger was, he wasn't working alone and his accomplices weren't going to stop after a single failure. Harvey had to assume his family in Ukraine was already on their radar.

That left him with only one choice: give his grandfather everything he had learned, and put the old man on the offensive before the enemy made another move.

Almost home, Harvey eased down to ten miles per hour. He reached into his pocket, pulled out his phone, and scrolled through his contacts until he stopped on his grandfather's name.

Pulling into the driveway, he waited for his phone to connect to Wi-Fi. He checked his watch early morning in Ukraine. With luck, he'd catch his grandfather before the daily routine began.

He pressed dial on WhatsApp video and listened as the line rang. Five … six times. Then the call went dead.

Harvey switched to text, his thumb hovering for a second before he typed:

Call me. We need to talk ASAP.

CHAPTER FIVE

(KYIV, UKRAINE)

Of all the calls Harvey had to make that week, this one worried him most. He'd spoken with his grandfather countless times, especially after his father's death, and the bond between them had only grown. Watching his father lose the battle to stage four cancer had forced Harvey to confront his own mortality and in turn, drawn him closer to Matviy.

Before that, his contact with the old man had been limited. Harvey had wanted distance, especially while pursuing a commission in the United States Air Force. Any questions about ties to a foreign government could have raised suspicion. But once he earned his wings, all bets were off. Matviy even flew to the States to watch him graduate from the Academy.

Now Harvey dialed his grandfather's direct line.

Matviy answered on the second ring. He was already suspicious of that night Harvey had taken the sedan to the club and returned with a busted window, then left in a hurry soon after. Still, Matviy had given his grandson the benefit of the doubt. Harvey was a decorated airman, after all.

"Hello, Harvey." His voice carried the strength of a man twenty years younger, the kind who could still jog a mile without slowing.

"Good evening, Papa." Harvey's tone, though, was that of a schoolboy about to face a strict teacher after forgetting his homework.

"I hope you're sitting," Harvey began. He paused, searching for the right words. "There's a problem you need to be aware of. It may involve"

"The car, yes," Matviy cut in. "I've been waiting to have this conversation."

"You're ready to hear what really happened that night?"

The words hit Harvey like a ton of bricks. He knows.

You're here now, Harvey. Tell him the whole truth.

Waiting for the attackers to try again this time targeting the people he cared about wasn't an option. He had one card left to play, though it was a long shot. If the man and woman from the club were accomplices, others could be waiting in the shadows.

Either they'd strike again soon, or vanish quietly out of the country. Harvey hoped for the former. Let them stay. Let them believe the Ukrainian government was already digging deep, launching a full-scale investigation that would leave no stone unturned.

Harvey steadied himself. It was time to tell his grandfather the truth.

"I got into a fight with a guy. He came out of nowhere and attacked me. During the scuffle, he landed face-first into the vehicle."

"That would explain the blood we found by the doorjamb and the gearbox."

"That's right. I did some research into my attacker and found some very interesting things."

Harvey wanted to tell his grandfather the full truth that the attack was about him and his ties to Ukraine and Russia but he knew he had to be tactful. The mugger and his accomplice hadn't cared about Harvey; they'd used him to send a message to Matviy, no matter how it played on the international stage. The thought twisted a knot in his stomach.

They had failed to kill Matviy many times. Harvey had become the easier target. They came, they missed and now he wanted payback. It was time to turn survival into an advantage.

"He was Russian," Harvey continued. "And he didn't seem to be working alone. In fact, I retrieved a cell phone from him and brought it back with me to the States. A friend of mine with impeccable skills managed to jailbreak it and crack the codes. Wanna know what we found?"

"Harvey, if this is as serious as it sounds, we should have had this conversation weeks ago."

"Right. I know. I just sent you an email with the findings. There are addresses, names, and surveillance photos linked to you and some of your colleagues. We think it's a hit list. If so, that means other operatives are already planning something big."

"This is a very big deal."

"Yes. And I'm sorry for not getting this to you sooner. Please, be careful, Papa."

"One more thing," Harvey added. "In the email, you'll find an address. I think that's where the attackers were staying. Look into it see what you can find."

"I will. And Harvey … thanks for telling me the truth. I really appreciate it."

"You're welcome. I'll be heading to Ramstein Air Base in the next few days. If you need me, send an email."

"Will do. Take care, Harvey."

The line went dead.

Matviy set the phone down on the coffee table, rose from the leather couch, and stepped onto the balcony. He had always been a resourceful man, not the type to run from a fight. Hell, he'd even crossed warlords across Europe and lived to tell the tale.

He returned to the table, picked up the phone, and was about to dial a number when he stopped himself. Instead, he flipped open his laptop, pulled up his email, and opened the PDF Harvey had sent. He enlarged the text, slipped a pair of readers from his breast pocket, and leaned in.

He was no longer accustomed to handling classified documents, but this one read like it. Harvey had put together a work of art lodging details on the attackers, with references pointing to others staying at the same hotel. Room 110, 111, and 112.

This is good, he thought.

With phone in hand, he pressed speed dial. A man's voice answered.

"Gather your men. We're taking a little trip."

He hung up.

Within hours, a Sprinter van rolled west on Interstate 40. Rain hammered the windshield. To the left, the Sheika River overflowed, twisting through marshland. The temperature had dropped into the low fifties as the sun slid behind the horizon.

Matviy rode shotgun. Beside him, his right-hand man Bilyk gripped the wheel. In the back, six men dressed head-to-toe in black tactical gear checked their weapons. These were no amateurs they toggled between burst and semi-auto, seated in silence, brims low and balaclavas pulled tight.

As the hotel came into view, Matviy turned in his seat. His men were locked in, ready for war. He gave them a sharp once-over, then said, "Hang tight." To Bilyk: "You're with me."

The van circled the hotel once before settling behind a row of overgrown hedges, sixty feet from the entrance. The two-story building brown and gray siding over a stone foundation stood on a hill. The lot was half-empty, a few scattered cars, no foot traffic.

Bilyk killed the engine. Matviy swung out, and the two strode toward the entrance, Matviy leading the way.

Behind the reception desk sat an older woman, late sixties.

In his best Russian accent, he said, "Hi. Some of my men are supposed to be staying here for military training. Is it this hotel or the one down the street?"

The woman blinked, confused. "Russian?"

"Yes," Matviy replied smoothly. "How can you tell?"

The woman chuckled without answering his accent said it all. Matviy gave her a polite smile.

While they spoke, Bilyk kept his head on a swivel. He counted steps from the front desk to the exit, scanned for fire escapes, and swept the ceiling for CCTV. Nothing. The man was detail-oriented, never stopped crossing T's and dotting I's.

"Right down that hall," the woman said, pointing. "Make a left and you'll see the 100s near the fire exit. They have the first three. Want me to give them a ring?"

"Oh no, don't bother. I'll use my phone it's in the car."

Matviy and Bilyk turned back through the front doors.

When they regrouped at the van, Matviy laid out the mission.

"Go into the rooms. Secure anything breathing. If they shoot first, neutralize the threat."

He studied his men. "Bilyk you take these two. Room 110. You two on me. The last pair 112."

He gave a final command. "Let's go."

By now, darkness had fallen. In black attire, they melted into the night as they crept toward the fire exit. Matviy's heart rate ticked upward. This could be an ambush. He hoped the targets were inside, unprepared for the shock-and-awe approach he demanded. These rooms were their only lead.

As they slipped through the side door, the thought nagged him how much he had missed this feeling. The rush of an operation, the edge of danger. He hadn't felt it in years, not since leading men into battle. Lunches with the President's advisors to talk war strategy hadn't scratched the itch. Civilian life dulled it, but here here it surged back in full force.

Through the dim-lit corridor, they followed the signs to the target rooms. At 111, Matviy drew his pistol, eased the slide back until the chamber glimmered with a silver round, then let it click forward.

The hallway was silent, save for muffled televisions behind closed doors. A black cat sat curled beside a potted plant near the fire exit, its eyes glinting in the low light.

Bilyk and his two men positioned themselves outside Room 110. Their eyes met, and Bilyk gave the signal.

The man on his left slung his rifle over his shoulder, letting it dangle by its strap. From his cargo pocket he pulled a multi-tool and a penlight. He clicked on the light, clenched it between his teeth, and angled the beam on the keyhole. After a quick inspection, he nodded familiar lock.

He snapped open the multi-tool, exposing a flathead screwdriver, and slid it into the keyhole. Moving slow, careful not to make a sound, he twisted until it caught on the latch. Click.

They were in.

The man stepped aside. Bilyk pressed the tip of his rifle against the door and eased it open. He froze, listening. Silence. A glance down the hall still clear. Then he slipped inside. The others followed.

Rifles up, they moved in formation. The suite was larger than expected, with four beds positioned at angles, each flanked by nightstands and lamps. Covers pulled up, but not neatly made.

In the center sat a round table with four chairs and a phone. Curtains were drawn, letting in a faint streetlight glow across the beige carpet.

As the men cleared space, the door swung shut behind them. Darkness pressed in, broken only by the thin glare seeping through the curtain. The room smelled of stale sweat and dirty socks.

It looked tidy, but lived in. Whoever stayed here had been moving constantly, traveling light, leaving almost nothing behind.

Bilyk moved to the curtains and tugged them shut completely. "Lights," he ordered.

The man by the door flipped the switch. A fluorescent tube flickered, then hummed to life.

"Now we toss the place." A glint of glee crept into Bilyk's voice.

One by one, the men snapped on latex gloves.

"Be careful. Look for notebooks, receipts anything with writing on it. I'll take the bathroom. You two, start here."

While the two men started in the bedroom, Bilyk headed down the narrow hallway. He checked the bathroom nothing but half-empty complimentary hotel shampoo bottles and used soap. The trash can beside the toilet was empty. They searched the closets and behind the fixtures. Satisfied that nothing was hidden in the bathroom, he returned to the bedroom and saw one of the men with half his body under the bed.

"Got something," the man called out.

He struggled for a moment, pulling hard on something, but emerged empty-handed.

"Nothing," he said regretfully.

Bilyk stood in the center of the suite, taking it all in. The space felt lived in, so where had they gone? By the look of things, housekeeping hadn't been through. The suite was special-ops tidy no personal effects left behind. No pocket change, no receipts, not even a used napkin. The occupants had been deliberate about leaving no trace. Some things were slightly out of place, but with the front desk kept out of the loop, it seemed the occupants had vanished into thin air and weren't planning on coming back.

The other men cleared their assigned rooms and also came up empty-handed. One of the men in Room 112 did a last-minute search of the bathroom closet and found a black backpack.

Matviy and his two men entered Room 110. Bilyk turned around, their eyes met, and he gave a disappointed shrug.

"Cleared?" Matviy asked.

"Yes, sir. All cleared."

Matviy folded his right arm across his chest, cupped his chin with his left hand, and rested a finger across his lips. Bilyk could see the old man's wheels turning.

Matviy sauntered over to the round table, picked up the phone, and pressed zero for the front desk.

"Front desk," a woman answered, giving her name. "How may I help you?"

"Hi, it's me again. I found my men, and we're leaving for military training. Can you prepare a copy of the charges?"

"Yes, of course. I'll have it emailed immediately."

"Heavens, no. We've shut down our computers, so a hard copy will do. I'm sending one of my men to pick it up."

"Okay," the woman said begrudgingly.

Matviy gave a nod to one of his men, who immediately exited the room. True to her word, the desk clerk delivered. Five minutes later, the man reentered with a detailed, itemized bill.

Matviy took it, scanned the page, and found the occupant information section. Only initials were listed no full name. Strange. No hotel would allow a reservation under just initials, unless it planned on running a charity.

In the payment section, he saw the last four digits of a credit card, but the balance was zero. How? If the guests had paid in advance, the clerk would at least have received a checkout notice. But she hadn't. Very strange.

The last two men entered Room 110 to rejoin the rest of the crew. Bilyk gave a dissatisfied shake of the head to the man in front. The man behind produced a black backpack, a 5.11 tactical model.

"Found this in the bathroom closet," he said, tossing it to Bilyk.

Bilyk placed it on the bed and began rummaging through it. Inside, he found a T-shirt, a pair of pants, black combat boots, and a folded sheet of paper. Opening it, he saw a layout of an airstrip marked with airplane hangars, the word Antonov-225 drawn inside a crosshair.

He laid the paper face up on the table, then turned the backpack upside down and gave it a violent shake. From a hidden compartment, a red passport dropped to the floor. A moment later, a pair of women's underwear slipped out beside it.

Bilyk pulled a pen from his pocket and used the tip to lift the underwear, earning chuckles from the men. He let it fall, then picked up the passport.

On the cover were the words "Russian Federation," embossed in bold letters. At the center gleamed the coat of arms: a golden two-headed eagle with wings spread wide, set against a four-cornered red heraldic shield with rounded edges. Two small crowns rested on each head, topped by a larger crown connected with a ribbon. In one claw, the eagle held a scepter; in the other, an orb. On the shield, Saint George speared a black dragon.

Matviy stepped closer, picking up both the paper and the passport. He studied them intently, immediately recognizing the document for what it was. Opening it, he scanned for the name.

It read: Nikolai Petrov.

Who are you, Mr. Petrov? Matviy thought. He didn't know the man, but he had learned one thing: Petrov was a Russian citizen.

And what business do you have in Ukraine, Mr. Petrov?

Matviy studied the diagram on the folded paper and gasped when he realized the plane in question the Antonov was indeed the target. It had been left behind by what could only be described as an enemy combatant. They were too late; the occupants of the hideout were gone.

Still staring at the markings, Matviy stepped into the hallway. Suddenly, a door creaked open at the far end. A man in a jogging suit and white sneakers appeared, his figure lit by the glow from outside. He froze when his eyes locked with Matviy's.

The man in the jogging suit took two quick steps back, reaching for something at his waistband.

"Hey! You stop right there!" Matviy shouted, but the man was already bolting through the door.

Bilyk and the rest of the crew rushed out with their guns drawn, but it was too late. By the time they reached the parking lot, a Toyota 4Runner was tearing out, gravel spraying as its tires screeched against the pavement.

Matviy caught sight of a silhouetted woman in the passenger seat. He couldn't see who else inside the vehicle.

Bilyk raised his assault rifle to take aim, but Matviy pressed his palm against the barrel, lowering it.

"No. He'll take us to the rest."

In one swift, practiced motion, Matviy and his men piled into the Sprinter van, with Bilyk behind the wheel.

The 4Runner sped east on the M03 highway, the van closing in to within 300 yards.

"Faster, faster!" Matviy barked.

Bilyk slammed the gas, the pedal flush to the floor, closing the gap to 200 yards.

Matviy opened the glove compartment and pulled out a revolver fitted with a tracker. With a flick of his wrist, the cylinder snapped open. Loaded. He spun it shut, rolled down the window, and leaned halfway out of the passenger side.

"Steady … yes, right there."

Matviy steadied his aim, focusing his sights on the back of the SUV and pulled the trigger. A black cartridge shot from the revolver's barrel and clattered against the bumper.

Lowering himself back into his seat, he told Bilyk to ease off the gas, letting the SUV create some distance. If they were lucky, it would lead them straight to the rest of the crew.

The Sprinter slowed slightly as the gap widened. Matviy pulled a small tablet from the same compartment and stared at the screen. One … two … three Mississippi. A red blip appeared. The 4Runner. It was headed northeast on the M03 toward Kharkiv.

Both vehicles wove through heavy late-night traffic, which was sparse at this hour. They tracked the SUV for miles until patches of snow began to appear in the roadside ditches and the asphalt grew slick. Signs for Kharkiv and Sumy flashed past. The terrain grew rural, thick forests pressing against either side of the highway.

Bilyk shifted in his seat. "Where the hell is he going? Belarus?" he muttered.

"He's a long way from Belarus. Just keep driving," the boss said flatly.

Bilyk gripped the steering wheel, his knuckles turning white.

"Tonight, justice will be served. How are we on gas?"

Bilyk glanced at the gauge half a tank.

"We're good, boss."

Matviy noticed the blip veer off course.

"He's getting off the highway just ahead."

Bilyk punched the accelerator, and soon the Sprinter's headlights swept across an exit sign. He took the turn, then veered north about fifty yards onto a dirt road.

The blip continued north.

The SUV had slowed to cross a shallow creek in the road when the Sprinter's headlights rounded a bend and lit up its rear end.

POP. POP. POP.

Shots rang out from the SUV, striking the Sprinter on the hood and the right side. The van swerved left as the SUV tore ahead at high speed, creating distance along the narrow, winding road by the Kharkiv River.

The Sprinter lurched over rocks embedded in the creek bed before climbing back onto the dirt road, resuming pursuit. Bilyk stole a glance at the tablet the blip still pulsed steadily on the screen.

By now the moon was at its brightest, hanging high in the night sky. Dark clouds drifted across it at a snail's pace.

Half a mile ahead, the SUV reached a fork in the road and veered left, its headlights sweeping across a weathered sign: CLOSED AIRSTRIP. Another sign in the same direction pointed toward POLTAVA LODGE, marked with the image of a cabin.

Inside the SUV, the driver pulled out his cell phone, scrolling through his contacts until he stopped at the name Boris. He hit dial.

"Hey, where are you?" he asked in a thick Russian accent.

"We've got company. Drop everything and head to the plane. Now!"

"Petrov, what's going on?" the voice on the other end demanded.

Petrov hardened his tone. "Boris, we have no time for questions. Get everyone to the plane now. Go, go, go!"

Beside him, the woman clung to the grab handle as the SUV bounced wildly down the dirt road. Petrov's eyes flicked between the windshield and the rearview mirror. He saw no headlights, but he knew the chase was still on.

Back at the fork, Bilyk checked the tablet, then turned left toward the airstrip.

"Faster, faster!" Matviy barked. He glanced back at the men in the rear seats.

"There's a dead end two miles ahead. Be ready."

He turned forward again, resting the tablet on his lap. Calmly, he unholstered his sidearm, racked the slide to check the chamber, confirmed a round was loaded, and slid it back into place. Satisfied, he reholstered.

The van jolted over ruts, the driver gripping the wheel tight, keeping pace despite the rough terrain. Silence settled over the crew as they scanned the trees and roadside. On both sides, the shoulders dropped into shallow ditches, choked with knee-high weeds dusted in snow.

The gravel glistened under the moonlight.

"I think he's turning again."

Matviy paused, eyes locked on the tablet.

"To the right this time!" he shouted.

Up ahead, Petrov drove hard for two minutes before catching a flicker of headlights in his rearview mirror.

"Sasha, we have to stall them."

She looked forward. The outline of a cabin loomed ahead.

"Look." She pointed to a leaning light pole, tilted at nearly seventy degrees above the road.

"Ram it."

Petrov considered the move, then nodded. She was right the pole would make a perfect barricade. He flashed a faint smile.

"Brace yourself."

He slammed the pedal to the floor. The SUV surged, the needle climbing past ninety. A quick glance in the rearview confirmed the Sprinter's headlights were gone, hidden by the bend in the road.

Sasha gripped the handle as the SUV slammed head-on into the pole. The impact jolted both of them violently, airbags bursting against their chests.

"Ouch," Petrov muttered, wincing as he touched his temple.

A low groan followed. Then another. The pole creaked under the strain, bending.

"Quickly!"

Petrov slashed his airbag with a pocketknife, then cut his seatbelt. He handed the blade to Sasha, and she followed suit. They forced the doors open and scrambled out barely a second before the pole toppled, crashing across the SUV and collapsing onto the road at a perpendicular angle.

Panting, they sprinted over a small hill and down into the cabin's parking lot. Behind it, a tower pulsed with a flashing red light.

Meanwhile, Bilyk glanced at the tablet. The red blip had stopped moving.

"Look they've stopped." He pointed at the screen.

Easing off the gas, he let the Sprinter's speed drop to sixty.

Two minutes later, the Sprinter rounded a corner and came to a halt. The road was blocked. Ahead lay the SUV they had been chasing, smoke curling from its wreckage.

Bilyk slowed the van by another twenty miles per hour before easing it to a stop. The men jumped out, weapons raised in ready-fire position. One by one, they slipped on their night-vision goggles.

In a single-file advance, each man stepped in line behind the other, closing in on the SUV and the massive log sprawled across the road.

Matviy suddenly raised his fist, elbow bent at ninety degrees. The squad froze. Eyes scanned the treeline, the mounds, the shadows.

Silence.

If their targets had set an ambush, they would be hiding behind trees, ridges even inside the wrecked SUV. The crew was ready for a firefight, but first they had to be sure they weren't already under watchful eyes.

Matviy lowered his fist and gestured them forward with a sharp sweep of his hand. The line resumed, slow and deliberate, eyes sweeping every angle.

A quick search of the downed SUV revealed nothing.

Then, faint at first, Matviy caught the whine of an aircraft engine. He turned toward the sound, but the view was blocked by the lodge.

It wasn't lost on him who they were dealing with. These men had already tried to kill his grandson and missed. If they got another chance, they wouldn't fail. And now, it seemed, they were making their getaway.

"Quick hurry!"

The boss shouted, and his men double-timed it into the foliage, skirting mounds, weaving between trees, then descending toward the lodge. They moved with precision and purpose, hoping to reach the airstrip in time.

The downgrade toward the lodge was slick with wet grass, forcing the men to watch their footing one slip and they'd be tumbling head over heels in pursuit of their enemies.

Fifty feet from the cabin's parking lot, they still hadn't taken sniper fire. The silence suggested their targets were already boarding the plane, but that didn't stop the men from scanning rooftops and storage sheds for a hidden shooter.

The engine's roar grew louder.

Truth be told, some of the men weren't sure what they would do once they reached the plane. Open fire? Risk hitting an innocent pilot? What if the pilot was just an unwitting accomplice?

Matviy, for his part, was ninety percent sure these were the same people who had tried to kill his grandson. But neither he, Bilyk, nor any of the others had laid eyes on the targets. If Harvey were here, he could confirm it in an instant. Even if he only identified the woman riding shotgun as the same woman from the club that night, it would give this entire game of cat and mouse a new dimension.

At a trot, they descended to the right of the lodge, pushing through two corrugated steel sheds before skidding to a stop. The tarmac stretched before them.

In the distance, a small plane was completing a U-turn on the runway. It paused briefly, then began taxiing toward the lodge, its engine spooling as it picked up speed.

Matviy raised his binoculars. Through the lenses, he could see the fuselage was bulkier than he'd expected, the wingspan broad and sturdy. The single-engine aircraft accelerated, gathering momentum.

It lifted gracefully into the night, climbing past the lodge, navigation lights blinking softly as it vanished into the midnight clouds.

Then it was gone.

CHAPTER SIX

(DOVER AFB, DELAWARE)

THE COCKPIT DOOR SLID open, and Staff Sergeant Daniels a Black woman in her late twenties with her hair pulled back in a tight bun poked her head inside, hesitant to step fully into the room. The air was thick with tension. Locking eyes with one of the pilots, she said,

"Sir, we're prepared for descent."

"Thanks, Sergeant," Captain Arnott replied.

She slipped back out as the door closed behind her.

Outside, the cargo plane with "USAF" emblazoned across its belly approached the runway. Harvey and his co-pilot, Captain Christopher Webb, thirty-six, already balding, and second only to Harvey on this flight (though first when it came to being the biggest pain in Harvey's ass), looked up from his phone to assist with the landing.

Night had fallen, but a fading band of light still lingered in the sky. The aircraft bled altitude as Harvey and Webb adjusted the speed, lining up for a straight-in approach. Both men worked through their checklists landing gear, flaps, air brakes confirming every system was operational.

During the final descent, Harvey kept his hand steady on the throttle, giving the engines just enough power to maintain control.

"Well, would you look at that," Webb said. "A standing ovation for us, Harv."

Harvey nodded toward the ribbon of runway below, his gloved hands steady on the controls. Raising his right hand to his helmet, he pulled the microphone closer to his lips.

"This is Galaxy, preparing for landing. All looks good on our end."

The intercom crackled. "Tower control here. You're all clear."

Harvey turned to his co-pilot. "If you mean the crowd on the ground, they're always there for these dignified transfers. It's their job."

"Geez, Captain Harvey, I was just making small talk."

"I need your full attention, man. We're trying to land a C-5 Galaxy in the dark on a strip the size of a popsicle stick. You want to fuck this up? Be my guest."

His words cut sharp, but his hands never wavered. No one runs a two-hundred-yard dash only to drop the baton at the finish. He'd done this a thousand times, and while it was never easy, it had become second nature. There was a reason he was named one of the best pilots ever assigned to the 60th Air Mobility Wing. He belonged to a small fraternity of men including his father, who had been the very best.

"Nah, I'll leave it to you," Webb said with a smug sniff. "That way, if you fuck it up, it's your ass, not mine."

Harvey didn't respond. He just rolled the toothpick in his mouth with his tongue, a wide grin spreading across his face. There were two things he never questioned about himself.

One: his innate ability to land a C-5 the largest cargo plane in the USAF arsenal on any strip, anywhere. Even with the tarmac below alive with airmen, fighter jets, Black Hawks, and other cargo planes, he rarely tensed as he threaded the behemoth into the middle of it all.

Two: his looks. Not arrogance just fact. Let's be honest. What are United States Air Force pilots if not a little vain?

You ever seen an ugly one? A pilot who didn't pinch a few nerves in the necks of every woman he passed by? Harvey looked like his father. And his father had been a looker.

The C-5 kissed the runway rear landing gear first, then the nose settling down for a clean finish. The massive frame jolted only slightly as the wheels gripped the concrete, Harvey easing it into a smooth rollout. In the cockpit, he threw the lever to engage reverse thrust, and the engines roared as the plane bled speed. Panels unfolded along the fuselage and wings; air brakes hissed in response. The whole maneuver was seamless just another day's work for two men who had done this a thousand times.

Through the windshield, Harvey looked out at a sprawl of hangars and service members in constant motion. Dusk had fallen, but the base still pulsed with life. Forklifts darted between cargo pullers, headlights crisscrossing like a laser show against the growing dark.

The C-5 rolled down the strip, made a U-turn, and eased to a stop in front of a massive hangar. The aircraft idled patiently as forklifts and belt loaders raced to the gangway. The refueling team swarmed with the precision of a NASCAR pit crew.

In the cockpit, Harvey slipped off his black leather gloves, folded them neatly, and tucked them into the outside pocket of his military-green coveralls.

"You see those knuckles?" Webb nodded at Harvey's right hand purple, swollen, mottled with bruises.

Harvey's lips tightened. It hurt like hell, but he wasn't about to show it. Not with Webb watching.

"Do you see your face?" Harvey shot back.

"Like you can talk," Webb sneered. "I should've clocked you in the mouth instead of the eye at least then you'd shut up for once."

"You hit like a bitch. I've taken worse hits from a"

Harvey stopped himself before the forbidden words slipped out. He adjusted the bandage over his left eye and winced. Webb had landed a solid sucker punch he had to give him that. Still, if they hadn't been mid-flight when it happened, Harvey would have finished him off.

Fights had a way of finding him. Once, back in training, he'd claimed to have fought a man in his sleep to dodge a reprimand from his drill instructor. To his surprise, the excuse had worked. Lucky bastard.

And here he was again. Two weeks ago, it had been a Russian operative in Kyiv. Now, it was his own co-pilot. Harvey was a magnet for confrontation, and trouble always knew where to find him.

Webb's cell phone buzzed, and he snatched it up. Meanwhile, Harvey ran through the post-flight checklist. Despite being a seasoned pilot both in the military and off-the-record settings Harvey was a by-the-book man. Not because he loved rules, he didn't. The rules of the sky were designed to keep you alive, and that' all he needed to believe. His pulsing, bruised right hand was proof enough of that. But Harvey had been trained by the best, and training at that level didn't come through soft words or passionate teaching. It came through militant expectation: demanded perfection, an eye for detail, and consequences for sloppiness. In short? Tough love.

Suddenly, Webb's phone rang again. "Yes, sir," Webb mumbled into the receiver, sinking low in his seat. If he'd been a puppy, his tail would've been tucked between his legs. "Yes, sir, I'll … yes, sir!"

He didn't need to say a word Harvey could tell from his expression that Webb was getting his ass chewed. When Webb finally hung up, Harvey locked eyes with him. Webb looked a little green around the gills. "And how did that go for you?" Harvey asked with a touch of sarcasm.

"How the hell do you think it went?" Webb shot back.

Harvey's mouth tipped into his signature grin as he rolled the toothpick in his mouth, waiting for Webb to continue.

"We have to tell them the truth."

"And what's that exactly?" Harvey asked.

"That you're an asshole, and I was defending myself."

"You know what? Fuck you, Webb." Harvey tore off his safety belt.

"Yeah? Fuck you too." Webb followed suit.

The hydraulics at the front of the C-5 Galaxy engaged, and the nose slowly separated from the fuselage, revealing neat rows of transfer cases. The C-5, a workhorse of the U.S. Air Force, can haul up to 270,000 pounds of cargo, making it one of the largest military transport planes in the world. It has carried everything from three hundred and fifty combat troops to trucks, MRAPs, even Minuteman ICBMs. Sometimes, though, the loads were smaller coffins, for instance. Today was one of those days.

Harvey would be the first to admit this was the hardest part of his job. Cargo drop-offs at Dover Air Base usually meant someone was coming home in a box. Still, he took pride in the solemn duty of returning his fallen brothers-in-arms to their homeland, where they could finally rest in peace.

A crowd had gathered at the opening of the plane, heavy-hearted and tearful. Harvey and Webb stood at attention, side by side, flanked by their aircrew and a few airmen on duty, all waiting to honor the arrival. This was standard practice: anyone present on the flight line when transfer cases arrived was expected to pay respects to fallen comrades. That was exactly what Harvey and Webb were doing saluting the American flag–draped cases before them.

Row by row, Marines, soldiers, airmen, and sailors lay in ice-cooled coffins, a stark contrast to the lives they had lived when they went to war. That night, the formation on the flight line included officers, enlisted airmen, NCO's, and civilian contractors. Together, they rendered a salute amid a heavy, respectful silence. Off to the side, a handful of bystanders family and friends, mostly clung to one another, grief written in their eyes.

Harvey kept stony eyes and a statuesque stance, though his jaw tightened and released in restless rhythm. He had to admit this was the part of the job he loathed. To most onlookers, it appeared clean and ceremonial: rows of perfectly spaced flag-draped caskets. But Harvey had been behind enemy lines with many of these men. With every unload, he saw not boxes but faces, names, and memories.

The air was thick with unspoken grief, broken only by hushed murmurs as the last transfer case was lowered. For the service members present, this was more than ceremony it was reality, a reflection of their way of life. At any moment, it could be their loved ones whose families stood on the sidelines, straining to hold back tears and cries. A dark part of them half-hoped their comrades would leap from the boxes, laughing, shouting "April Fool." But this was no joke. It was final. These men and women had paid the ultimate price they had sworn to accept.

Harvey and his partner Webb had done this too many times to count. Harvey once confided to Webb that he hoped he'd never grow numb to it. Better to feel this side of it, he thought, than the other. The pristine, heroic image of American sacrifice was good for optics. But behind it lay a harsher truth.

What the crowd did not see were the original transfer cases, stacked in the rear of the previous C-5. In the theater of war, nothing was neat. Nothing was perfect. After removal, the cargo bay had to be scrubbed down blood and water swept away with stiff utility brooms. The stench of death clung to the cavernous space long after the bodies were gone.

When soldiers went to war, they crossed oceans as warriors, fresh-faced and restless, brimming with grit. The night before, they drank with their comrades, tossing back shots of Patrón, laughing, hiding their nerves. None of them imagined they would return as cargo in the belly of the C-5 Galaxy.

Once the ceremony ended, Harvey and Webb headed into a briefing room in the Wing Building for the standard debrief. It was late, the crew was exhausted, but Harvey sensed trouble from a mile away. There was an elephant in the room.

At their level in the USAF, there was no room for overthinking or for indulging the human side of things. Everything was work. Mechanical. Robotic. Any deviation from protocol had to be dealt with immediately. Harvey had been turning this over in his mind, knowing the odds were good that sooner or later someone would press him about the incident with Webb in the cockpit. He hadn't expected it to come up so soon.

He was right.

The officers and NCOs gathered, running through the usual list of mission successes and failures. Not a word, however, was spoken about Harvey and Webb's altercation outside the cockpit. It had been a silly clash born of misunderstanding. Webb was as much a hothead as Harvey, and the two of them bickered like an old married couple every chance they got. But underneath it, there was trust. Respect.

Harvey drifted in and out of focus during the debrief, careful not to draw attention. Only one thing occupied his thoughts: sleep. But before he could rest, he'd have to make the long trip back to California this time as a passenger, not a pilot.

CHAPTER SEVEN

(THE O-CLUB & THE SCIF)

Back at Travis Air Force Base, Harvey woke from an afternoon nap to the sound of his smartphone pinging. Still half-asleep, he squinted at the screen: We're heading to the O-Club.

He checked the time 1400 hours. A few of the other pilots were already making their way to the officers' club for food and drinks before the afternoon briefing. With only a few minutes to spare, Harvey jumped to his feet.

He splashed his face with cold water, shook it off, and grabbed a towel from the rack above the sink. After drying off, he smoothed his hair into place and pulled on an olive-green Nomex flight suit from the closet. He double-checked that his captain's insignia was properly fastened before heading out.

At the O-Club, his buddies were gathered in a large booth, eating and trading stories about "fly-boy and fly-girl stuff." Most were dressed in workout gear, ready for physical training later in the day. Across the room, a group of field-grade officers looked sharp in full dress uniforms, while the company-grade officers opted for lighter attire tied to their duty stations.

"Whassup, guys?" Harvey leaned over the booth, towering above the group. Seven pairs of eyes turned toward him. Among them was Christopher Webb. Beside Webb sat First Lieutenant Juanito Jamison and First Lieutenant Abby Smith both F-15 pilots out of Keesler Air Force Base in Biloxi, Mississippi.

"Glad you decided to join us," said Captain Christian Fingerle, a German American and a damn good pilot something he loved to remind anyone willing to listen. His spiky blond hair and chiseled jawline gave him a boyish look, even with his German ancestry. Christian could push an F-16 to its absolute limits better than most. A seasoned dogfighter, he had flown combat missions in Iraq and earned several ribbons and commendations.

"Hey, Christian. Hey, gang," Harvey said as he slid into the edge of the booth beside Captain Teddy Mezyoire, who sat next to First Lieutenant Grant Seymour both from Holloman Air Force Base, home of the F-22 Raptor. Across from Harvey, at the opposite edge, sat First Lieutenant Morgan Hale.

Harvey had interrupted a heated debate over which jet reigned supreme: the F-16 Falcon or the fifth-generation F-22 Raptor. The consensus leaned toward the Raptor, praised for its stealth, supercruise capabilities, and advanced avionics. Still, the Falcon had its defenders, valued for its versatility, cost-effectiveness, and rugged durability.

The real question, bouncing around the booth, was simple: in the chaos of battle, would you rather fly a nimble machine striking from a distance, or a scrappy dogfighter weaving through the weeds?

Webb, not being a fighter pilot, stayed quiet, nursing his drink while the so-called alphas pounded their chests.

"What do you got there?" Hale asked.

Harvey picked up the can and turned the label toward Hale.

"Monster Energy. I'm gonna need it to stay awake through that briefing."

He took a sip, then set the can back on the table.

"So, what'd you all order?"

One by one, they went around the table, calling out their meals until the attention landed on Webb. The booth fell silent. After a long pause, he muttered,

"Caesar salad."

"Geez, was that so difficult?" someone said.

"Yo, what's with you two?" Christian cut in, eyeing Webb and Harvey. "All this bickering like some old married couple."

Morgan smirked. "Are they ever going to pair you two up again?"

Christian shook his head. "After what happened last time? I'd be surprised if one of them doesn't get reassigned."

"You two have got to learn to work together," Morgan said firmly.

"He started it I just finished it," Webb shot back with a smirk.

"This isn't over," Harvey muttered.

Webb let out a long, persecuted sigh.

"You act like you didn't sign up for this. Maybe the stress is getting to you," Christian said, trying to play peacemaker, though his tone was indifferent.

"I mean, I could've walked away from it by now," Webb replied, his voice low. "But at this point … what else would I even do? This is the only life I know taking orders, flying planes, and putting up with his bullshit."

Harvey wagged a finger in Webb's direction. They were starting to draw the attention of the higher-ranking officers in the room attention Harvey didn't need right now.

"Cocky son of a bitch," Webb muttered under his breath.

Harvey didn't give him the satisfaction of a response. Instead, he clenched his fist under the table, wincing at the pain in his bruised knuckles. One more crash into Webb's face and his hand would probably break and a pilot without hands wasn't a pilot at all. If not for that minor inconvenience, he'd gladly risk the fracture just to watch Webb hit the floor.

Abby leaned forward, giving Harvey a once-over.

"Why are you all dressed up?"

"Got a call from Jim. Told me to be in uniform."

Lieutenant Jamison let out a sigh. "You in some kind of trouble?" He barely got the words out before adding, "Oh yeah that's right."

Not in the mood for Webb's games, Harvey pushed back from the booth. "Hey, Abby, can I talk to you for a sec?"

Abby slid past Jamison and Webb, following Harvey out of earshot. Nearly six feet tall, she had a lean, athletic build, thick brown hair, and deep-set, steel-gray eyes that matched her California tan. She carried the whole surfer-girl package, complete with six-pack abs she wasn't shy about showing off especially during squadron PT sessions.

"You gonna let him take your girl like that?" Christian teased, turning toward Webb.

"She's not my girl!" Webb shot back, his voice sharp. Christian was clearly getting under his skin.

"That's not what I heard," Christian pressed, unrelenting, unconcerned about Webb's rising temper.

"Just shut up. Everybody shut the fuck up!" Webb exploded. He'd had enough.

A few hours later, they all sat in the briefing room on their best behavior. With his hands clasped in his lap, Harvey stayed quiet, focusing on the man at the podium. Abby, Grant, Teddy, Christian, Jamison, and Morgan were spread across the room inside the Sensitive Compartmented Information Facility better known as the SCIF.

At the front stood retired aviator James Vanderbeer, the American flag draped across the back wall behind him. Jumbo screens lined every available wall, though all were currently dimmed in sleep mode. Every seat in the room was filled, with late arrivals forced to stand in the back.

This wasn't the usual snooze-fest junior officers had come to expect from daily briefings. This one was different this one was special. And Harvey was the man of the hour.

"We are gathered here today to make right what we were unable to do last month," Vanderbeer began, his voice carrying across the room. "Some of us were on leave during the last promotion ceremony, so today we correct that.

"Let me speak quickly on what promotion means. Promotion is not a reward. Promotion is recognition of an officer's ability to accept higher levels of responsibility. We are asking this young man to shoulder a heavier burden than he already has over the last ten years of his career. Going from captain to field grade is a major transition, and we are honored today to have with us General Higby."

Mr. Vanderbeer stepped away from the podium and motioned for Harvey to move to the front of the room. The hoots and hollers from the junior officers quickly died down when Jim raised a single fist in the air.

Turning to the commander, Vanderbeer said simply, "General."

Brigadier General Thomas Higby was a man among men tall, with golden-brown hair and a chiseled jawline. He looked every bit the part, down to the wire-rimmed glasses perched on the bridge of his nose. He was the kind of man you noticed when he entered a room and not just because military bearing demanded it. His presence commanded attention.

He wore his battle dress uniform, a single silver star gleaming on each lapel and one set prominently at the center of his chest.

General Higby and Captain Harvey Arnott stood at attention, facing the audience, as a lieutenant colonel stepped forward and read from the orders in her hand.

"Attention to orders. The President of the United States has reposed special trust and confidence in the patriotism, valor, fidelity, and abilities of Harvey Arnott. He has demonstrated potential for increased responsibility and is hereby promoted to the rank of Major."

Webb snickered. Harvey swallowed hard as the words trailed off, becoming background noise. He had done it. He'd told his dad, long before his passing, that he would one day take command of a flying squadron and now, he was on his way. But his father wouldn't be there to see it.

Harvey drifted back into consciousness just as the General stared into his soul while pinning on the rank of major. This time, the hooting and hollering from friends and colleagues went unchecked.

The room gradually emptied, and only those with a need to know were allowed to remain. Once the doors shut, the screens flickered to life, and General Higby stepped up to the podium.

The General began outlining recent world events across the Middle East, Southeast Asia, and Europe. Webb, however, was distracted, contemplating the new dynamic of their relationship. After all, Harvey was now his superior officer, and Webb knew he'd have to dial things back sooner rather than later.

Abby stole a glance at the brand-new major. Harvey met her gaze with a grin. Webb noticed.

General Higby had been speaking for about five minutes, addressing the drawdown of U.S. forces from Iraq and Afghanistan and what that would mean for future flying missions. Then the screen behind him lit up, revealing the most magnificent flying machine the room had ever seen: the Antonov An-225.

Eyes widened in amazement.

"Ladies and gentlemen,"

General Higby addressed the room full of aviators some were fighter pilots, and then there were the others. The others were those who, more often than not, didn't quite make the cut to fly one of the high-speed racers.

Fighter pilots were the cool guys. Everyone with a silver wing on their uniform aspired to be one of them. Those who didn't pass the brutal selection process or failed to meet some near-impossible standard during evaluations ended up flying C-5s or other cargo airbuses.

Harvey had always wanted to be a strike pilot, just like his father and grandfather. But due to vision issues, he was relegated to cargo planes. The bitterness he once felt about missing out on fighter jets had long since faded. He only wished his wingman and partner in crime, Captain Christopher Webb, could say the same.

"Maybe we still get to have a little fun after all," the General said, lightening the mood.

Seeing the General give the briefing himself meant it was a big deal. Harvey knew that.

The General or "Tommy," as Harvey's dad used to call him was top dog when it came to anything that mattered. If you saw his face, it meant business. It meant something was going down something few people could know about. Something that threatened national security.

Standing at attention at the front of the room beside the commander, Harvey could only think of his father. He remembered all the stories his dad used to tell him those wild tales of the old flying days with his buddy Tommy. They'd served together back in their prime. And though they'd butted heads and occasionally knocked fists, they were tight.

Maybe there's hope for Webb and me after all, Harvey thought.

He refocused on the image projected on the screen.

The massive structure before them was the largest and heaviest cargo aircraft ever built capable of transporting ultra-heavy, oversized freight of nearly any shape and size. It had been designed to haul components for the Soviet-Russian space program.

The plane's frame was stark white, its belly wrapped in blue and gold stripes that ran the full length of the aircraft. A modern marvel. That much was clear to every eye in the room.

"Welcome to Operation 225," the General said, continuing the briefing.

"If you're in this room, you've been selected and cleared for this intel. You're the best at what you do even if some of you still have a little growing up to do."

The General tilted his head downward and peered over the frame of his glasses, locking eyes with the new major. Harvey shifted uncomfortably in his seat. Jim noticed the other pilots snickering.

Webb and Harvey felt the attention in the room zero in on them just as an image of Ukraine's maritime territory appeared on the jumbo screen. The calm, blue body of water filled the display.

"Two weeks ago, a Ukrainian boat crew encountered a Russian warship the Admiral Kuznetsov in the Black Sea."

Hearing this, Harvey perked up and glanced around, checking to see if anyone was watching him. He was well aware of the incident. What he didn't know was which version they were about to be told the unvarnished truth, or the Washington D.C. spin.

"We have reason to believe Russia intends to destabilize this region starting with Ukraine. This is more than intimidation. Washington believes an attack is imminent. Ukraine is a U.S. ally, and we've been tasked with protecting a highly valuable asset on the ground. Jim." he called out.

Vanderbeer clicked the remote. Another image appeared this time, the Antonov, sitting outside an airplane hangar.

"This is Ukraine's crown jewel in the aviation world and now, she's a sitting duck in what's about to become hostile territory if Russia succeeds. President Zelensky needs our help to get her out.

There have been previous failed attempts by the Russians to seize or destroy this aircraft but things have changed. This time, we believe they'll succeed if given another shot.

Two of our own will be selected to lead the mission. It's a quick exfil get in and get out, fast. The Pentagon will be running point on this one. Your mission is to learn the Antonov An-225 like the back of your hand. Good luck."

He nodded toward the team. "Jim will fill you in on the rest. Any questions?"

He waited. When no one spoke, the general said, "Good luck, ladies and gentlemen."

The room snapped to attention as the general exited the SCIF. Once the door closed, Vanderbeer resumed the briefing.

"This mission needs 110% from everyone. A lot is at stake. The asset is currently on the ground in Kyiv."

Vanderbeer clicked the remote, and the screen changed. Gasps and low whistles echoed through the room as everyone stared at the interior photo of a gargantuan aircraft. It was, without question, a thing of beauty.

"Jesus Christ," Webb muttered. "What in God's name is that?"

"That's the ANTONOV-225. You could damn near fit a C-5 in that belly," Jim said.

Harvey had to admit it was a sight to behold. It made the Galaxy, or any other aircraft he'd ever flown, look small. Vanderbeer continued.

"A plane that size, with that kind of cargo capacity, could deliver a catastrophic amount of weapons to the wrong people. We can't let the Russians get their hands on it."

"So why don't we just blow the damn thing up?" Christian asked.

"Because our taxpayers and the United States Congress say otherwise," Vanderbeer snarled, scowling.

It all made sense to Harvey. A plane that massive could cause untold destruction or do incredible good, if kept in the right hands. And somehow, he felt a connection to the beast, unlike any other pilot in the room. Around him, the others murmured and exchanged hushed remarks, eyes fixed on the massive aircraft.

"Quiet down," Vanderbeer snapped, casting a sharp look around the room.

Harvey leaned forward, fully tuned in. The Antonov-225 was a rare beauty. At 84 meters long with an 88.4-meter wingspan, it was larger than a football field and weighed 640 metric tons. On a single trip, it could haul more than 250,000 kilograms of cargo that's like carrying 50 fully loaded semis through the sky, he marveled. Six thunderous engines powered it, and it rested on 32 of the largest wheels ever engineered. She was a flying fortress an aviation machine on steroids.

"We're going to fly her out away from prying eyes. Namely, Russia," Vanderbeer said. "It's a quick exfil, just like the General said. Stand by for your assignments. Some of you will be flying her out. The rest will be on standby in case something goes wrong."

Vanderbeer tried to rally the group, reminding them as if they needed reminding that the United States Air Force was the best in the world. If a mountain needed moving, no other group of men and women was more qualified. Whispers rippled through the room as pilots quietly speculated who would be doing what.

"Imagine trying to get that thing off the ground while taking fire," Webb chuckled. "It's fucking colossal. Gotta take at least a dozen men to fly it."

"… Or women," Abby added.

"No way a chick is flying that thing," Christian muttered.

Christian was known for his off-color, sometimes sexist remarks. Everyone knew he didn't mean harm, he was just a jerk. They'd long since learned to ignore him when he said things that could raise eyebrows.

Trying to regain control of the room, Vanderbeer pressed on.

"Yes, it is colossal, Captain. But we fly…"

And in unison, the entire room recited the Air Force mission statement, finishing Vanderbeer's words:

"… fight and win."

The room erupted in enthusiastic shouts and applause.

Harvey, meanwhile, was lost in thought. The AN-225 was easily the most impressive aircraft he'd ever seen. With Russia pressing in on Ukraine's borders and potentially seizing control of the capital this mission was practically suicidal. You couldn't exactly sneak something that massive into the sky unnoticed. It was going to draw eyes the moment its wheels lifted off the ground.

But this was exactly the kind of mission that drove Harvey. He hadn't joined the Air Force to loiter around garrisons, polishing aircrafts and clearing birds' nests out of engines. Risky or not, this was what he'd signed up for.

He didn't know the plan. But he knew one thing: he had to be the one flying that plane.

Then again, there was the promise he'd made to himself never to set foot on Eastern European soil again. Not after what happened the last time. Not if he wanted to avoid becoming a footnote in a cold case file the U.S. government wouldn't or couldn't touch for decades to come.

Jim brought the meeting to a close with a final reminder about the upcoming dress rehearsal.

"You'll receive your orders tomorrow morning at 0900. Then report to San Diego Naval Station for Joint Task Force training. Understood?"

"Yes, sir," the room echoed.

And just like that, they were dismissed.

CHAPTER EIGHT

(ASSIGNMENTS, IRON HORSE)

As the target came into view, a cluster of instruments lit up, accompanied by radio chatter confirming multiple threat locations. For a moment, the cockpit needles spiked brief flashes of radioactivity contrasting sharply with the otherwise silent light show outside the canopy.

Abby gripped the stick tightly between her legs. With her right thumb, she flipped the cap and raised the master arm switch.

"Come on … steadyyyyyyy," she whispered to herself, eyes fixed on the HUD as it locked onto several emerging targets. Right on time, she thought.

The radar cursor bounced across the display like a metronome. Pulling the trigger now would be useless it would send a guided missile straight into dense forest.

"Hold on to your seat," she said into the headset, warning her co-pilot seated in the rear of the F-15E Strike Eagle.

"Roger, Holly," came the response.

Harvey responded quickly, leaning over her left shoulder just as Moscow came into view. It was the first time he'd used her call sign seriously until now, he'd only said it in bed.

She squeezed the trigger. With a lurch, Harvey felt a missile detach from the jet. It ignited with a roar, giving the F-15 a subtle jolt before streaking toward its target like a jaguar with a fiery tail. Through his goggles, Harvey tracked it dead on.

A sudden flash lit up the sky, briefly blinding them. A muffled boom followed, jolting both pilots in their seatbacks. Abby nudged the stick, rolling the jet right, then leveling as they passed over a burning warehouse below. The Strike Eagle surged forward into the cold night, Moscow now off their left wing.

"You okay back there?"

Harvey leaned forward, straining against his harness. He raised a thumb above Abby's shoulder just high enough for her to catch in her rearview mirror. She nodded.

He shifted, trying to relieve the stiffness from hours in the seat. It wasn't easy for him, being second in command. He was used to being in control. But this wasn't a cargo plane this was a supersonic jet, and Abby was the only fighter pilot onboard.

Harvey admired her. Even staring at the back of her helmet, he imagined she looked fierce bringing death from above. They were alone, with one more target near Moscow before returning to the U.S. Navy carrier in the Black Sea.

Abby scanned her fuel gauge and swept the horizon for threats. Her eyes locked on a mesmerizing confusion of distant, moving lights. Harvey, parched, realized his mouth was dry. He reached into his G-suit, pulled out a small canteen, and took a swig before sealing it and placing it back in its pocket.

Suddenly, flashes from five miles below drew their attention. Through the windscreen, the lights grew larger as the altimeter ticked lower. Moscow, from up here, was beautiful.

Then a blip on radar.

A pre-recorded female voice filled the cockpit.

"Flight control, flight control."

A pause. Then: "Engage. Engage."

Warning lights exploded across the panels. Red strobes, alerts, and sirens overwhelmed the digital displays.

WARNING. WARNING.

Sweat beaded on Harvey's forehead. Panic rose.

In the distance, a cluster of flashing red lights approached fast. Bogeys, he realized. Gaining.

He whispered a prayer and opened his eyes just in time to see a miniature sun racing toward them.

Abby locked on to her radar. Three tight blips. Rotating scatter lights climbed from the ground below. They were closing in fast.

Sensing imminent danger, she slammed the afterburner. The jet vomited thick red and blue flames, rocketing forward like lightning.

But the missile was faster.

Just before it struck the underbelly of the Strike Eagle, Harvey squeezed his eyes shut then opened.

When Harvey opened his eyes, adjusting to the hint of daylight peeking through the curtains, the first thing he saw was a mass of thick brown hair resting on his right arm now completely numb.

He took a deep breath. The strike mission had only been a dream.

Just a dream, he thought.

Still, better than the others the ones where he was being interrogated by Ukrainian agents for murder. Even in his sleep, it seemed, he was crushing on Abby. They weren't officially a couple, but he had a feeling it wouldn't be long.

Carefully, he shifted to free his arm from beneath her head. As he raised himself slightly, his eyes caught a glimpse of her bare hip peeking out from beneath the covers. He was reminded, not for the first time, why he found her so attractive.

Gently, he slid his arm away, and as blood rushed back into his fingertips, he rolled over.

"Good morning."

The soft voice came from behind him. He turned to face her. They shared a grin, then both glanced at the desk clock with its glowing red digits: 0600 hours.

Two hours until the morning brief.

Harvey was a night owl. He was used to sleeping in, especially on deployed missions, when he flew nighttime ops for troop movements. But this wasn't a war zone. He'd need to report to the ready room like everyone else.

Abby kissed his shoulder before gracefully sliding out of bed. She pulled on a pink robe and disappeared into the bathroom.

Harvey grabbed his phone and tapped the screen. It lit up instantly, headlines and news tickers flooding in everything he'd missed while asleep. He scrolled absently. Deals. Sports. Politics.

Then one headline made him pause: UKRAINIAN PRESIDENT TO VISIT WHITE HOUSE.

He reached for the lamp on the nightstand and clicked it on. Light filled the room. Scanning the floor, he found what he was looking for. His t-shirt and pants were still there. He pulled them on, sat up against the headboard, and opened the article.

He got so caught up in reading that he didn't notice twenty-five minutes had passed.

Abby stepped out of the bathroom without the bath robe. Her hair was tied in a tight military bun, her face brushed with light makeup. She was the type who wore it occasionally, though she never needed it.

She walked to the closet and stood in front of a flight suit hanging on a hook, her back to him.

"Are you coming to San Diego?"

She asked the question while unbuttoning her pajama top.

Harvey glanced over. He knew exactly what she meant. She was asking if he'd come watch the Joint Task Force exercise, even though he wasn't required to be there. It wouldn't hurt to see his face in the crowd, she thought.

Abby had curves. Not too little, not too much just enough.

"Do you want me to?" he asked, already knowing the answer.

She shot him an *are you serious?* look over her left shoulder, then turned back to the closet. As she undid the last button, she peeled the shirt off her back. Harvey's eyes followed the shape of her V-tapered frame down to her narrow waist. Her shoulders and triceps were sculpted, thanks to all those pull-ups she did in the gym, he figured.

She could feel him staring but didn't turn around. Vanity wasn't her thing.

When the shirt came off completely, he caught a sidelong glimpse of her breast. She slid off her pajama bottoms in a smooth, left-to-right motion. As the fabric pooled at her feet, she stepped out with one leg and kicked the pants into the closet with the other.

Now wearing only a black thong, she reached for her flight suit and stepped into it. She pulled it up to her waist before grabbing a black bra to match. Once the suit was over her shoulders, she zipped it closed, turning to face Harvey as she did.

He didn't look away. He wanted to, but thought it might be weird if she caught him doing so.

"Hurry up, man. You're gonna be late."

Harvey glanced at his watch.

"Nah, I still have forty-five minutes to make it to the morning briefing."

He stood, adjusted his clothes, and headed for the door.

"See you in the ready room," he said softly.

In his khakis and low quarters, Harvey opened the side door to the ready room. His eyes landed on Abby, then on Lt. Jamison, who sat beside her. Across from them were Captain Webb and Lt. Grant Seymour.

Harvey's gaze shifted to Vanderbeer, who was busy adjusting the audio-video equipment at the front of the room. The space was quiet now; most of the pilots had taken their seats and were flipping through manila folders they found tucked into the seatbacks. The squadron's colors blue and black were echoed in the patterned cushions. Emblazoned on each seatback was the squadron emblem: a fighter jet escorting an Airbus, lightning bolts radiating around it.

Harvey chose the row directly behind Abby and Jamison. Easing his way between two rows of high-back chairs, he dropped into a seat next to the German-American.

"Hey there."

"Hey," Christian replied, handing Harvey a manila folder with his name on it.

Captain Christian Fingerle carried an assortment of nicknames, all gifts from his squadron mates when the mood turned rowdy: the Germanator, the Germerican. Sometimes even Drago, since he was a dead ringer for the villain in Rocky IV. Christian was a good sport and he played along, better that than drawing unwanted attention from the comrades.

The fighter pilots wore flight suits and looked mission-ready. Tanker and cargo pilots, by contrast, sported khakis and variations of their squadron T-shirts.

When the last pilot entered, Vanderbeer secured the room and projected a status update onto the big screen. Heads bent as pilots searched for their names to confirm their assignments.

Harvey spotted his and Webb's names slotted for the Antonov mission. They exchanged a quick glance; Webb forced a smile. Harvey leaned back in his chair, stretching his legs, bracing himself for another snooze-fest.

It didn't take long for James Vanderbeer to break the silence.

"Listen for your call sign."

Vanderbeer began reading aloud, giving the pilots a chance to change their identifiers if they wished. Most stuck with the ones they knew.

"Whiskey One." "Affirmative!" Lt. Jamison shouted.

"Whiskey Two." "Affirmative!" Lt. Hale responded.

"Hollywood."

"Right here!" Abby called out.

"Moneybag."

"Right here!" Lt. Grant replied.

"Drago."

"Negative, sir. It's Rocky."

Vanderbeer peered over his glasses, his look saying: Pick a call sign and stick with it.

"Rocky it is," he said, annotating the correction on the screen.

"Teddy Bear." "Affirmative!" Captain Theodore Meczoire replied.

Finally, Vanderbeer wrapped up. "Major Arnott and Captain Webb, your call signs are as follows. Major, as team lead, you are 225-Alpha. Captain, you are 225-Bravo. Any questions?"

No hands went up. Vanderbeer clicked his remote, and the screen shifted to a slide stamped in bold red letters: TOP SECRET. The slide was divided into two sections: Eastern Europe and Southeast Asia.

"Major," Vanderbeer continued, "you and your team are tasked with delivering munitions and weapons systems authorized by Congress to Ukraine. Afterward, you will retrieve the package and bring her to safety."

He pointed to the image of the Antonov, An-225 projected on the adjacent screen as he finished.

"Teddy Bear is team lead for Southeast Asia. But remember once you're aboard the carrier, the skipper is in charge. You take orders from him. North Korea has been emboldened by Russia's actions outside Ukraine, so be prepared for an act of aggression."

Vanderbeer tapped a button on his computer, and the screens went dark.

"You are all to report to Naval Base San Diego for JTF training. That's Joint Task Force training, in case any of you have forgotten. Now go fly, fight, and win."

With a single, thunderous burst, the room erupted:

"HOAH!"

CHAPTER NINE

(USS MIDWAY. TRAINING DAY-1)

At thirty-eight, Harvey was at the pinnacle of his flying career as an air mobility pilot with a spotless record but the upcoming assignment to Ukraine weighed heavily on him. With more than 4,000 flight hours logged, he was seriously considering a move into the private sector.

For fifteen years, he had lived in the cockpits of the C-5 Galaxy and the C-17 Globemaster. He sometimes regretted not pursuing the fighter track after flight school, but over time he'd grown to love the mission: hauling heavy equipment and personnel across the globe whenever duty called. He dreamt of flying one of those rockets more times than he would like to admit.

As he dragged the razor down his right cheek, stripping away a swath of shaving cream and rinsing it into the sink, his thoughts drifted to Abby. He shaved in silence, his mind oscillating between the upcoming naval training where his friends would be risking their lives in supersonic machines and Webb, his co-pilot and constant thorn in his side. Maybe I'll just pull rank, he thought, smirking at his own mock indignation.

For now, the focus was training with the Navy's fighter community in San Diego Bay. Competition was their lifeblood: squadron against squadron, pilots against outside groups, each sortie a relentless pursuit of greatness. Whether in Super Hornets, Strike Eagles, F-16s, F/A-18s, F-22s, or any fourth- or fifth-generation stealth fighter, their ethos was the same— who can do it better.

Most pilots welcomed feedback from both senior and junior officers. Those who didn't were quickly taught humility the old-fashioned way: ready-room mockery.

The dress rehearsal scheduled for today was designed to measure performance, humility, and above all mission capability and readiness.

As Harvey stepped aboard the carrier, he was greeted by the familiar roar of jet engines and clusters of pilots gathered around the closed-circuit flight deck monitor known as the Pilot Landing Aid Television, or PLAT. Every pilot, regardless of experience, had their eyes drawn to the PLAT whenever it flickered on.

From the speakers, Harvey caught the cockpit radio chatter from last week's training flights. The voices were unfamiliar, mostly Navy and Marine aviators but the tension coming from the cockpits were clear. One pilot strained through a final approach. Another landed, missed the arresting cable, lit his afterburner, and clawed back into the sky. Landing on a carrier was always life-or-death. A jet that rolled too far and toppled overboard meant another seventy-million-dollar loss for the taxpayers.

Beneath his boots, Harvey felt the carrier sliding into open waters. By sunset, it had gathered speed, barreling down the Pacific, its massive hull rising and falling with each swell. He had half-expected calmer seas this time of year. With storm clouds gathering overhead, he hoped the thunderstorms would hold off for just one night.

He threaded his way through the carrier toward the stateroom where his buddies and the Air Operations Officer (OPSO) in charge of the exercise were waiting. He ducked through bulkheads, stepped over knee-knockers, and pressed down the passageway as jet blasts thundered above deck.

Halfway there, the ship rolled hard to starboard. Harvey steadied himself against a bulkhead, bounced off the opposite wall, and pushed forward. When the rocking eased, he spotted a familiar face: Major Reginald "Fastball" Ellis.

Ellis had earned the call sign back in officer school, thanks to his endless stories about semi-pro baseball and his reputation for quick decisions. His motto was always the same: Do it now. Ask questions later.

"Sir." Harvey greeted the OPSO.

"Congrats, Major. I heard the news. Why don't you come fly for us?"

Harvey caught the snark in his tone. "No one goes from Air Force to Navy— it's the other way around, sir," he shot back with a quip he knew had to sting. But Fastball had a tough hide.

The OPSO led the way to the ready room. They covered nearly the length of a football field before reaching the Air Ops unit, where Colonel Gregory "Speed" Sanders was already mid-brief in front of the assembled pilots.

Lieutenants Abby, Jamison, Seymour, Hale, and Captain Fingerle sat listening intently to the skipper. Hale was the odd one out. A nugget pilot, she had spent her first six years enlisted in the Army before cross-training, commissioning into the Air Force, and finally earning her wings. She needed exercises like this to sharpen her edge and build confidence.

The room was filled with aviators from the Air Force, Navy, Marines, and Coast Guard. The Coasties were present only as a precaution in case something went sideways. All wore flight suits, the shared uniform of the day.

The skipper's briefing focused on contingencies and the heavy-weather patterns that could produce pitching decks. A pitching deck in the middle of the ocean at night was every pilot's nightmare. The violent rise and fall of the carrier driven by massive swells turned the flight deck into a shifting target. Pilots compared landing in those conditions to threading a needle while power-walking.

Harvey sat in the back beside Fastball, eyes darting between the skipper and a whiteboard covered in grease-pencil markings: pilots' names, call signs, and aircraft assignments. He spotted what he was looking for, Hollywood, Strike Eagle–5. The "5" marked the tail number.

When the briefing wrapped, the skipper swung the door open. A blast of sound hit them jet engines at full roar. "Godspeed!" he bellowed, his voice climbing above the thunder.

An F-14 Tomcat screamed off the flight deck, spitting blue flame and throwing up a rolling mist from its exhaust. The sound tore through the ship in a chest-rattling WHOOSH.

One by one, the officers filed out, heading topside. Fastball glanced at Harvey. "Wanna grab some coffee before heading up?" "Absolutely."

Harvey answered with enthusiasm. The other pilots had already filed out, but the skipper remained hunched over his desk, rifling through a stack of papers.

Fastball and Harvey made for the exit. Before leaving, Harvey paused at the PLAT to scan the flight schedule and weather conditions and, more importantly, to see if he could reach the deck before Abby launched. He studied the acronyms and numbers on the status board, committing them to memory. Abby, Jamison, and Seymour were already checked into Marshall, the holding pattern aft of the ship at 10,000 feet. Strike Eagle, tail number 5, was assigned to CAT-3. Harvey filed it away.

They reached the elevator just as the familiar THUNK of a jet locking into catapult tension echoed through the bow. Coffee steaming from their cups, Fastball and Harvey stepped topside.

A crowd of spectators ringed the deck. Harvey and Fastball joined them in time to hear the click-clack, click-clack of the catapult mechanism retracting. An F/A-18 Hornet crouched on CAT-2, connected to the shuttle. Two massive pistons slid into place. With a hand signal from the deck crew, the cylinders detonated under the pressure of scalding steam, hurling the Hornet forward like a slingshot just as Abby had once described it. The jet roared skyward, noise and fire engulfing the air.

Harvey's expression betrayed his thoughts. Why isn't the skipper or air boss calling this off? The carrier was rolling hard in the swells, the sky black with low clouds, lightning was a real threat within the hour. Still, one by one, fighters were shuttled into the cats.

Why risk it? Harvey asked himself, even though he knew the answer: it wasn't the pilots' call.

Light rain fell as the dark horizon closed in.

"Gonna be a rough night," Harvey muttered. "Yes, it is," Fastball replied. "I'm just glad I'm not the one up there."

The ship banked starboard, the roll sloshing coffee onto Harvey's flight suit. He brushed it away and looked up just in time to see the F-15 Strike Eagle, tail number 5, easing into launch position.

Clickity clack. Clickity clack. Clickity clack.

Harvey's heart sank for Abby. The sky had gone dark, conditions ripe for a mishap. And mishaps carried a price: ridicule, harsh judgment from the LSO, and the cutting mockery of squadron mates.

Tonight's exercise was blue-water ops, and Harvey found himself calculating divert fields in his head. He recalled seeing them posted on the status board in the ready room. A divert was the last resort: if a pilot failed to trap aboard the carrier, they faced a long solo flight to a distant field or, in an emergency with a Mayday call, they'd have no choice but to eject. Then survival depended on luck: avoiding sharks, resisting hypothermia, and hoping rescue came fast enough.

By now, the carrier had launched two F-14 Tomcats and two F/A-18 Super Hornets from the Navy and Marine units. Harvey watched them climb into an overhead diamond, peel into a flawless barrel roll, then vanish into the night sky, inverted and defiant.

"Prepare for butterfly we're riding the blade on the next one." The lead Tomcat's voice crackled over the radio, a mile out from formation.

"Angels on the right. Roger last traffic."

The lead Hornet pilot responded. With that, all four aircraft pushed their throttles to military power and broke away for a final engagement before returning to the carrier.

This was a battle-formation sortie designed to showcase American fighter-jet maneuverability. The planes climbed hard, the horizon rolling beneath them as they reached the apex of a looping climb, lifting with precise vector control.

When they had stretched far enough apart, the lead Tomcat gave the signal. Instantly, they rolled back toward each other cockpits spinning through water, sky, water, sky before leveling off. The flight path traced in the maneuver resembled butterfly wings. Hence the name: butterfly.

The Hornet lead glanced at his temperature gauge holding just below sixty degrees. The formation leveled at 1,800 feet over the ocean. On command, all four slammed their throttles into afterburner, ripping across the horizon while keeping visual and radar lock on one another. Each pilot held the opposite aircraft square in the HUD, radar locked, boxing the opponent in.

Now they were nose-on, closing at over 800 knots. In combat, this would be the instant of missile release, a heat-seeker to annihilate the enemy, or a Sidewinder to finish the kill. But tonight was only rehearsal, a violent ballet disguised as a friendly sparring match.

As they converged, the formation tightened, skimming over the sea and carrier deck. For a moment, each pilot could see into the dim-lit cockpit of the aircraft across from him, even the helmets of the others as they knifed past.

On deck, Harvey drew a sharp breath, mouth agape as the fighters roared overhead, rattling the steel deck and bulkheads. The jets climbed away, contrails carving opposing streaks of white across the dark sky.

"Alright, bring it in," the ops officer called over comms. The pilots understood immediately.

"Roger, Midway. Coming in."

One by one, they bled down to a hundred knots, arcing wide into the landing pattern. Within ten minutes, all four fighters were in glide path. Everything was unfolding by the book, and Harvey liked what he saw. We truly are the best, he thought.

Fastball caught the eye of Captain Louis Phelps, the LSO for night ops, and gave a nod. Phelps stepped over to join them.

"Hey, Ellis, how's it going?" "So far, so good. You've met Harvey, right?" "I can't say that I have."

The LSO extended his hand, and Harvey met it with a firm shake.

"Air Force, right?"

Harvey nodded.

"Any deployments coming up soon?"

"Something like that."

He knew he couldn't reveal much, so he quickly steered the conversation elsewhere. Are we launching all of these guys tonight?"

"Something like that," Phelps answered with a grin.

Well played, Harvey thought.

"The weather looks to improve with the frontal passage, and the Colonel wants every G-suit in the air."

"And recovery?" Harvey asked.

"Haven't had a mishap yet. We've got tankers on standby just in case. What are your concerns?"

"Nothing."

"He's concerned about the pitching deck and the weather," Fastball cut in.

The LSO glanced at the gathering of spectators ducking under cover from the rain. "Hey, wanna join me on the bridge? That's where the real action is."

"Of course."

Fastball and Harvey answered at once. The bridge was the place to be especially on a night like this. Here, dozens of decisions shaped the carrier's course and the performance of every aircraft in the air or on deck.

From the bridge, you could watch safely as a 37,000-pound Hornet slammed into the deck at a descent rate of 700 feet per minute. In the instant the wheels struck, the tailhook snatched a steel arresting cable, stretching it across the deck until the jet screeched to a halt slowing from over 140 miles per hour to zero in seconds.

If the pilot missed coming in too high or too long the Hornet would spark across the deck in full afterburner, clawing skyward again. The alternative was unthinkable: tumbling off the side into the dark abyss below.

Harvey knew all of this, and the knowledge set him on edge. But he also trusted that his squadron mates were trained, capable, and ready. Some cheated a little by taking extra fuel. Two or three more minutes airborne could mean another shot at the trap or a chance to link up with a tanker. This is why in most operations, the fuel gauge is the single most important instrument in the cockpit.

When they reached the bridge, Harvey and Fastball found leaders from other squadrons already gathered. Marines, Navy, Coast Guard. Greetings and head nods were exchanged where appropriate.

The bridge commander didn't budge. A former linebacker with blond hair and a jutting chin, he was the ship's Executive Officer, or EXO. His eyes stayed locked on the PLAT. The other officers were there mainly to provide expertise or to absorb his wrath if a pilot screwed up in the air or on landing.

Harvey passed behind the EXO and offered a quick greeting. The only reply was a growl, the man's gaze never leaving the screen.

Around them, officers critiqued every flicker of movement on the PLAT, judging some of the world's finest pilots as they fought through the night's rough conditions with almost no margin for error. At times, they even joked or laughed. Harvey thought it wrong, but he kept that thought to himself.

The rest of the crew aboard ship had no idea what was happening above them.

A loud ROAR filled the bridge, cutting off conversation and pulling every eye to CAT-3.

On the PLAT monitor, Harvey saw the jet being locked into catapult tension at full power. He recognized the tail number Five. The catapult machinery screamed in reply.

"They're really going through with this," he muttered, more to himself than anyone else.

The Strike Eagle's engines thundered, the rising pitch forcing Harvey and the others to cover their ears. The blast deflectors shook as the jet's twin afterburners spat cones of fire against them. The deck trembled.

The shuttle made its sharp zip, locking the fighter in place. Abby flicked on her external lights, the pulsing glow bathing the deck around her aircraft. She was ready.

On the PLAT, the LED clock ticked down. The Strike Eagle strained against the catapult, guzzling fuel at an unforgiving rate.

Then POP!

The Eagle leapt forward, afterburners clawing at the deck as the catapult hurled it down the track. At the end, a bone-rattling THUNK released her into the sky. The ship shuddered as the jet tore free.

Harvey realized his throat was parched from hanging open in awe. He drained the last sip of his coffee and tossed the cup away.

Abby's voice came crisp over the departure frequency: "Eagle Five airborne. Call sign Hollywood."

She sounded like a pro.

On the PLAT, Harvey watched her climb, banking into her first turn before cutting afterburner to conserve fuel.

Four more to go, Harvey thought.

CHAPTER TEN

(USS MIDWAY. The Recovery)

THE ROAR OF A Hornet recovery above snapped Harvey back to reality he had been on the phone for nearly five minutes. With the Hornet safely aboard, a Super Hornet and two Tomcats were next in line for recovery. Harvey hadn't been present for the launch of his squadron mates, but he half remembered the violent tremors that shook the carrier at least four or five times.

"Yes, ma'am. I won't leave the country without talking to you," he said to his grandmother.

"Please call me back … and promise me."

"I promise," he assured her before hanging up.

The room glowed under fluorescent lights, banks of monitors surrounding them in every direction. Everyone sat on pins and needles as the recoveries continued.

"Anyone care to go flying tonight?" the LSO asked the group of mostly senior aviators.

"No, sir," one aviator answered with a smirk, his voice carrying across the room. "You'd need a letter from Congress to get me back up in that thing."

The others laughed, the tension finally breaking. They needed to relax, to trust that everything would go as planned that the carrier wouldn't lose a $70 million asset to the hungry ocean.

Just then, a heavy swell slammed against the bow. The ship rolled hard, and the XO grabbed his clipboard before it slid off the desk.

Over the loudspeaker, a voice rang out: "BOLTER, BOLTER!" followed by a deafening VHRROOOOM.

The aviators exchanged knowing glances as Super Hornet tail number 101 shot off the angled deck and clawed its way back into the air. The failed trap meant the pilot would have to try again.

The XO turned toward the room, scanning for anyone with a high-and-tight. "Who's up there?"

"It's one of ours, sir," a Marine officer answered, his regulation haircut leaving no doubt of Semper Fidelis.

The XO's grim expression tightened as he nodded and turned back to his monitor. On the radar screen, the Hornet had already shrunk to a tiny blip. With no discernible horizon, sea and sky blended into one vast, featureless black.

He sat in a razor-edged state of concentration mirroring the pilots above the clouds monitoring airspeed, descent rate, and sequence. Five jets circled in the night, waiting for clearance to return to the deck. Right now, fuel states dominated his thinking as he ran manual calculations.

Tension filled the room, bordering on fear. The commander knew they all felt it, though none dared speak when optimism was so desperately needed.

The XO adjusted his headset and spoke into the mic. "101, say fuel state."

Three seconds of static passed before a voice broke through the radio. "4.1."

The young Hornet pilot in 101 had answered. The XO ran the numbers in his head enough fuel for one more pass.

"Okay, 101, call the ball when you're on glide path."

"Roger that. 101 commencing approach."

"101 replied. Finally. Get everyone back down here so we can go home," Harvey thought.

Darkness had fallen, and his mind replayed all the things that could go wrong in conditions like these catapult failure, ramp strikes, electrical malfunctions, ejection. The list went on. Pilots who suffered brake failure while landing had one choice: yank the ejection handle fast, or ride the jet into the frigid sea. This time of year, the water was cold and unforgiving.

But these were United States fighter pilots trained to handle anything.

On the PLAT screen, the view switched to approach. The room now stared into the black void as four aircraft made wide loops before lining up with the carrier. Four green lights flickered on Harvey's radar: a Marine Hornet, two F-15s, and a Raptor. Strike Eagle Five was last in the stack, its blip trailing behind.

Get home safely, Harvey whispered in a silent prayer.

The others had already landed some smoothly. others with a hard catch on the wires but they had all made it. These four were the last still burning fuel in the night sky.

The XO noted they were all left of the radar crosshairs. He lifted his clipboard, jotted a quick mark, then set it down again. The glide slope and wind speed worried him.

The approach controller's voice crackled over the radio, relaying coordinates. The XO cross-checked them against the status board. Everything matched.

"How are we looking on fuel?" he asked.

"We've got a tanker on standby if we need it," came the reply.

The approach controller's voice came steady, confident. The ship always kept a tanker nearby for a moment like this. The last thing anyone wanted was an aircraft low on fuel with no chance of landing safely. It didn't happen often, but when it did, protocol called for a barricade unless a Viking or Rhino refueler was in sight.

An unknown voice broke over the radio, asking the commander for his twenty. "In the bridge," the commander replied. "Roger that." The channel went quiet.

Harvey caught the XO's attention, pointing to flashing lights on the horizon. The XO nudged his headset microphone closer to his lips. "Hornet, you're a quarter mile. Call the ball."

"Roger, Midway. Working ball at forty-five knots."

The voice made Harvey freeze. He hadn't expected to recognize it not from a Hornet, not from a Tomcat. He'd been listening for Eagles and Raptors, not this.

Every head turned toward the PLAT. The feed showed Hornet 101 on final, making its second attempt. The jet loomed larger with every heartbeat, its strobe lights blinking like a metronome.

"101, you're coming in high and fast. I'll keep the deck steady just listen to my voice."

On the horizon, the cluster of inbound aircraft swelled, their lights rising in unison.

"101, slightly above glide path."

The Hornet corrected, dropping altitude to match the carrier's rhythm.

"101, call the ball."

"Roger, ball. Thirty-five knots."

When the ball was called, every officer in the room fell silent. Side conversations stopped, and radio traffic was restricted to the landing craft alone.

"Lined up a little right," the XO said, eyes on the glide slope crosshairs. "Move to center. You're on glide path."

"Roger that. 101," came the reply.

The Hornet corrected, then dropped hard toward the deck. It slammed onto the carrier, the tailhook catching an arresting wire with a violent jolt. The sound echoed through the ship. Freed of the wire, the pilot advanced throttles and taxied forward to clear the landing area.

On the PLAT screen, the feed shifted to the next inbound: an F-22 Raptor. The XO scanned the call signs, blinked twice, then shook his head.

"Moneybag, call the ball. You're on glide slope."

"Moneybag?" someone muttered.

The aviators chuckled, but a stern look from the XO silenced them. Harvey didn't share the joke. He'd already had his laugh at Lieutenant Seymour years ago at Holloman Air Force Base.

On the monitor, Moneybag's Raptor drew closer.

"You're on glide slope. Stay the course," the XO directed.

He stole a glance at the deck to ensure it wasn't foul, then refocused on the PLAT. Harvey studied the status board to ensure everything lined up. He was impressed by the XO's composure. He sounds good on the radio, Harvey thought.

The XO had orchestrated countless recoveries. His calm tone reflected experience more than confidence.

"How many left to recover?" Fastball asked, hanging up the phone.

"Three more," Harvey answered.

The XO nodded. Another set of flickering strobes appeared on the PLAT.

"Two miles out," he said, anticipating the unasked question.

Every aviator in the room silently pulled for the young pilot on approach. Moneybag drifted slightly left of the glide path but corrected immediately. As if sensing the next call, Lieutenant Seymour announced the ball and made fine adjustments as he drew closer.

The XO calculated he had half an hour to bring in four more fighters before launching a tanker became unavoidable. The thought made him uneasy. He wiped sweat from his forehead, noticing how the room had fallen silent except for the steady hum of the air vents.

"Moneybag, hold steady. You're on glide slope."

Seymour gripped the sticks tighter than he should have, sweat dripping as he kept the jet locked on course. When he called the ball, he was committed to putting his wheels down on that pitching deck, no matter what.

Harvey watched the monitors intently. Suddenly, the Raptor dropped out of the sky, charging toward the deck at full speed. Wheels struck with a thunderous WHOOM as the number one arresting wire snapped taut on the hook.

A collective sigh swept through Air Ops. So far, so good. No mishaps yet, the XO thought.

"Who's next?"

The XO glanced at Harvey, who assumed the question was for him. After a quick look at the status board, he answered: "Whiskey-One, sir. That's Lieutenant Jamison. Hollywood's last."

All eyes in Air Ops and on deck shifted to Whiskey-One. Time to bring her home. The pilots had been circling for what felt like hours, their fuel gauges warning that the window was closing fast.

Whiskey-One slid her F-15 into glide path and called the ball.

"You're on glide slope, Whiskey-One. Keep her steady."

A bolt of lightning struck the F-15's wing, jolting Lieutenant Jamison off course. For a moment, she was distracted then realized she was outside the crosshairs. She tried to correct, but overcompensated.

"Wave off," the XO ordered.

Whiskey-One lit her afterburners and roared over the carrier, the jet's shock rattling the ship.

"Whiskey-One, say state."

"Two-point-zero and bleeding fast," she replied, her voice betraying the urgency. If she didn't land soon, she'd run out of fuel.

"Hollywood, keep clear for Whiskey-One," the XO said into the mic, voice low and steady.

Seconds later, Abby's voice crackled over the comm. "Roger, Midway. Coast is clear."

And just like that, Hollywood banked left, pulling away from the carrier.

Harvey didn't know how to feel. Relief washed through him at the sound of her voice. It felt like hours since he'd last heard it. But if Lieutenant Jamison was low on fuel, Abby likely was too. Why hadn't she called her fuel state? Harvey wondered. And why hadn't the XO asked?

He couldn't shake the thought that Whiskey-One might have landed without the wave-off. Was the carrier losing faith in the Air Force nugget pilot? The irritation rising inside him made him stop. He chastised himself for letting intrusive doubts slip in.

Whiskey-One circled wide, looping back for another attempt. Harvey needed a distraction. His eyes swept the room until they landed on a shelf stacked with old magazines. He walked over and grabbed the one on top—Navy Times. Beneath it, he spotted the Air Force Times.

He chose the Air Force magazine and thumbed through nervously. Articles covered new uniform standards, deployment life, PCS guides, pay and benefits. Then he reached a section marked by photos of American service members killed in recent weeks. The magazine was three months old.

Most portraits showed soldiers, airmen, Marines, and sailors in formal poses at their duty stations. A few were boot camp shots. Many of the faces looked heartbreakingly young. Harvey searched for familiar names but found none.

One photo caught him: Captain Analise Hernandez, a helicopter pilot, her build strikingly similar to Abby's. She had died during a rescue mission. Harvey swallowed hard.

Suddenly, Abby's voice crackled over the comm system.

"Hollywood to Midway, amber lights are on. I need blood, ASAP!"

Air Ops understood instantly: the low-fuel light had flashed in Strike Eagle Five's cockpit.

"We're launching a tanker. Stand by for max conserve," the XO told Hollywood, then spun and barked into the room. "Launch that tanker now!"

"Yes, sir," an officer snapped, grabbing his LMR.

The XO's attention snapped back to Whiskey-One. "You're on glide slope."

"Roger," came the reply.

The XO's voice stayed calm, steady, as if nothing was wrong. The room, however, was dead silent every eye locked on the F-15 drifting in and out of the crosshairs while the carrier's bow pitched and rolled.

"We're going to barricade," the XO muttered.

He seized the mic and issued the order that thundered across the deck. Rig the barricade now!"

The muffled command echoed over the loudspeaker, and the deck crew moved instantly.

In Air Ops, aviators exchanged uneasy looks. Many had seen a barricade before but it was never something you wanted to watch.

"But sir," Fastball tried to protest, "she still has fuel."

"Deck won't cooperate. We're rigging it."

Fastball fell silent. He knew the XO was right, but the call still stung.

The XO's gaze locked on Whiskey-One, holding glide path with perfect discipline. She had maybe twenty minutes of fuel left. Any longer, and it would be the ocean.

"Hold for five mikes," he called. "Prepare for barricade."

Lieutenant Jamison couldn't believe what she was hearing, but there was nothing she could do. The ship had already made the call.

Harvey dug his heel into the floor as he stared at the deck monitor. He watched sailors rigging the barricade running, shouting orders, jumping across the deck, yanking heavy-duty straps, and locking connections into place.

He had never witnessed a barricade setup firsthand and was eager to see it in action. The barricade itself was a massive web of reinforced nylon, slung vertically from steel cables across the landing area to trap an aircraft during an emergency recovery. Once engaged, the net would wrap around the jet like a blanket, killing its forward momentum. The aircraft might be damaged but the pilot would live. If it failed, the fighter would slam into the deck in a violent, fiery wreck.

"You're rock-solid, Whiskey-One," the XO called. "The deck just isn't cooperating."

The XO had taken only five minutes to review the barricade manual. When the time was up, he grabbed the mic and guided Whiskey-One into position.

"I'm going to walk you through the barricade brief. State your configuration, approach speed, and gross weight."

"120 knots, 25K," Whiskey replied.

"Roger that," the XO answered. He drew in a long breath and exhaled hard through his nose.

Within minutes, the F-16 was back in the crosshairs. The room stayed silent everyone rooting for the two jets still airborne. From her vantage point, Hollywood could see her squadron mate aligning with the ship.

The barricade was ready. Lightning tore across the sky, casting the carrier in a flash of blue before darkness swallowed it again. Whiskey-One held steady.

Suddenly, the XO remembered something. He snatched the mic.

"Whiskey-One, do you have any ordnance onboard?" "Negative." "And the drop tanks?" "Negative, sir. Already jettisoned. I'm clean." "Remember no negative G."

For the first time, the XO flashed a grin, careful not to show teeth. He was glad she had taken the initiative.

"You can all learn a thing or two from the Air Force," he told the room. Silence met his words.

Harvey appreciated hearing the Executive Naval Officer speak of the Air Force with such respect.

"You're doing great, Whiskey-One." "Thank you, sir."

Jamison pulled a small canteen from her flight-suit knee pocket and took a long gulp. Through the canopy she could now see the ship racing up fast.

From her headset came the calm voice again: "Bingo. Fly the ball. Keep your throttle under control." "Roger, sir." "Deck's moving a little, but remember small corrections only. I'll be right here with you. Got it?" "Roger, sir."

He sounded like a father teaching his daughter to drive a Volkswagen Beetle.

Jamison double-checked her glide path, then touched the hook handle to confirm it was down. I'm good, she thought. She dropped the gear switch and eased the flap lever to half. A roar filled the cockpit as the landing gear locked into place.

She was due on deck in minutes.

The loudspeaker crackled across the ship. "Strike Eagle approaching deck. Prepare for barricade impact."

The crew didn't flinch. They were ready.

"Come left . . . a little more left."

The F-15 corrected, then dipped its nose for a steep view of the carrier before leveling off to hold the picture. Jamison just managed to keep the ship in sight over her jet's nose.

It felt like staring into a chasm as sheets of rain hammered the windscreen and canopy. The carrier rushed toward her, fast and furious, and there was no turning back.

The jet drifted then corrected again.

On deck, the Landing Signal Officer caught it on his monitor just in time to see the fighter drop from the sky, slam into the deck, shear the main mount, and vanish into the barricade's heavy nylon netting. The hook grabbed a wire as the aircraft struck, dragging the jet to a bone-rattling stop just short of the platform's edge.

Relief swept through Air Ops. Pilot and asset were both down safely aboard.

Deck crew scrambled to douse a small fire sparked by the brutal landing. A cheer erupted across the ship, booming through every space where eyes had been glued to the monitors.

One more to go, Harvey thought.

"Come in, Eagle-Five." "I'm still here, sir," Abby's voice crackled over comms.

"Deck is foul. Hold your position. How are you looking on fuel"

Before the XO could finish, the cockpit screamed:

FUEL LOW! FUEL LOW!

Amber lights strobed across Abby's instrument panel.

"Not good," she replied flatly. "I'm dry, sir."

She killed the amber warning lights but kept her eyes glued to the needles as they crept toward empty.

Rain hammered harder now. Strike Eagle Five was the last jet still in the sky and just a lone blip on radar, floating in space, waiting for her turn to dive on the carrier.

A green pulsing beacon marked the ship's aft position.

Suddenly, the loudspeaker erupted across the platform. The XO snatched up the LMR and bellowed: "Where the hell is that tanker?"

"Angel's airborne, sir," Fastball replied.

The XO stared at the deck monitor, unimpressed with the crew's pace. He stabbed the intercom and barked loud enough for everyone in the landing area to hear: "Barricade Eagle clear the deck! Chop-chop!"

Sailors and paddles scrambled, working frantically to clear the space for another possible barricade recovery.

From Air Ops, Harvey doubted it could be done in time. Twenty-five minutes that's all the fuel Abby had left.

He watched her icon drift toward the glide path, the green pulsing light locked in the crosshairs of the landing system.

From her cockpit, Abby focused on the HUD, nudging the velocity vector left and watching her jet drift. She rolled her wings slightly an instinct most pilots had then glanced down.

Below was nothing but a void. The carrier barely showed through the rain.

She had never been this low on fuel. Breathing through her mouth, she could hear her own heartbeat. A dull ache at the base of her skull spread into her shoulders. She reached up and massaged the knot, the pain like a needle driving into her neck.

She felt utterly alone.

A bolt of lightning split the sky nearby, and her headset crackled to life.

"Listen up, Eagle-Five. Angel is up there with you. Rendezvous for a quick plug and get some lifeblood."

Harvey felt encouraged by the calm authority in the XO's voice.

Abby scanned her radar. Another aircraft appeared at her six. Oh, thank God, she thought.

Less than three minutes of fuel remained.

The Strike Eagle leveled at two thousand feet, sliding into position behind the tanker. Abby eased the throttle, steady hands, determined to connect on the first try.

Flashing strobes under Angel's belly revealed the silhouette of the tanker as the refueling probe extended into the storm.

Abby gave the left rudder a few pumps to align the fuselage. She tried to anticipate the basket's sway but it whipped in the airstream, taunting her.

The probe missed. Again.

She backed off, frustration mounting, as the lights on her fuel gauge shifted from amber to red.

Then her cockpit exploded with warnings.

REFUEL NOW! REFUEL NOW!

Her voice cracked over comms: "Eagle-Five is pulling out. Negative on the plug."

The ship's comm system broadcast the final warning, and every pair of eyes locked onto the radar and monitors. They watched the jet back away from the refueling tank, its probe extender trembling in the wind and rain. A patch of cloud swept past, followed by a bolt of lightning, and Abby knew she had to get out of this plane now.

Somewhere below, her friend Harvey was equally worried about her safety. The pulsing lights grew larger as the Strike Eagle executed a wide loop and nosedived toward the ship. From that steep angle, it looked like a dive-attack. Suddenly, a frantic voice cut through her headset:

"Eagle-Five, the deck is foul … you're not clear for landing. I repeat, the deck is foul."

The aircraft shook violently as she held the glide path, the ship looming fast beneath her. The landing gear dropped into the airstream with a dull roar. Abby focused on landing the jet, pushing away the disaster unfolding in her mind.

"Eagle-Five, abort! Abort!"

The EXO's urgent commands echoed in her headset, each one sharper than the last. On deck, aviators and crew froze, bracing for impact. Then chaos erupted as they scrambled for cover ducking into catwalks and crouching behind barricades as the jet roared closer to the platform.

"Oh my God."

Harvey braced himself, dreading the worst. On the PLAT screen, the familiar strobes of the Strike Eagle grew larger, sliding right to left across the crosshairs. The jet held a conservative speed, but it was still too fast for a clean landing. Harvey felt the ship lurch as the strobes dropped sharply, the F-15 had reached the wave-off point.

Suddenly, the fighter yanked its nose up, afterburners igniting as it screamed above the ship, rattling the entire vessel. In Abby's cockpit, the lights went dark, and an impersonal warning tone blared through her headset.

"EJECT! EJECT!"

On deck, the crew watched in shock as twin fiery plumes roared past and vanished into the night.

Abby reached into the left pocket of her G-suit and pulled out a small canteen. If she was going into the water, the last thing she wanted was to be thirsty. She twisted off the cap, unclipped a fitting on her oxygen mask, and drank deeply. The fitting dangled against her cheek as she drained the canteen dry. Tossing it aside, she snapped the mask back into place.

Sweat poured down her face. Her breathing came in ragged bursts, and she fought the temptation to tear the mask off again. The engines sputtered and rolled back fuel starvation. The time had come.

Her fingers closed around the ejection handle. She took a deep breath, pulled hard, and the cockpit exploded around her. Abby rocketed into the cold night air. A second blast fired, deploying the parachute. Suspended between earth and sky, she looked down and saw the F-15 tumbling helplessly into the abyss. Seconds later, a distant splash signaled the jet's end as the ocean swallowed it whole.

Guiding the chute with practiced pulls, she steered toward the carrier, homing in on sodium flares from the tower and a cluster of yellow lights shining against the black. The ship held steady, every eye on deck fixed on her descent.

After what felt like enternity, her boots hit the deck. In an instant, crew members swarmed her, their cheer erupting like a release valve after unbearable tension. A medic with a red reflective cross emblazoned across the chest reached her first, shining a penlight into her eyes and shouting over the noise:

"Are you okay?" "Yeah, I'm okay." "Welcome aboard, Lieutenant."

He gave a thumbs-up to the others and helped Abby to her feet as the deck erupted in relief.

CHAPTER ELEVEN

(MEMORY LANE)

HARVEY STEPPED OUT OF the Travis Air Force Base convenience store with a bottle of Palmer's iced tea in one hand and a receipt in the other. He stuffed the slip of paper into his pocket, pulled open his car door, and sank into the warm leather seat. The sun had only been up a few hours, still climbing, but its heat was already sharp.

He drove half a mile before turning onto Commander's Boulevard, stopping beside the Wing Headquarters building. The structure of reinforced concrete and brick rose with an imposing façade, designed for longevity and projecting strength. A massive Air Force insignia with a flying crest dominated the exterior. Out front, a flagpole bore Old Glory, while a smaller flag jutted from a wall-mounted bracket near the entrance.

Harvey got out, crossed the pavement, and entered the Wing Headquarters. A young lieutenant sat at the duty desk, fingers clattering across a keyboard. She paused as he approached. The lobby was meticulous and orderly, lit bright and spacious. A directory showcased military honors, while framed photographs and displays celebrated past and present might. Offices branched off in precise rows, divided by department and function.

Though Harvey wore civilian clothes, sunglasses hooked into the collar of his T-shirt, the lieutenant knew him instantly.

"Good morning, Major," she said with a smile.

"Morning, Ashlee," he replied.

"You here to see the boss?"

"Has he had his coffee yet?"

"Yes, sir."

"Good. I'll see him then. He asked for me but didn't say why. Did he tell you what this is about?"

"No, sir."

He returned the smile as the lieutenant pointed him "that way."

General Higby's office was enclosed by thick plexiglass, its surface etched with squadron, group, and wing patches. Harvey grabbed the door handle, pulled it open, and stepped inside. A second glass door marked Commander's Office stood ahead. He knocked twice, paused, then entered.

"Sir," he said.

General Higby sat sideways at his desk, leaning back with his legs crossed. He closed the blue folder he had been reading and looked up. Dressed in his blues, his ribbon rack precise and gleaming, he gestured toward the couch.

"Please, have a seat."

Harvey did as instructed, settling at the end of the three-seater, feet planted firmly on the floor, hands folded on his lap. Higby rose, folder still in hand, and moved to the visiting area. He lowered himself onto the opposite couch, crossed his legs, and reopened the folder. For five long seconds, he silently scanned its pages.

To Harvey, the pause felt like ten. Uneasy, he let his eyes wander the immaculate office. The solid oak executive desk matched the polished coffee tables. A silver-and-gold-plated sword rested behind a name placard that held pens and pencils, likely a gift from an overseas posting. From this distance, Harvey couldn't make out the engravings.

A desktop computer sat on the far left of the desk. Behind the high-backed leather chair, four flagpoles carried the American flag, the Wing flag, the Group flag, and a squadron flag. A muted television on the wall streamed a 24-hour news feed. On the coffee tables, a model cargo plane and a fighter jet stood on display, silent witnesses to the tension in the room.

"Major, I'm looking at the record of a stellar pilot who isn't happy where he is. Help me understand that."

Stacks of papers came into view as General Higby spun his chair. Harvey shifted uneasily.

"Sir, come again? What exactly do you mean by 'not happy'?"

"Well, the Group Commander said she spoke with you. You mentioned something about wanting to hang it up, leaving the United States Air Force. To go and do what, exactly?" Higby's questions piled up, sharp and direct. "Fly for Delta? UPS? FedEx? Where to? Are you seriously considering an early separation?"

Harvey drew in a deep breath. The last thing he wanted was to lie, or even shade the truth to the man he admired most. Higby wasn't just a commander; he was a family friend. And right now, he was speaking with a calm, measured tone that carried far more weight than anger ever could.

"Yes, sir."

Higby lifted his eyes from the folder, set it aside, and fixed Harvey with a hard stare. The young pilot stirred memories of the General's own flying days days long past. He gave orders now; he didn't take them. And seeing Harvey was like seeing the ghost of his late wingman.

The kid tested his patience, sure sometimes he deserved a fat lip but his presence also carried a wave of nostalgia Higby couldn't shake. It blurred, at times, the line between commander and protégé.

"You're leaving the Air Force?" he asked, indignation breaking through. "You're one of our finest young pilots, well on your way to commanding your own Group or Wing someday. Your father would be so proud of you."

"He already is, sir."

Higby realized his words hadn't come out the way he intended. He quickly apologized and pressed on.

"I promised your old man I'd look after you. I'd consider myself a failure if I didn't see you become everything you can as a commissioned officer. Do you really want to resign?"

Hearing it spoken aloud hit hard. Harvey had only been toying with the idea for a few months, but now it felt heavier than ever. He fought to stay composed.

"No, sir."

The answer was technically true, though lately he had given serious thought to the next chapter of his life.

"Come with me."

They crossed the room to a large bookcase against the wall. Higby pointed. "Look at that."

Harvey's eyes settled on an old Polaroid his father and Higby as young lieutenants, standing beside a fighter jet in their G-suits, helmets cradled at their waists.

"When the orders came down for this mission, I had you in mind all along," Higby said. "Because you're the best. The apple doesn't fall far from the tree, son. Your old man and I got into worse trouble than you and Captain Webb. So if you were worried about that incident a few months back, just know that I took care of it. It won't appear in your record."

Harvey knew exactly which incident the commander meant. He prayed it would never resurface.

"Thank you, sir."

"Don't mention it. How's your grandmother?"

"Fine, sir. Relatively speaking."

"There's no substitute for aging, it comes for all of us. That's why we have to make the most of the short time we're given."

Harvey clung to every word, as if the pep talk was exactly what he needed.

"I flew thousands of sorties with your father," Higby continued. "We were the good guys in an evil world. And good always wins … even if it takes a thousand years."

Higby turned to face Harvey. Now they were eye to eye. Harvey looked away for a moment, only to return his gaze as a large hand settled firmly on his shoulder.

"A lot is riding on this mission," Higby said. "It's career-defining. With its success, you could be wearing your bird sooner than you think. And I don't doubt you for a second. With your family's heritage and your connection to Ukraine, you're the best man for the job. That's why I chose you. The asset was purchased with taxpayer dollars."

He caught himself realizing he had already said more than he should have and let the point hang.

"The American people are depending on you. You understand what Russia would do if they got their hands on that plane, right?"

"I do."

Harvey kept his head lowered, and the General could tell something else weighed on him. Higby gave him a slight nudge.

"What is it, son? Just say it."

Harvey hesitated. The last thing he wanted was to sound disloyal, but he couldn't keep quiet.

"What about Webb?"

"What about him?" Higby asked. His expression softened; the smugness drained from his face.

"Does he have to be on this detail? I like the guy, but he's a pain in my neck. Every time we're together, we argue like an old married couple."

"Except now, you outrank him. Correct?"

"That's correct."

The General turned toward his desk, Harvey trailing behind, matching his pace. Higby leaned against the desk, one cheek resting on the edge, one leg planted firmly on the floor. He held the Major's gaze for several long seconds.

"This assignment was sanctioned by Congress and the DoD. Everyone with a need to know already has clearance. The window is too tight to brief a new crew and issue new clearances. You make do with what you have. That's an order."

His voice carried a sharp edge no longer the tone of a family friend, but of a commander making it clear the discussion was over. Harvey got the message, though it didn't mean he was satisfied. Drawing a deep breath, he forced out a "Yes, sir."

He wanted to bring up the incident in Ukraine but knew this wasn't the time. Harvey had promised himself he would never step foot on Ukrainian soil again. Yet here he was, being ordered back to deliver a package that could tip the balance in the confrontation with Russia. He didn't need to be reminded how crucial this mission was; he knew it was the most important of his career.

Harvey was a warrior, and Eastern Europe held a complicated place in his heart. He respected it. He hated it. It had nearly killed him. But could he walk away now, after everything that had happened?

"You're also on the hopper, I heard," Harvey asked.

"You heard right," Higby said. "The Pentagon wants me running point on this mission. I'll be in Qatar for about six months. I'll deliver the final brief before you launch from the AOR."

A brief silence followed as Harvey processed the news. Knowing the General would be close by gave him both courage and reassurance of a trusted partner if things went wrong.

"If nothing else, you're dismissed."

The general gave him his orders. Harvey snapped a salute, and his boss returned it. At the door, Harvey paused, stealing one last glance at the photo on the bookcase before letting it shut behind him.

The midday heat pressed down, turning his vehicle into an oven. The leather seat scorched against his uniform, and he cranked the air conditioner to full blast, letting the cold air rush over his face. As he drove, his thoughts drifted to Abby. What was she doing right now? Maybe packing her bags, saying her final goodbyes.

They were bound for opposite ends of the globe, he to Europe, she to Southeast Asia, assigned to a naval carrier flexing its muscles near the Korean Peninsula to deter North Korea from more rocket tests. He wondered what their lives together might look like. He wanted a family, wanted to settle down now, but Abby lived in a different world. She thrived in deployments, constant motion. Deep down, Harvey wanted to marry a civilian woman, someone who would always be home with the kids, not gone as often as he was.

His phone rang. Whiskey-One flashed across the screen.

"Hey, I was just"

He stopped himself. Was he really about to admit he'd been thinking about her?

"You were just what?" Abby teased.

"Nothing. What're you up to?"

"Laundry. Nothing much. You?"

"I just left Higby's office. I'm really doing this."

"That's good. Do it for God and country. In your case, countries."

She chuckled. Harvey pictured her smile, bright even through the phone.

"Hey, I gotta go. My mom's calling."

When the call ended, Harvey thought about his grandmother. He'd promised to call her last week and hadn't. Scrolling through his contacts, he found her number and pressed dial.

"It's my favorite grandson!" the old woman exclaimed.

"I'm your only grandson, Gigi," Harvey said matter-of-factly. He chuckled.

Georgina, seventy-five, wasn't about to let age slow her down. The silver-haired matriarch sat in a rocking chair on the wide, wraparound porch of her cottage-style farmhouse. Beyond her stretched two acres of farmland, nearly ready for harvest. Her hair was mostly white now, streaked with the last traces of brown. The warmth in her voice made Harvey smile as he leaned back in his seat.

"So, Gigi, how are things? Been keeping out of trouble?"

"Oh, you know me, Harvey. I'm a saint."

Her playful lilt made him laugh as he turned onto a busy street.

"But enough about me. You've been busy, haven't you? Your mother says you're preparing for something big. Tell me what is it?"

Her voice had a giddy bounce, like a high school girl fishing for gossip. Harvey hesitated, rubbing the back of his neck.

"Yeah, it's been a lot. But I can handle it."

"Spill the beans already."

"You know I can't give you too much detail about my work, Gigi."

She sighed, surrendering with mock defeat. Wind chimes tinkled faintly in the breeze behind her.

"That's what you always say. But don't forget have a little fun, too. Life's too short to be all work and no play."

Harvey turned onto his street and coasted down to the cul-de-sac beside his base housing. He already knew where Gigi's questions were headed. Whenever she started talking like this, it usually ended with a tongue-lashing about his broken promises to visit or her nagging him about settling down.

He had promised to come by soon maybe even bring her favorite chocolates but that promise was long overdue. A pang of guilt struck him for not calling sooner.

"Are you seeing anyone yet?"

Harvey had predicted this.

"Something like that."

He regretted the cheeky response the moment it left his mouth and tried to recover.

"I'm working on it, Gi."

He pulled into his driveway and shut off the engine.

"You need to get over Trish."

"Geez, Grandma, where did that come from?"

"It's been five years. She's not coming back. I never believed for a second that a city girl like her would take to farm life. Besides, you're not getting any younger."

She paused, choosing her next words carefully.

"You're still coming to take over the farm, right?"

"Working on it."

"Okay, all I can say is don't show up for Thanksgiving by yourself."

"I'm going out of the country for a short while, but I promise I'll be back by Thanksgiving and I'll bring a plus one."

She didn't answer, but Harvey could almost feel her smiling on the other end, her rosy cheeks glowing.

"Deal?"

"That's a deal."

She hung up. Harvey slipped his phone into his pocket and leaned back in his seat. He pressed a button, and the panoramic roof slid open. Tilting his head back, he wasn't looking at anything in particular he just wanted a moment of calm.

CHAPTER TWELVE

(AL UDEID, QATAR)

WHEN THE TIRES OF the Lockheed C-130 Hercules kissed the ground, the plane bounced slightly before regaining control and making full contact with the tarmac at Al Udeid Air Base. The flaps on the wings extended and retracted as the hiss of the air brakes grew louder. The four-engine military transport aircraft rolled forward at cruising speed before gradually slowing down under a massive gray-and-brown tent designed to house American flying machines.

The land surrounding the airfield was flat and barren, with sand-colored structures that blended into the desert floor. When the aircraft doors opened, they revealed a cavernous underbelly from which hundreds of service members disembarked via the gangway and into a building labeled "CUSTOMS." Harvey wore his battle dress uniform, as did the other men and women deployed to the Middle East.

The customs check was routine: the familiar "Show me your ID and military orders" barked by representatives of the Qatari government. They're always so friendly to us, Harvey thought as he moved through the zigzagging line, hauling his duffel bag and weapons case.

After clearing customs, he proceeded to the commander and first sergeant's briefing, something he had done dozens of times before. Two hours later, he had showered and changed out of his uniform. He now wore jeans and a black polo shirt as he made his way to the section of the base where service members gathered in the evenings to unwind and socialize.

Hip-hop music thumped from stereo speakers as Harvey stepped into the community center. The pounding rhythm came from the Fox Sports Skybox, a favorite venue where personnel relaxed after a demanding day. The Skybox sat beside the Kasbah and Memorial Plaza, where thousands of troops lounged in the warm evening air eating, drinking, playing cards, and listening to music. Others watched Rocky IV on a giant projector next to the fitness and wellness center.

"Hey, stranger."

A voice called from behind. Harvey turned to see Abby. Before he could say a word, she wrapped him in an embrace that lingered just a second longer than expected. He didn't protest.

"We're sitting at the bar over there." She gestured toward the makeshift sports bar where other officers had gathered. Harvey was parched and could use a drink even if it had to be non-alcoholic, in deference to the host country's laws.

Everyone stationed here knew that under Islamic law, alcohol was prohibited. Sparkling water, soda, and mocktails served as the stand-ins. Harvey grabbed a barstool and slid it between Abby and Jamison before taking a seat.

"Why do they still call it a bar when they don't even serve beer?" he asked no one in particular, grabbing a can of Coca-Cola from the ice bucket as he surveyed the scene. Several groups of officers lounged nearby, chatting about flying. Occasionally, the topic shifted to wives and girlfriends back home, but it always circled back to flying.

Harvey sipped his soft drink at the shaded bar, taking in the scene and enjoying the evening breeze. The bartender a young airman wearing a Navy squadron T-shirt spent most of his time mixing colorful, alcohol-free drinks.

"Did you get my email?" Abby asked.

"The one about Doha?"

"Yeah."

"You in on this?" he asked Lieutenant Jamison.

"That's all her doing," Jamison said, raising his hands. "I've got nothing to do with the planning."

"C'mon, guys. Live a little," Abby said with a smirk.

The following day, the late September sun blazed overhead, a harsh reminder that they were far from home. The bus carrying U.S. service members to the city of Doha crawled through the heat, its weak air conditioning offering little relief. Abby sat near the front, quietly wishing the tour guide would just shut up. To be fair, the man was only doing his job but she'd heard his speech three times already and had no patience for it today.

The journey spanned thirty miles, but it felt twice as long under the stifling heat. Doha, the capital of Qatar, stood as the country's financial center, one of the wealthiest cities along the Persian Gulf, north of Al Wakrah and south of Al Khor. Americans usually came here with a purpose. Today, Abby's was simple: to have fun before shipping out on a U.S. carrier headed to the East China Sea in preparation for Kim Jong Un's shenanigans.

As the bus reached Doha's outskirts, the newer arrivals began to gawk at the skyline and industrial sprawl. The piers were packed with loading cranes, warehouses, stacks of shipping containers, and all manner of modern port equipment. The area buzzed with activity, a testament to Qatar's growing trade dominance.

Airmen, soldiers, sailors, and Marines filed off the bus when it stopped in the business district. Officers and enlisted personnel alike wore neutral clothing, careful not to display anything overtly marked "USA." Avoiding the more obvious tourist destinations, Harvey, Abby, Jamison, and Christian peeled away from the crowd and headed in the opposite direction.

Harvey had been here once before, but the city still amazed him. The skyline was a patchwork of architectural ambition, huge skyscrapers, each different from the last, rose among ever-present construction cranes. On his last visit, he had marveled at the variety: sleek towers, lavish hotels, and shaded gardens carved into the urban sprawl.

German-made cars zipped through the streets, but traffic never felt as choked as in downtown Los Angeles or New York. Locals dressed in a mix of traditional Arab robes and Western casual wear. So far, the visit looked much the same as before.

Then he saw two young boys wearing Milwaukee Bucks Conference Finals Championship T-shirts and matching caps.

Harvey smiled.

"The kids got taste."

He said it loud enough for his comrades to hear. The kids spoke Arabic, but the signs they were reading were in English. Two Arab men in traditional garb walked past the Americans holding hands, prompting Abby to reach for Harvey's right hand. He instinctively jerked his hand away, causing her to abort the gesture.

He wasn't sure why he reacted that way to such a simple, beautiful touch. Reflex, maybe? The thought lingered as they crossed a busy intersection.

On the other side of the street, Christian and Jamison marveled at the contrast between tribal customs and 21st-century modernity. Towering skyscrapers surrounded them, and the entire area seemed to radiate wealth. It was Christian and Jamison's first time in Doha, and they snapped photos at every opportunity.

An hour after stepping off the bus, the group stood in front of the Four Seasons Hotel in downtown Doha. As they stepped into the opulent lobby, Jamison's eyes darted around, trying to take it all in.

"What do you boys have an appetite for this afternoon?" Abby asked.

"Let's see what they've got on the menu," Harvey replied.

"You boys go have a look around. My girl and I are headed to the spa for massages," Abby added. "We'll meet you at the bar in exactly one hour."

In under twenty minutes, the women had discovered the in-house boutique, purchased two cute dresses, found the spa, and were now half-naked on parallel massage tables in a private room. The oohs and aahs were all the proof needed they were thoroughly enjoying themselves as the masseurs worked knots out of their muscles.

"Make sure you get all the knots out," Abby instructed her masseur.

He responded with a firm deep-tissue roll along her upper back, prompting her to let out a drawn-out, "Ooooh, yes."

"Yep. I feel the same way over here," Jamison chimed in from the next table.

After a brief silence, Abby spoke again.

"So, where are you from?"

"The Philippines," her masseur replied in a soft but masculine voice.

"You are Americans, yes?"

"What gave it away?" she asked, smiling.

"We see a lot of Americans this time of year," he said with a knowing grin.

"Touché," Abby murmured. As long as he doesn't identify us as fighter pilots, we're fine. Some things are better left unsaid, she thought.

She rolled onto her back and adjusted the towel to allow access to her abdomen and legs while remaining modest and appropriate. The masseur resumed his work.

"I'm going to perform tonight, you know," Abby said suddenly.

"I'm sorry … come again?" Jamison asked, slightly confused.

"There's a spot not far from here where foreigners and some locals gather for karaoke. I'm going to sing tonight."

Jamison spun her head toward her fellow officer, shooting Abby a look of surprise. Abby replied with a smug smile.

"Umm, what are you going to sing and how long have you been planning this?" After a beat, she added, "Are you any good?"

"You'll see. Don't tell the boys I want it to be a surprise."

Forty-five minutes later, both masseuses stepped out of the room after giving a few final instructions. Once the door closed behind them, Jamison leaned in and whispered

"It was a little weird having that man all over me like that."

"Who? The masseuse? Oh, girl, don't worry they're both gay. How else do you think they got this gig?"

The women dressed quickly, getting ready to meet the boys for an early dinner. Their outfits were modest, intentionally so they made a conscious effort not to show too much cleavage, mindful of their surroundings in a foreign country. Still, the dresses flattered them in all the right ways, hugging curves at the edges without being overt.

The two were stepping outside their comfort zones and were glad to have each other for support. When they entered the crowded lobby, heads turned. Harvey and Christian took notice immediately.

By the door, two bellmen began arguing in Hindi over which one of the American women was hotter.

After dinner, they hailed a cab and departed the hotel, heading down a wide boulevard before turning left between towering buildings. Harvey considered haggling with the driver but resisted the urge, opting to pay the fare without argument.

Twenty-five minutes later, the cab pulled up in front of a popular nightspot on the boulevard. Following a small crowd, the pilots entered the nightclub.

The venue boasted sleek, modern décor hardwood paneling, velvet seating, and low ambient lighting. In one far corner, a caged platform hung suspended, where a clothed dancer swayed lazily to the beat. A disco ball spun overhead, scattering light across the polished floor, though no one was dancing. Businessmen and women mostly foreigners lounged at tables, sipping drinks and enjoying the vibe.

It was karaoke night, and the place was packed.

Suddenly, a group took to the stage for their rendition of YMCA, made famous by the Village People. Christian and Harvey chuckled along but would never have guessed what was coming next. The officer with the most conservative reputation in their circle was about to take the stage and take it she did.

When the Village People act wrapped up, the stage sat empty for a solid three minutes. Then Abby stood up, excused herself, and walked confidently to the DJ booth. She leaned in, whispered something to the DJ, and remained near the stage.

Harvey and Christian exchanged glances, then looked to Jamison who suppressed a knowing smile. She'd been playing with her hair all evening, laughing at every one of Christian's corny jokes. She could tell he was into her. All he needed now was his wingman to stick the landing.

The DJ gave Abby a nod once he'd found the track. She was ready.

The DJ's voice boomed through the sound system:

"Ladies and gentlemen, please welcome ... Miss Abby!"

She had prepared for this moment for months and now was her time to shine.

As she stepped onto the stage, she took a moment to absorb the spotlight, scanning the silent crowd before the music hit. Then, a sudden cheer erupted from the audience as the first beat dropped.

The song: "Shake It Off" by Taylor Swift.

CHAPTER THIRTEEN

(AL UDEID, QATAR)

Harvey slid both feet into the warm water as he sat on the pool deck. He wore red, white, and blue swim shorts and no shirt same as the other guys around the pool. After partying in Doha the night before, everyone was feeling the aftereffects.

Today's mission was simple: relax with friends and colleagues, maybe rehash last night's escapades or, as usual, shift the conversation back to flying.

Harvey sat beside Christian and two other fighter pilots they'd met on this hop. In the pool, Abby and Jamison stood waist-deep, wearing one-piece swimsuits and jean shorts over their bottoms to keep things modest on base. Around them, enlisted personnel lounged in the sun or splashed in the water, some attempting a disorganized game of water volleyball.

Harvey took a sip from his water bottle, then poured the rest over his head to combat the oppressive heatwave.

The two pilots next to him, dark sunglasses in place, were clearly eyeing the women in the pool but Abby and Jamison paid them no mind.

At a round table nearby, Webb sat with their loadmaster, Master Sergeant Daniels, and a few other personnel who'd be joining them on their next mission to Ukraine in about

48 hours. Even in relaxation mode, the conversation kept drifting back to flying.

"Been anywhere interesting lately?" Master Sergeant Daniels asked Captain Webb.

"Yeah … well, not recently. But Balad was interesting if you can call it that."

"What happened?" Daniels asked, leaning forward.

"We were in Iraq picking up human cargo mostly remains out of Mosul and Kabul."

He nodded toward Major Harvey, sunbathing by the pool.

"Then that genius over there decided we should go outside the wire you know, for research purposes or whatever. Against my better judgment, I went along with it."

Webb leaned back and continued.

"Around 0200, we got the green light to roll out. We boarded the MRAP and joined a convoy already in progress. The moment we rolled out, the roads went black—I mean pitch dark."

He paused, eyes narrowing.

"What we didn't know at the time was that Al-Zarqawi had placed a million-dollar bounty on any American convoy …"

Master Sergeant Daniels shook his head, and a brief silence followed.

"It was supposed to be a three-hour convoy," Webb said. "They blew the lead vehicle, and we saw this giant fireball tracer rounds flying in every direction, and then the flares started going up. It looked like a fuckin' Star Wars movie. My balls were in my throat."

An enlisted man a navigator by trade shifted uncomfortably in his seat and asked, "How'd y'all get out of there?"

"The 69th Infantry out of New York came through and saved our asses. If it wasn't for their gun truck, I'd be dead right now."

"So why are you mad at him?" Sergeant Daniels asked, his voice low.

"Because he's an asshole who still hasn't apologized for dragging me onto that damn convoy. We had no business being on the ground. We're aviators, for Chrissakes!"

Webb caught himself he'd gotten too loud. He reeled it in. He was talking about a superior officer, after all, even if they used to be best friends.

The navigator cleared his throat, trying to shift the conversation. "I had a somewhat similar situation involving surface-to-air missiles"

"Not now," Sergeant Daniels cut in sharply, his voice edged with indignation. He could see Webb was still shaken still haunted.

Webb let out a groan and looked across the pool.

Harvey and the others were now playing water volleyball, laughing like nothing in the world could touch them.

Daniels made a mental note: when the time was right, he'd tell Harvey a little secret about his wingman.

"Your boy's having the time of his life over there," he muttered.

Sergeant Daniels glanced at the women surrounding Harvey in the pool. "Your boy's got it made."

"Sure does," Webb said, nodding slowly.

The afternoon sun was dipping low. One by one, people were leaving the pool area, some heading back to the barracks, others drifting toward the community center to keep the evening going.

"Got a moment?"

The question caught Abby off guard.

Watching her in the pool was something else. She had all the right curves in all the right places, and somehow, the water only enhanced her hourglass figure. Harvey knew he had to make a move because in less than 48 hours, they'd be going their separate ways. He to Ukraine. She to the DMZ.

He reached for her hand and gave a subtle nod toward the far end of the pool. She understood. As he backstroked away, she dove beneath the surface, trailing him like a shadow. When they reached the edge, Harvey stopped and glanced around but she was gone. Then, in an instant, she popped up behind him with a grin.

Finally, they were alone or as close to it as they could be. A few people still lingered nearby, but in that moment, it felt like the rest of the world had faded.

A fire had been smoldering between them for a long time, and Harvey knew he'd been a fool for not making it official. She didn't owe him anything. She could've been swept up by one of the other sharp-looking officers around base and if that happened, he'd have no one to blame but himself.

Harvey had always played the role of officer and gentleman when they were in public. It was an unspoken understanding between them: the tension, the connection, it was real, but never voiced.

It had to be hard, loving someone in silence. Not being able to say it. Not being able to show it.

Still, it wasn't the threat of fraternization that worried him. It was what such a relationship might do to the unit back home. But they weren't stateside anymore. Did those rules still apply?

That was the kicker.

Harvey wasn't the kind of man to think only of himself. If they were any other couple with the kind of sexual tension they had they probably would've crossed the line back when he was her instructor.

He had met her at Keesler Air Force Base, teaching a war college course to young officers. She was brilliant. Confident.

Sharp as hell. And the fact that his best friend, Captain Webb, had a crush on her made things even more complicated.

As the water drifted them closer together, Harvey reached up and gently brushed her hair back, wiping water from her face. Her nose was puffy, her eyes red from the chlorine but to him, she'd never looked more beautiful. Heartbreakingly so.

She sniffled and dabbed at her cheek, gaze lowered.

He placed a finger under her chin and tilted her face toward his.

"What are you doing?"

She tried to turn her head to see who might be watching, but his finger gently held her chin in place.

"What does it look like?" he asked in return though he wasn't expecting an answer, and she knew it.

She hiccuped and smiled, her face glowing with the soft radiance that had captivated him from the very first day in the classroom back when he'd stood silently, listening as everyone introduced themselves.

"This is really happening," she said softly.

"It's really happening," he echoed, his voice low.

He was caught in a magnetic pull he didn't want to resist. From the moment they met at Keesler, something had felt inevitable like they were meant to collide. He couldn't explain it. And whether Captain Webb liked it or not, First Lieutenant Abby Smith was his. It was time he made that clear.

"I'm about to kiss you," he said.

A cool breeze swept past as she let out a soft, shuddering breath and nodded.

"Yeah ... yeah, okay."

She moved closer until their lips were just a hair's breadth apart. Her lips parted slightly, her cheeks flushed against her sun-kissed skin. He lowered his head and kissed her without caring who might be watching.

She tasted sweet, soft, supple plump.

With a soft moan, Abby's hand slid around the back of his neck as she kissed him back. His left hand traced down her side and came to rest on her hip. This moment was theirs and they had both imagined it, maybe even dreamed it.

Abby had thought about it more.

Behind the steely-eyed, GI Jane exterior of the fighter pilot was a softness only Harvey had seen until now.

With his free hand, he cupped her chin again, savoring every second. Their lips pressed harder together, breath merging. They held each other tightly for nearly a minute then slowly parted.

Jamison wasn't far off, holding court with another officer near the deck.

"What took you so long?" Abby asked, her voice a near whisper.

Harvey held her gaze for a moment and replied, "I'm here now. I'm not going anywhere."

Truthfully, he wanted to take her back to his lodging and make love to her all night. But duty called. The mission was less than 28 hours away, and protocol demanded full rest and mental readiness.

He said goodnight to Abby and Jamison. The moment had ended, but it had changed everything.

The night passed.

Harvey listened intently, a rising sense of unease creeping in.

What is that? he thought.

"This is a cargo plane," he said aloud, voice tightening. "So why does it sound like someone's out there banging hammer to nail?"

He thought.

He looked outside the cockpit window. Dark clouds rushed past. Harvey set the instrument to autopilot, got up, and pushed through the cabin door. The plane rattled beneath his feet. He steadied himself and reached for the flight manifest hanging on the wall. Slightly crooked he straightened it. He listened for the strange sound, but it had stopped.

Suddenly, the plane dipped, then leveled out violently shaking. Harvey was thrown against the wall. He grabbed the door jamb to hold himself upright as a frantic garble crackled from the cockpit radio. Everything turned hazy and out of focus. For a few seconds, he felt like he'd been binging. Weakness spread through his torso and legs. He forced an exhale as the cabin tilted and twisted.

Rows of cargo, strapped down with FedEx-branded nylon, held firm until one broke loose with a harsh slap. Then, from the shadows of the back row, a figure emerged. He held something sharp Harvey decided it was a blade. The figure wore a dark hoodie.

"Sergeant, is that you?"

No reply.

"Hey, man. Quit screwing around. This isn't funny."

Still nothing.

It felt surreal like a nightmare. Harvey's face floated in a cloud of fear. Is this really happening? he thought. He stood frozen in the dimly lit cargo hold, surrounded by crates stamped with the FedEx logo.

The man advanced, blade pointed at Harvey.

Harvey stepped back. It felt like wading through sand in heavy boots. Pallets shifted and groaned. One snapped free just as the hooded man stepped aside, letting the massive crate slam into the fuselage and burst open. The man kept moving forward, closer his face still hidden.

Just the two of them now. Red warning lights pulsed from the wings, casting eerie flashes across the interior.

Harvey patted his body, searching for a weapon. Nothing.

Suddenly, the hooded figure launched himself. A powerful leap he was airborne. Their bodies collided, slamming into the cockpit door just as the jumbo jet plunged.

Up close, Harvey finally saw the man's eyes bright red, empty, inhuman.

The plummet sent the plane into a vicious spiral. The two men were tossed like rag dolls. Harvey reached for something anything but his arms felt like lead.

Then impact. The crash. Water.

Harvey's eyes flew open. He was breathing hard, deep and ragged. He touched his forehead it was drenched in sweat. He rolled over and reached for his watch.

05:45.

CHAPTER FOURTEEN

(THE DELIVERY)

By mid-afternoon, the C-5 Galaxy had already been rolled out of the hangar bay for loading and inspection. The aircraft was opened from nose to tail. Its massive front end tilted skyward, perpendicular to the heavens, while the rear ramp lay extended onto the tarmac ready for vehicle loading.

It was time to go over the preflight checklist.

The preflight safety check was more than routine it was the cornerstone of military aviation operations. By rigorously inspecting every detail, from structural integrity to cargo security, the process ensured that the aircraft was fully prepared to transport weapons and equipment across the globe safely and efficiently. That was exactly the kind of mission Harvey and his crew were about to embark on.

A forklift hoisted a container to the cargo door. Another forklift, driven by an airman first class, zoomed off the ramp with a larger box loaded into the Galaxy's belly. It was a seemingly endless line of airmen, soldiers, and marines working in coordinated motion. Cargo sat stacked both inside and outside the hangars. Three cargo planes were being loaded simultaneously, each bound for a different part of the world.

The C-5 Galaxy bound for Ukraine carried massive military-grade crates packed with a wide array of weapons.

Harvey leaned over a wooden pallet, inspecting a tightly wrapped bulk load covered in military netting. He was squinting at the faded labeling when he heard that familiar pain in the neck.

"You gotta be fucking kidding me," Webb shouted over the roar of engines.

As usual, the tarmac was a circus ground crews servicing planes, forklifts darting in and out, loading belts feeding cargo into the bellies of aircraft. Harvey sighed. Here we go again.

He straightened up just in time to see Webb trotting toward him.

Harvey adjusted his flight gloves casually. They fit a little looser now the swelling in his knuckles had finally gone down.

"I take it you've got something to say?"

"You tried to get me nixed from this mission."

"Look, man, I inquired about a different wingman but I didn't force the issue or try to get you removed."

Harvey responded to Webb. They were out of earshot of the nearest airman, and he didn't mind having this conversation even though his first instinct was to ignore his hot-headed co-pilot.

Harvey tugged on the cargo netting. A flap came loose. He knelt beside the pallet, adjusted the netting, and tightened it until he was satisfied it wouldn't budge.

"Okay, I'll tell you what. On this mission, you stay outta my way, and I'll stay outta yours. Deal?"

His jaw clenched. He was getting really annoyed.

"I'm your superior and the flight lead. Have you forgotten how this works? You will do as I say. Deal?"

Webb knew Harvey was right. It didn't matter how long their friendship had lasted. In the military, rank was king and the king made the rules, or at least bent them to his will.

"Again, I don't make the rules."

Harvey knew he had Webb by the balls. He didn't feel like dealing with him, not now. He was about to spend a lot more time with him than he cared to, doomed to share the same cockpit soon enough. He kept his head down, hands fussing with the loose ends on the pallet.

"That's bullshit and you know it. You've got way more leverage than any other junior officer in the unit, and we all know why."

He was grinding Harvey's last nerve.

"Look, I didn't ask for this either. You definitely weren't my first choice."

Harvey stood up sharply and started walking away.

Like a puppy trailing his master, Webb caught up.

"You had a choice? What makes you so goddamn special? Just because you're the son of"

Harvey stopped cold. Furious.

"I'd be very careful how you finish that sentence if I were you."

He raised a finger in Webb's face, letting the threat hang in the thick, hot air between them for a beat then turned and kept walking.

Webb kept following.

"You wanna know what I think?"

"Not really. Just drop it. Okay?"

Chest to chest, the two men stared each other down. It was clear there was still bad blood surging through their veins. But it wasn't just that. Neither of them wanted to admit they'd wronged the other.

Everyone in the unit knew the comparison Harvey was to his father. And it was no secret that many believed Higby favored Harvey because of it. Webb, of all people, had heard the gossip. He also knew what people said about him.

Harvey was an Arnott through and through. Webb, despite being Harvey's reluctant right-hand man, was no Higby.

By now, their shouting had drawn the attention of nearby airmen. Eyes were turning. Heads were tilting.

Harvey noticed the stares. He had to stay focused.

Higby is counting on me. Everything depends on me, he thought.

"We'll settle this later," he barked.

As much as he wanted to take Webb to the ground, he couldn't. There was a plane to inspect.

Captain Webb exited the cargo area and moved toward a pallet outside the aircraft.

Harvey craned his neck to survey the cargo already locked down inside. A large crate wrapped in cargo netting was stamped with the word JAVELIN. Another box read STINGER. Beside it sat a crate marked NASAMS all secured and strapped tight.

Harvey tapped the nearest load. It didn't budge.

"How are we looking?"

A voice called out from behind, followed by approaching footsteps. Harvey turned and saw Master Sergeant Daniel coming his way, clipboard in hand, checking off a list.

Sergeant Daniel wore battle dress camouflage with his cap stuffed into his right cargo pocket.

"Good. What do we have left out there?" Harvey asked.

"A couple of Switchblade kamikazes and some small arms munitions. I think .50 calibers and night vision goggles," Daniel replied, walking past Harvey toward the small ladder leading to the cockpit.

"If this doesn't even the fight, maybe we give them some fuckin' planes," Daniel yelled, grabbing the ladder and planting a foot on the bottom rung.

"I'm thinking F-35s. That'd put fear in the Russians."

By the time he finished, Daniel was already halfway up, climbing into the cockpit.

Harvey turned back to the cargo, eyes tracking the airmen still working feverishly loading, strapping, tying everything down. In his mind, he could already picture Ukrainian fighters using the Javelins and FIM-92 Stingers to knock Russian helicopters out of the sky if they crossed enemy lines.

He remembered watching CNN the night before. The newscaster had reported on Russian forces launching a ground operation near Ukraine's border. The images of conscripts in tanks rolling into Ukrainian territory lingered in Harvey's mind, adding weight to this mission.

He felt uneasy but not hesitant.

Helping the underdog always felt right. And Harvey hated bullies. Deep down, he felt a strong sense of patriotism for Ukraine, even though he was, through and through, all-American.

A food truck pulled up next to the plane, and a catering container was quickly whisked aboard the C-5. Thank God for the Services crew, Harvey thought. They keep us fed on these long flights.

The meals were mostly ham and turkey sandwiches with cheese and sodas. Still anything beat MREs.

He hated MREs.

The bustling activity around the cargo planes was a symbol of coordination and precision. These were military-grade weapons being loaded, and every imaginable safety precaution was taken. One damaged weapon system showing up on the battlefield could leave its user caught in a gunfight with their pants down.

Airmen, soldiers and marines carefully aligned the pallets with the plane's massive cargo hold. Supervisors barked updates into handheld radios, ensuring every item was accounted for and securely stowed. A forklift rolled out from the aircraft's belly and came to a stop beside the gangway. The airman at the wheel waited for further instructions.

When it was all said and done, Harvey was just glad he no longer felt Webb's eyes burning into the back of his neck. He knew that sooner or later, he'd have to pull rank in a way that made him uncomfortable but not today.

Standing at a distance, Harvey watched as the C-5 prepared to seal up. On the underside of the nose were the words AIR MOBILITY COMMAND, painted against the dark gray and black of its military-grade hull. With a loud hiss of hydraulics, the nose descended slowly, lining up flush with the rest of the fuselage. A heavy click echoed across the tarmac as it locked into place.

They entered the cockpit side by side, tension between them hanging in the confined air, a silent reminder that trust, once cracked, takes more than orders or rank to repair.

There, seated in front of them, was an older gentleman in a pristine navy-blue suit with a neatly trimmed white beard. He flipped through a flight manual, seemingly absorbed. He was big and burly, likely in his fifties, though not quite at the tipping point of obesity. His thinning white hair was combed with care, giving some cover to a steadily retreating hairline.

When he noticed Webb and Harvey entering, he stood with a smile.

Harvey extended his hand.

"Let me guess. You must be the expert."

"The name is Pavlyuk…"

The man replied. Harvey picked up the faint Ukrainian accent.

"…and I only flew the Antonov-225 for about a hundred years or so," he said, as they shook hands and exchanged greetings.

Harvey let out a hearty laugh and turned to Webb, giving him a playful smack on the chest.

"You see that? That is humor. That's how you have fun on the job. Take notes."

Webb shot him a look that could kill, but Harvey ignored it and turned back to the man.

"Call me Harvey."

Webb cut in.

"First-name basis? You just met him."

He muttered something under his breath.

Keeping his eyes on the bearded man, Harvey gave a casual side nod in Webb's direction.

"…and call him Asshole."

Pavlyuk cracked a grin. It took him a moment to register that this was some kind of inside joke but he wisely chose not to ask.

"What else do I need to know about this Antonov?" Harvey asked.

The three men made their way deeper into the aircraft and stopped at the galley. Pavlyuk poured himself a cup of coffee and launched into his speech.

"Gentlemen, observe the aircraft you are standing in. The C-5…she is something to behold, no? But the Antonov-225…" he paused, lifting the cup with reverence, "…how do you say — it is a step up."

He was proud of what he knew about the Antonov. In the realm of the mighty AN-225, Pavlyuk felt superior.

As he spoke, Harvey and Webb poured themselves cups of coffee, adding cream and sugar.

"Just bigger?" Webb asked.

Pavlyuk nodded. "Much bigger."

"And better, I guess," Harvey added, with a hint of sarcasm.

Pavlyuk smiled. "Much better. The Antonov-225 has survived many attempts by the Russians. Ya nenavydzhu tsykh vyrodkiv."

His eyes drifted for a moment, then refocused.

"Viktor Bout. You've heard of him, yes?"

He clearly expected the military men to know the name if not, it would've disappointed him.

"Of course," Webb replied matter-of-factly. "Biggest arms dealer the world's ever seen."

"The Merchant of Death," Harvey added.

"That's him," Pavlyuk nodded in agreement, then continued.

"Before his arrest, he attempted to steal the Mriya. That's what we call her."

Webb let out a low whistle. "Ballsy."

Pavlyuk went on. "Ukrainian intel stopped him. But now he's a free man. And with Russia threatening to overtake Ukraine…"

Harvey took a sip of coffee.

"You think he'll try again?"

Pavlyuk nodded once more. "Yes. Viktor is a very dedicated and very evil man. If he were to gain access to that plane, he could supply weapons to all of Europe. And Africa."

Harvey popped a toothpick between his teeth.

"Damn, Potluck. That's some scary shit."

The bearded man narrowed his eyes, and Harvey knew he wasn't going to ignore the fact that the American had just butchered his name probably on purpose.

Pavlyuk was used to people mispronouncing his name. He wasn't fond of it. Especially not when he suspected it was done with intent.

"The name is Pavlyuk," he said firmly.

But Harvey was already lost in thought stuck on the idea of Bout and the Antonov coming together. It didn't sit right with him.

Things had been serious before, but now they'd taken a darker turn. This was starting to feel like a suicide mission.

And it was one the good guys as Higby had labeled them, had to win.

CHAPTER FIFTEEN

(CROSSING THE RUBICON)

HARVEY REACHED FOR THE folder hanging on the wall just above the stairwell leading down into the cargo bay. He scanned the manifest, paying close attention to the load descriptions.

He went down the list

- M777 Howitzer check.

- MRAP check.

- Javelin check.

- Stinger check.

- Switchblades check.

- Night vision gear, small and large arms ammo check.

He handed the manifest to Webb and proceeded down the ladder. As he reached the bottom rung, he looked up and saw the fat man descending one step at a time. Webb followed.

Soon, all three men were walking the cargo bay for a final inspection.

Webb snickered at the sight of the neatly packed payload. "The Russians have no idea what's in store for them."

Harvey glanced at Pavlyuk's face as he took it in.

"Indeed," Pavlyuk replied. But something in his expression didn't read excitement maybe he was tired. Or maybe something else.

Once satisfied that everything matched the manifest, the three men climbed back up into the cockpit.

Harvey dropped into the left seat. Webb took the right. Pavlyuk settled into the jump seat behind Webb.

Harvey pulled out the pre-flight manual binder and was about to speak when Webb cut in.

"Do we really have to use that every time?" he asked, watching Harvey flip through the checklist.

"We've got this shit memorized like a fucking Zac Brown Band song."

"It's protocol," Harvey said with a smile.

Webb responded with a middle finger.

Harvey handed the manual to Pavlyuk, who thumbed through it quickly. He clearly wasn't absorbing much already sweating.

"Nervous, Potluck?" Harvey asked, grinning.

"No, no. Not at all."

Harvey looked out the window. Darkness had fallen, and the lights along the runway stretched for miles ahead of them. An airman stood in front of the plane, holding two red light cones as if waiting for a signal. Before long, he raised both hands, forming an X with the cones.

Pavlyuk pulled a small three-by-four photo from his shirt pocket and pinned it to the wall where he could see it from his seat.

Harvey squinted, noting the young woman in the picture. She looked to be in her late twenties, maybe early thirties. Even though the photo was slightly faded, her honey-blonde hair still caught the light. Her smile was perfect. Her eyes if Harvey had to guess were the color of the morning sky.

The C-5 rumbled backward, then began taxiing forward across the tarmac with a woozy kind of momentum. Harvey and Webb shifted into expert mode. Ahead of them, a sea of runway lights glowed like stars guiding the way.

"Tower, Halo is ready for takeoff," Harvey said calmly into his mic.

"Halo, the runway is yours," came the response from the air traffic controller.

A deep rumble echoed from the belly of the C-5. It belched exhaust, then surged forward. The engines roared, the turbines screamed, and the 190-ton plane picked up speed, lifting off from the asphalt and into the air. The landing gear folded into the belly with a satisfying thud.

Behind him, Harvey saw Pavlyuk wink at the photo on the wall as he buckled his seatbelt.

Harvey couldn't help himself.

"Damn, Potluck. You like 'em young, huh?"

Harvey shook his head, wearing a sheepish grin as he waited for the fat man to respond but Pavlyuk said nothing.

"I knew the suit and manners were all an act. You're just a dirty old man at heart. Not bad, my friend. Not bad at all."

Pavlyuk opened his mouth as if to reply, but thought better of it. He refocused on the manual he was halfway through.

The plane banked left and continued its climb. Pavlyuk folded the manual, leaned toward the small cockpit window, and peered into the night sky. Red lights blinked from the massive wing and fuselage.

After a steady ascent to nearly 28,000 feet, the C-5 began to level off while navigating Qatari airspace. A half moon hung high, haloed by streaks of dark clouds. The temperature outside was forty-nine degrees. The red blinking lights on the wings danced, bleeding into the rain-slick darkness as moist air streaked across the glass and metal.

Only a few scattered lights far below maybe ships at sea hinted that the Qatari coast was still beneath them.

General Higby stood by his window, a cigar in his right hand, his left tucked into his pants pocket. He watched as the C-5 flew high overhead and slowly disappeared, leaving behind only faint red glimmers in the night.

He turned away from the window and faced his desk, eyes settling on the paused footage on his laptop screen.

He sat down, hit play, and the video resumed.

Grainy footage played two figures locked in a scuffle outside a cockpit. His pilots. Harvey and Webb.

"I'll be fucking damned," he muttered.

He tried to process what he was seeing. How could his two top junior officers pull something this stupid? Frustrated, he slammed the laptop shut and walked back to the window, staring into the night.

Out there, only the faintest twinkling lights remained like stars from a galaxy far, far away.

The C-5 was long gone.

For what it was worth, the two officers hadn't been grounded, not yet, at least. Not figuratively. Not literally. Instead, they were en route on a covert mission to a distant land.

Maybe this mission will be their saving grace.

The United States government was counting on them.

"Don't let me down, kid. Don't let me down."

He said a quick prayer to the heavens, then took a long swig of his drink.

A wall-mounted TV quietly played CNN in the background, but nothing caught Higby's interest. He stole quick glances at the screen now and then, but it was just the same recycled stories from earlier in the day.

His phone buzzed on the table. He picked it up.

"Hey, Mark. What's up?"

He listened, nodding slightly.

"Yeah. Of course."

He glanced at the clock on the wall. 1950 hours.

"Yeah, I'm in. Tell the fellas to wait for me."

Meanwhile 30,000 feet above the Persian Gulf

The C-5 was shaking violently.

The night outside was a vast, inky canvas starless and stretched above a churning, angry sea. Inside the cockpit, Harvey gripped the yoke, his knuckles bone white. Webb reached for the radio, fumbling to send out a distress signal. Pavlyuk clung to his seat, bracing against the turbulence.

In the cargo hold, airmen manned their stations. The full crew: two pilots, two flight engineers, a loadmaster, a crew chief, two staff sergeants from the Security Forces Squadron and the Antonov expert, known (jokingly) as Potluck.

He hated that nickname. Juvenile, he thought. Unnecessary.

The rhythmic thrum of the four massive engines was usually a comforting lullaby at this point in the flight. But not tonight.

Tonight, it sounded like a prelude to disaster.

The weather briefing had promised smooth skies over the Gulf. But radar now showed something else entirely: a sprawling, angry splotch of red and violent purple directly in their path.

"Looks like someone lied about this weather!" Harvey shouted over the roar of the engines, his eyes glued to the instrument panel.

"Halo to Tower One, come in," Webb called, his voice tight into the mic.

He paused, waiting.

The plane suddenly bucked hard. A violent jolt.

Pavlyuk's spine snapped upright in his seat.

"Ouch."

He cried out.

Down in the cargo bay, the heavy chains securing the MRAP groaned under sudden strain. Master Sergeant Daniels the flight's loadmaster, a man whose career had weathered more turbulence than most pilots felt his stomach lurch.

He watched as the MRAP and the two Stinger crates beside it shifted slightly. Just slightly.

But it was enough.

A ripple of unease moved through the crew.

Pavlyuk could no longer hide his fear.

"Are you going to make it?" Webb asked, turning to see him fidgeting with the straps on his jump seat.

"Potluck, get your vest on."

"What did you say?" Pavlyuk cupped a hand around his ear.

"He said get your vest on in case we have to dump the bird!" Harvey shouted.

"What about you?"

"Don't worry about us, Potluck."

This time, Pavlyuk didn't correct him. He was too busy retching into a brown paper bag.

"Holy shit, Potluck. Don't you die on me," Harvey snapped. "I need my Antonov expert alive and well."

Webb glanced back, one brow arched. "He's alive..."

"...but I don't think he's well."

Harvey almost laughed. Almost.

Pavlyuk struggled with his vest, fingers fumbling to align the straps. The plane was shaking violently now like it might break apart mid-air.

Webb turned to Harvey.

"Harv...if we die...here...together..."

"Oh, shut the fuck up, Webb!" Harvey barked.

"No one is dying today. Jesus."

Harvey switched frequencies on his headset and called for the loadmaster but just as he did, lightning lit up the sky and thunder shook the aircraft. The cockpit rattled violently against the chaotic currents of the approaching storm.

Pavlyuk kept vomiting, while Webb wiped sweat from his brow.

Harvey tried again.

"Sergeant Daniels!"

A few seconds later, Master Sergeant Daniels' voice crackled into his headset.

"Yes, Major?"

"How's the cargo looking down there?"

"Solid as a rock, sir!"

Daniels tried to sound calm measured. No need to alarm the pilots. They had enough to deal with up there.

Strapped into his jump seat, Daniels gripped the safety bar beside him.

Then it hit.

Not a gentle rock but a violent, upward thrust that slammed him hard against his harness. The cabin lights flickered, casting eerie shadows across exposed panels and bulkheads.

Outside, darkness pressed against the plane black, endless broken only by flashes of lightning that lit up monstrous, anvil-headed clouds.

"Whoa! Rapid descent!" Harvey yelled, eyes locked on the altimeter needle as it danced wildly across the gauge cluster.

He and Webb fought the controls, muscles taut, trying to keep the aircraft level.

Warning lights flared across the dashboard a frantic cascade of red and amber.

Garbled radio chatter filled their headsets as the aircraft twisted and tilted, caught in a nightmarish spiral.

This is scary, Pavlyuk thought. Is this really happening?

The plane groaned a tortured symphony of stressed metal while rain pelted the fuselage like a thousand tiny fists pounding to be let in.

In the cargo bay, airmen clung to their harnesses. The MRAP, nearly 40,000 pounds was holding, but the restraints groaned and creaked, their protest nearly as loud as the storm outside.

"We're entering the core of it, Captain," Daniels shouted. "Keep holding onto that stick!"

Harvey gritted his teeth, sweat beading on his forehead. He wiped it away with the back of his hand and regained a firm grip on the yoke.

His eyes narrowed, locked in fierce concentration as he scanned the instrument panel.

They could feel the strain on the C-5, the immense power of the engines struggling against the violent, invisible air currents. For a horrifying moment, the aircraft seemed to hang suspended in midair.

Then it dropped.

A stomach-lurching freefall that felt like it lasted forever.

A collective gasp filled the cockpit.

Harvey fought the rising urge to panic. Webb wasn't so lucky the freefall had rattled him.

"Don't give up on me, Captain. I need you to focus," Harvey snapped.

Webb gave his best tough-guy impression, swiping the panic off his face, trying to recompose himself.

Harvey focused on the feel of the aircraft, the subtle resistance in the controls, the feedback through the stick, the heartbeat of the plane.

"We're almost through it, fellas. Just a little more," he murmured, almost to himself.

A blinding flash of lightning tore through the sky, illuminating the ragged, swirling edges of the storm and just beyond, a glimpse of calm.

The madness had an end.

"Okay, here we go. We're almost in the clear, boys."

"Hang tight."

He reassured everyone, then signaled to Webb.

Together, they pushed the throttles forward.

Slowly painstakingly the C-5 clawed its way out of the maelstrom. The violent shaking eased into a series of diminishing bumps, and finally, a return to that familiar, steady thrum.

Harvey let out a long, shuddering breath one he hadn't realized he'd been holding. His hands still trembled on the yoke.

At last, the C-5 Galaxy emerged from the storm. The night sky began to reveal itself again, stars piercing slowly through the receding clouds. The moon, a thin crescent, peeked out from behind the last ragged traces of rain.

Harvey was glad he had his gloves on. He wouldn't admit it out loud, but his palms were sweaty. He'd felt every pulse of that squall.

With every breath, every shake, every jolt the trick was to ride with the storm, not try to outrun it. Work with the air around you, not against it.

That, he knew.

And just like that, everything leveled out. The chaos behind them. The plane flew steady now like they'd been catapulted through Earth's turbulent shell and reached the stillness of zero gravity.

The only sound was the low, comforting drone of the engines finally, a lullaby again.

The cabin erupted in nervous, triumphant laughter.

"Not bad, asshole. Not bad," Webb offered.

"You were shaking in your boots for a second," Harvey shot back.

"Yeah, well … you're still in charge, so I'm still not done saying my prayers."

"Fuck you too, Webb," Harvey muttered, and they both laughed again.

Even Pavlyuk let out a sigh of relief, a soft smile forming as he pulled the small photo from the wall and pressed it to his chest. He closed his eyes in quiet thanks.

They had faced the night's fury and emerged. Bruised, maybe. But unbroken.

Harvey stole a glance at the radar cluster.

Nothing but green and black.

CHAPTER SIXTEEN

(HIGH STAKES POKER)

A POKER GAME WAS in full swing. All the big wigs not currently on duty were gathered in the day room, the unofficial hangout spot for senior officers stationed at Qatar Air Base.

The fellas called it "high-stakes," but in reality, it was nothing more than a pressure valve blowing off steam after a grueling day. Their roles were among the most demanding on base, and not many envied them for that reason.

"Let me know when you boys want to play for real money," said Major General Mark Curry, speaking around a fat cigar clenched between his teeth as he raked in the poker chips.

Curry, Higby, and a handful of other Field Grade Officers, aka FGOs, sat around an octagonal poker table, winding down from the day's events as they usually did most nights. Some wore Air Force PT gear as their dress-down choice, while others had opted for good old-fashioned civilian pajamas.

General Curry, head of Air Force Central Command, or AFCENT was a man whose formidable handsomeness seemed to defy his fifty-something years. His close-cropped hair, now more salt than pepper, only served to highlight a career spent making hard calls.

Right now, he was the man responsible for all U.S. air operations in the Middle East.

"Maybe when you don't show up to the game in your jammies, we'll talk," Higby quipped.

The room burst into laughter.

"What's wrong with my PJs?" Curry asked, raising an eyebrow.

Higby grabbed the deck and began to shuffle, taking a long pull from his cigar.

Curry cleared his throat loud enough to quiet the chuckling officers.

"For starters the Avengers," Higby said, nodding at Curry's pajama pants.

"What's wrong with the Avengers? My son loves Iron Man. He bought me these."

"Okay, whatever you say, Mark," Higby said with mock disbelief, shaking his head. "Hey who's on call tonight?"

"Colonel Wiggins."

Another FGO chimed in as General Higby dealt five cards around the table, one at a time, clockwise. Each player received two cards face down. He dealt himself last, then stole a quick glance at his hand.

"What do we know about Wiggins?" Higby asked.

"Tough as nails, that sonofabitch. I was deployed with him in Kuwait, back in our early days," Curry replied, just as the table started placing wagers. Players eyed their cards, developing strategies and negotiating bets.

"Good to know the Air Force has a fine line of replacements for us old farts," Higby muttered, nodding toward the oldest FGO in the room a thinning, grey-haired man who somehow still wore his battle dress uniform every single day.

"Simmons is old as dirt."

Another round of laughter erupted as General Simmons became the butt of yet another joke. He was used to it by now. All he could do was smile and take the burn.

Sometimes, he wished the burns came from a junior officer at least then he could throw his rank around a little. But here? A grin would have to do.

"I'm going to grab some coffee. Gotta stay awake somehow," Simmons said, not playing a hand at the moment. He pushed back from the table and shuffled into the kitchen.

"With what's at stake," he added over his shoulder, "I couldn't fall asleep if I wanted to."

Higby raised his hand of cards to eye level and admitted, "This mission's like nothing I've ever handled. The Antonov is so rare and so delicate that if this thing goes south, I'll be in deep shit."

"Why so extreme?" someone asked.

"Well, I bet the house money on Major Arnott and Captain Webb. While I've got faith in the Major, the kid scares me a little. He's a hothead, like his father." Higby paused. "I miss the sonofabitch."

They kept playing into the night until the room was suddenly flooded with sound from the wall-mounted TV.

BREAKING NEWS CNN

"Welcome back. We have a developing story this hour," the anchor announced. "Explosions and air raid sirens are being reported across Ukraine's capital and several neighboring cities in what officials confirm is a missile attack launched from Russia."

The poker game froze.

Everyone turned to the screen, now displaying a map of Ukraine: Kyiv, Kharkiv, Crimea, and the Black Sea.

The reporter continued.

"Air defense systems have been activated. Cruise missiles are inbound from multiple directions. In Odessa, emergency power outages have been implemented to protect key infrastructure."

The senior officers were silent, eyes locked on the TV as footage began rolling columns of Russian tanks rumbling through Crimea, pushing north in a coordinated formation.

"Sources tell our sister station in Washington that the Pentagon and the White House are currently finalizing a military aid package for Ukraine. What's in that package hasn't been disclosed yet, but hopes are high it brings some strength to our allies."

The reporter's tone dropped.

"It's starting to feel like another Chernobyl."

She ended the segment with a deadpan look straight into the camera.

There was a long pause.

"Jesus Christ. Can you believe this?" someone muttered.

Simmons let out a breath, cradling his coffee between both hands.

"Tell me about it."

Higby took one last drag from his cigar and stubbed it out in the ashtray.

"I just sent two of my boys down there."

General Curry, sitting across the poker table from Higby, stiffened.

"Russia is playing with fire. We get on the horn with the Pentagon at 0600hrs."

At thirty thousand feet above, the skies were finally smooth. The storm had passed, and with turbulence behind them, Harvey, Webb, Pavlyuk, and the rest of the crew cruised the C-5 Galaxy on autopilot.

But there was no banter. No back-and-forth. Not this time.

Everyone was locked onto the screen in the crew area, watching CNN's live coverage of the unrest in Ukraine the same report their commanders were watching back at Qatar Air Base.

"You've gotta be shitting me," Harvey barked.

"As if the storm wasn't enough … now this shit," Webb muttered, his frustration simmering. After a beat, he added, "I say we turn this thing around."

He wasn't serious, Harvey knew it was just the anger talking.

"What do you think the United States is going to do?" Pavlyuk asked. His face was still pale and damp from being sick earlier.

"If the Russians take over Ukrainian airspace … we will be flying ducks."

"Don't you mean sitting ducks?" Webb asked, confused.

"No," Harvey said quietly. "He's right."

Harvey answered. Pavlyuk looked razzled like he might be sick again.

"They'll blow us clear out of the sky."

But Harvey wasn't about to accept that. Serious options needed to be weighed, sure but assuming they were already dead? That was never his go-to move. He rotated the toothpick between his teeth, thinking.

"I say we gotta make a call here, Harv," Webb said. "No point in dying for nothing. What happens if we change course?"

"The mission fails," Harvey replied. "Just let me think."

Pavlyuk asked something but it was ignored.

"And what happens if the mission fails?" Webb pressed.

"Just let me think," Harvey repeated, sharper now, almost pleading.

"Just listen to this," Webb continued, undeterred. "I mean, I'm no quitter, but the odds are not in our favor, not even close. So, what's the point? We're flying into hostile airspace, and this time the enemy isn't the Iraqis, it's the formidable Russians."

He leaned forward.

"So I repeat what happens if the mission fails?"

Harvey's voice rose.

"Then Russia gets a new fuckin' plane!"

He paused, eyes locked on the dim radar glow.

"The Antonov-225 is not just a plane. For us it's more than that. Without it as a bargaining chip, we can't pay for the weapons to fight the Russians."

Pavlyuk finally spoke, his voice low but clear.

"Without the Antonov, Ukraine dies."

He reached for the photo again pressed it to his chest.

"Vira dies."

He spoke softly almost a whisper but loud enough to be heard.

Harvey had to look away. He couldn't bear to see a grown man cry.

Webb pulled up an aerial map of their location, and they all huddled over it.

"This is where we are," Webb said, pointing to a spot over the Gulf. "And we have until here…" he slid his finger along the route "… to change course, avoid Ukraine's airspace, and save our asses."

"You mean Russian airspace, if we lose the Antonov," Pavlyuk added somberly.

A brief silence settled.

"I wouldn't underestimate the heart and fight of the Ukrainians," Pavlyuk continued.

"And I wouldn't underestimate our odds with Russia," Webb snapped. "Especially not if we're in the sky right now with a hundred of their SAMs locked on us!"

He turned to his co-pilot.

"It's your call, Harv. But we have to act now."

Harvey stood and walked away from the cockpit area, heading toward the open hatch that led down to the cargo hold. He leaned his back against the sliding door to a lower compartment, facing the open hatch.

From where he stood, he could see the front end of the MRAP in the hold below.

He closed his eyes.

His mind raced.

This wasn't the first time he'd faced a situation that could cost lives. He wasn't a rookie and this wasn't his first rodeo. But still … this mission felt heavier than the rest.

He didn't make decisions without thinking them through. Well most of the time.

But this? This wasn't just about crew morale or fear of what might lie ahead.

This was bigger.

To abort a mission like this, orders would have to come from someone far above his pay grade.

He wondered what his father would've done in this situation.

He knew exactly what Higby would ask him to do.

For a moment, Harvey's mind drifted back to the phone conversation he'd had just before boarding the plane.

He could still hear the gentle creak of the wooden chair on the porch, facing rows of late-summer crops. He could still hear his grandma's voice warm, teasing, timeless.

"So, are you dating anyone yet? I can't wait forever for a grandchild, you know?"

She wasn't too focused on his work. She hadn't mentioned the news. She just wanted to know about him.

"That's not how that works, Grandma. I need time to get to know her," he had replied, smiling to himself hoping she wouldn't press further.

She didn't.

She was sweet and loving in every sense of the word. And Harvey had needed that moment, needed the distraction from the mess he knew he was flying into.

"You need to get over Trisha … it's been five years," he recalled her saying, her voice firm with gentle insistence. "It's over, and she's not coming back. I never believed a city girl was going to take to farm living anyway. Besides, you're not getting any younger."

He sighed.

But it was her final words that stuck with him the most:

"All I can say is don't show up for Thanksgiving alone, Harv."

Harvey blinked hard, snapping out of the memory.

He glanced toward the crew area and saw the others still huddled together, talking in hushed tones. His eyes landed on the map Webb had pinned beside the computer monitor. For a second, everything stilled.

Then he realized they were all looking to him now.

Waiting.

The weight of the moment settled fully on his shoulders.

This was the decision.

He stepped back into the crew area, locked eyes with each member of the team, and said with steady conviction:

"We stay the course."

CHAPTER SEVENTEEN

(POINT OF NO RETURN)

BUILT DURING WORLD WAR II, the Pentagon stands as a symbol of American military power and global influence. With five concentric pentagonal rings connected by ten spokelike corridors radiating from a central courtyard, it remains one of the largest office buildings in the world. Located in Arlington, Virginia, just across the Potomac River, the massive structure was hosting a meeting that could reshape the European geopolitical landscape.

Inside the Joint Chiefs of Staff Conference Room known as The Tank, a gathering of top brass and high-ranking civilians with top-secret clearances sat in high-backed leather chairs around a U-shaped table. Spider phones were positioned strategically between each seat.

"Russia has violated the United Nations Charter by attacking Ukraine and illegally annexing territories belonging to our ally. Our multilateral system is under greater strain than at any time in recent history."

The voice of Vice Chairman of the Joint Chiefs of Staff, Christopher Milton, echoed across the room. Concern crept over the faces of those in attendance. After a brief pause, the admiral continued.

"I'm sure you boys have a television over there in Qatar and saw what happened last night."

Thousands of miles away, in a similarly secured meeting space known as a Sensitive Compartmented Information Facility, or SCIF on Al Udeid Air Base, commanders sat around a large oak table. A central speakerphone transmitted the Pentagon's words. Though it was night in Qatar, the room was brightly lit.

General Simmons sat across from Higby. Calm and composed, Higby steepled his fingers, absorbing the information transmitted through the spider phone.

"That's correct, sir. We were watching as it unfolded," came the voice of General Higby through the intercom speaker embedded in the center of the U-shaped table.

Admiral Milton continued.

"I've already spoken with POTUS. He wants to know the sitrep and our operational capabilities if this escalates further. Mark, that's your domain. What do you have for us?"

They waited for a response from the speakerphone. The room was stuffy not just from poor air circulation, but from the thickening tension as Milton and his colleagues awaited General Curry's reply.

"Sir, we're maintaining secure airspace over Ukraine to prevent any aerial surprises. We also have a rapid-response unit ready in Poland and Moldova in case things spiral. Higby, want to weigh in?"

General Higby didn't appreciate being put on the spot. General Simmons found it amusing he stifled a chuckle and perhaps even a tear. Higby shot him a cold look and straightened in his seat.

"We've trained alongside the Ukrainian military, and I'm confident they can hold their ground against the Russians. We may not need to engage directly. The mere presence of American forces both on the ground and in the air could be enough to deter any reckless moves."

The Secretary of Defense nodded, clearly reassured.

"Thanks for the vote of confidence, Tom."

But Admiral Milton had something else on his mind. He leaned forward, speaking into the slim microphone in front of him.

"Are you suggesting we put boots on the ground, General?"

Higby replied without hesitation.

"No, sir. I was referring to the package en route as we speak."

General Miguel Arajillo, Commandant of the Marine Corps, leaned into his mic.

"What package?"

A collective gasp rippled through the room. He glanced at Admiral Milton just as the question left his lips. The fact that some members weren't aware of the operation was already raising alarms. The Commandant looked genuinely confused.

General Higby's voice crackled over the speaker.

"I take it everyone in that room has the highest clearance?"

"That's right, Tom. Go ahead," Milton confirmed.

General Higby cleared his throat before continuing.

"As we speak, a C-5 Galaxy is entering Ukrainian airspace. It's carrying weapons systems authorized by Congress to support our allies in the region against any Russian aggression. We foresaw this possibility but not this soon."

"What's in the package?"

The Marine Commandant pressed for details, but Vice Admiral Milton cut him off with a wave of his hand.

"Don't worry about that. I'll brief the rest of the team here. Thanks, Tom. Thanks, Mark."

And with that, the conference call ended. Higby and the other deployed commanders rose from their seats, breaking off into quiet side conversations. Those uninterested in small talk filed out of the SCIF.

Only then did Higby release the deep breath he'd been holding. Did he have confidence in his troops if things went south? Absolutely. But did he believe the Ukrainians could withstand a full-scale Russian assault alone? That, he could not say. All he could do was hope for the best while keeping his eyes and ears locked on the mission at hand.

He had promised Congress a successful delivery, and the stakes were climbing by the hour. Quietly, Higby offered a prayer for both the C-5 Galaxy and the massive Antonov, An-225 carrying its share of the burden.

The C-5 Galaxy glided smoothly through the night sky. Outside, the air was calm; inside the cockpit, the mood was anything but. Harvey, Webb, and Pavlyuk sat in silence, eyes fixed on a small TV broadcasting CNN. From behind his desk, Anderson Cooper polished as ever was trying to connect with a reporter on the ground.

"We're seeing movements across the border into Ukraine. Fred, tell us what you're seeing."

Webb shook his head and muttered under his breath.

"A shitshow. That's what he's seeing. A motherfucking shitshow."

Pavlyuk chimed in, his voice heavy.

"It's all so sad. So very, very sad."

He shook his head, wringing his weathered hands in his lap. Harvey's eyes stayed locked on the screen, sharp and unblinking. He wasn't taking this development lightly. Whatever unfolded here would affect them, affect the entire mission. Leaning forward, he grabbed the knob and turned up the volume.

"I just want to explain where I am…Anderson," Fred began.

"I'm at the last checkpoint before the frontline near Belgorod. People here are fleeing from as far as Kharkiv. It's a harrowing sight. Men, women, children running for their lives. They're terrified, and rightfully so. Russia is raining missiles down on them, stripping away everything they know in an act of menacing destruction. Back to you, Anderson."

"A heart-wrenching sight, indeed," Anderson Cooper said somberly. "And what's that behind you, Fred?"

Fred turned, glanced at the distance, then faced the camera again, his eyes sharper, more worried than before. "Anderson, there's a column of T-72 battle tanks moving in."

"Where are they headed?" Anderson asked.

"Deep into Ukrainian territory," Fred replied, shaking his head.

In the cockpit, Pavlyuk lowered his gaze, fixating on anything but the news. He pulled out his phone, scrolled aimlessly, then paused typing something into a note. Harvey, meanwhile, had heard and seen enough. He jabbed the mute button on the TV, then turned and strode back toward the controls, Webb and Pavlyuk following close behind.

Harvey and Webb resumed full command of the plane. "Enough of that. We need to keep our focus. Russia will do what it's going to do, and we'll do what we must to ensure this mission doesn't fail. It's more crucial than ever, and turning back is no longer an option. Potluck, get on the horn with tower and alert them of our presence. It's time to put this bird down, make the swap, and get the hell out."

Pavlyuk pocketed his phone and reached for the radio while Harvey began preparing for descent. The C-5 sank through the cloud cover, breaking into the hazy skyline as the crew steadied for approach.

From the cockpit, Webb narrowed his eyes. Something was coming into view. "Are you guys seeing this?"

"Fucking hell," Harvey muttered. "What are they doing?"

Below, a massive crowd surged toward the airfield, thousands of civilians carrying signs and light belongins, less than half a mile from the runway.

"They'll be slaughtered," Pavlyuk whispered, his eyes wide with terror.

"Looks like they're trying to make a statement," Harvey said. "Let's bring her lower."

Webb shifted in his seat, adjusting his headset. "Out of the frying pan, into the fire," he muttered as the C-5 pushed into final descent.

The fact they hadn't been shot down yet meant one thing, Russia was not yet controlling Ukrainian airspace. And for now, that was the best outcome they could hope for.

Engines whirred and thundered as the C-5 dropped steadily, its green silhouette cutting through the dusk. The colossal wingspan dwarfed everything in sight, its four turbines emitting a deep, resonant hum that rippled through the air. With a hydraulic groan, the underbelly opened and the landing gear deployed, locking into place like the legs of a massive insect.

Flaps and slats extended, trading speed for lift, as Harvey and Webb guided the beast with surgical precision. Air rushed across the fuselage, the nose lifting slightly as speed bled off. The giant aircraft gave a guttural growl.

The ground rushed upward. Then impact. A heavy, satisfying thud as the main gear slammed onto the runway. Smoke hissed from the tires before they bit into asphalt. The nose dropped gently, followed by the roar of reverse thrust. The engines howled with concussive force before spooling down.

The C-5 lumbered off the active strip, turning onto a taxiway and into a predesignated hangar.

Minutes later, Harvey, Webb, and the crew descended the gangway. Outside, chaos reigned crowds scattered, moving without direction, the air buzzing with fear and confusion.

Pavlyuk trailed behind, his eyes glued to his phone. He checked it over and over, like a schoolboy waiting for a message from a crush. Whether he was avoiding the chaos around him or shaken from the news footage, Harvey couldn't tell. But something about Pavlyuk felt off in a way Harvey couldn't quite place.

Once they were on the ground and deplaned, The two Staff Sergeants from the security forces squadron emerged, hauling a large black box secured with a heavy lock.

A Ukrainian officer in dark shades approached. He removed them, slipping the pair into his pocket.

"Major," he greeted, extending a hand to Harvey. "We've been eagerly awaiting your arrival. I'm General Melnik, and this is Lieutenant Koshani."

They shook hands briefly.

"Follow me."

General Melnik was a man of few words until he needed to drive a point home. Today was one of those days. An architect of many of Ukraine's ground offensives, he was often considered one of the country's greatest generals. His build was heavy, his graying hair thinning, but his eyes a striking, ice-blue were his most commanding feature.

At his side stood Lieutenant Koshani, six-foot-four with a lean, wiry frame and a week's growth of beard.

The general led the group across the asphalt toward a massive hangar. His lieutenant stayed close at every step.

"Damn, Potluck," Harvey called over. "The general's English is better than yours. What part of Ukraine did you say you're from again?"

"This from a man who still can't pronounce my name," Pavlyuk shot back. He had been waiting for the perfect chance to return the jab.

Harvey just grinned and kept pace with Melnik. The others followed close behind until they reached the east end of the flight line, where two helicopters roared overhead. Their rotors thundered so loudly that Melnik had to shout.

"I should probably mention there's been a slight change of plans, Major!"

Harvey didn't like last-minute changes. Especially not on missions like this one. But he wasn't green. He knew military operations were unpredictable.

"Yeah, that would've been nice to know earlier," Harvey shouted back. "What's the change?"

"The president and his family will be coming aboard the Antonov."

Harvey froze. He ripped off his shades, his face twisting in shock. Webb's eyes widened beside him.

"What did he just say?" Webb asked.

"You've got to be fucking kidding me, General," Harvey snapped. "With all due respect, that wasn't part of my orders. Washington will never approve a deviation like this."

Melnik stopped, turning to face him. For the first time, their eyes locked.

"I don't kid, Major. No president, no Antonov. Besides, we don't need Washington's permission. Zelensky and your president are friends. I'm sure they'll understand."

Without another word, Melnik turned back toward the hangar.

Harvey glanced at Webb and silently mouthed: What the fuck.

CHAPTER EIGHTEEN

(CHANGE OF PLANS)

Harvey stalked after Melnik and Koshani, who hadn't slowed their pace for nearly a minute. Ahead loomed a massive, fully enclosed hangar, soldiers with long rifles stationed around its perimeter.

"I'm sorry, General," Harvey called out. "Maybe I've still got dust in my ears from all that commotion back there. But I could've sworn you said we'd be transporting the Ukrainian president."

"You heard right, Major. Congratulations." Melnik didn't break stride, eyes fixed forward.

"What the fu" Webb began, but Harvey cut him off. "You've got to give me some time to"

"Take all the time you need, Major," Melnik interrupted smoothly. "Just don't take too long. The president has a plane to catch."

"General, with all due respect," Webb said, half-grinning at the absurdity and shoving his hands into his pockets, "that wasn't part of the mission. And under these circumstances, Washington would never approve"

Melnik stopped abruptly, turning to face them. His ice-blue stare pinned both Webb and Harvey in place. Beside him, Koshani folded his arms, silent and imposing.

"The circumstances," Melnik said evenly, "are exactly why we must deviate. You've seen the news. The president is in danger. The Antonov is the only way for him, his family, and his aircraft to leave safely and discreetly. The Russians won't even know where to look."

Before Harvey could respond and he had plenty to say the massive hangar doors began to move with a low, rumbling groan. The grinding of metal mixed with the whir of motors, echoing through the cavernous space.

A sliver of light cut through the seam where the doors met. As the gap widened, dust motes swirled in the air, giving way to the sleek metallic fuselage that emerged from the shadows painted white, yellow, and blue.

There she was. The Antonov, An-225 Mriya, in all her glory.

The air inside was still, heavy with the scent of hydraulic fluid and jet fuel. The men tilted their heads back, eyes wide, taking in the colossal machine. She was breathtaking dwarfing even a Boeing 747. Painted in Ukraine's national colors, her tail bore the proud mark: AN-225.

"Goddamn," Webb muttered. "I knew she was big, but…goddamn."

"The grandest aircraft ever built," Melnik declared, grinning as he admired the plane. "Take good care of her."

"Jesus," Harvey breathed, mouth agape. In all his years as a pilot, he had never imagined flying anything this enormous. To him, it looked more like a spacecraft than something bound for Washington, D.C.

Then he noticed Potluck again, hunched over that damn phone. It irritated him the expert seemed more consumed by the little device than by the monster of steel in front of them.

"Potluck," Harvey snapped. "Did you know about this?"

Harvey fixed his gaze on Pavlyuk, but before the man could speak, Melnik cut in again.

"It's irrelevant, Major. The Russians have been tracking President Zelensky's plane for some time. We have intel that if it takes to the sky, they'll bring it down by any means necessary. So we hid it inside the Mriya."

The words caught Harvey and Webb completely off guard.

"Wait wait, wait." Webb shook his head, throwing up a hand in disbelief. "Are you serious? There's a plane … inside this plane?"

Melnik gave a curt nod. "Does that surprise you?"

"Fuck yeah. Show me." Webb started toward the cargo hold, almost eager now.

"Get President Zelensky and his family out of here," Melnik said, "and Ukraine will owe you a debt of gratitude."

Harvey clenched his jaw. He was beginning to realize this was an argument he couldn't win but that didn't stop him from trying.

"I have clearance to fly the plane," Harvey snapped, "not to smuggle the president out of his own country in the middle of a goddamn war!" His voice rose, sharper with every word.

It was the question both he and Webb had been suppressing until now.

"Why would the president even want to leave at a time like this?" Harvey demanded. It would make him appear like a coward, Harvey thought.

Harvey's question came out harsher than anything he'd yet said to the general. Koshani shot him a cold, warning glare but unfolded his arms to answer a buzzing cell phone. He stepped a few paces away, out of earshot. Whatever he heard on the other end wasn't good, his face made that clear.

"It's none of your business," Melnik barked at Harvey. "You're the pilot. You fly and do your job."

By the time Koshani returned, he looked like he'd seen a ghost. Webb, sensing the tension thickening between the men, tried to cut it with a joke.

"Careful, General. He's got a mean left hook," Webb said with a grin.

For a long, heated moment, Harvey and Melnik stared each other down, the American balling his fist and gritting his teeth. The air hung heavy between them, until Melnik finally spoke.

"You have your orders, Major. Now I suggest you orient yourself with the functions of the plane, because the president will be here in one hour."

Suddenly, Melnik's radio chirped on his hip. He unclipped it, raised it to his lips, and spoke in rapid Ukrainian before reholstering it. When he turned back to Harvey, his tone had shifted quieter, more deliberate.

"Like I said. The president will be here in one hour."

Koshani leaned in close, whispering something into Melnik's ear. The general's face stayed blank, unreadable.

Concerned, Harvey asked, "What's the matter?"

Melnik answered flatly. "We have a problem outside the gate. A mob is forming. We need to move now."

Melnik led the way up the massive metal ramp, already angled into position. His boots clanged against the ribbed steel with each step. After a stubborn pause, Harvey followed, then Pavlyuk, and finally Webb still muttering under his breath.

Inside, the sight that greeted them was staggering: the fuselage of a modified Boeing 747, stripped of its wings and horizontal stabilizers.

Melnik gestured toward it. "The wings and stabilizers were removed and carefully stowed within the Antonov's walls."

The jet was a palace in disguise. Its exterior and interior gleamed with ultra-luxury, often described as a flying mansion customized for the Ukrainian president with unmatched space, range, and refinement. The letters VZ were etched proudly on the vertical stabilizer, the one feature left in place.

"Well, I'll be damned." Webb let out a low whistle. "It does fit. And yes that's what she said."

He chuckled at his own joke.

"Who's she?" Pavlyuk asked, frowning.

"Don't worry about it, Potluck." Webb shook his head.

The Americans circled the fuselage, their awe plain on their faces. Melnik raised a hand, directing their attention toward the nose.

"Gentlemen, I give you the Z Plane, a Boeing 747 private jet. This is where the president and his family will remain for the duration of the flight."

Standing in the cavernous belly of the Mriya, Lieutenant Koshani pointed toward the upper deck, just beneath the nose of the embedded jet.

"So," he asked, "are you ready to see your cockpit?"

Pavlyuk, who had been quiet for some time, finally shut off his phone and slipped it into his pocket. "Yes, I'll lead the way," he said, guiding them toward the stairway to the upper deck.

"The plane has been retrofitted to meet your American standards," Koshani explained.

"That's right," Melnik added. "The cockpit has been completely redesigned to give it a modern look. We even installed a table to play Angry Birds."

He had hoped to break the tension with humor, but the attempt fell flat.

Pavlyuk and Koshani were nearly at the top of the stairwell when Harvey spoke up.

"So, I gotta ask," he said as he climbed after them, "what about all those people outside the walls? Is that going to be an issue when we try to get this thing off the ground?"

Melnik shook his head, his response clipped. "Don't worry about them. They pose no problem."

At the cockpit door, Koshani stepped ahead and swung open a reinforced, five-inch-thick steel door.

Despite his mounting concerns about the mission, the mob, everything Harvey couldn't hide his intrigue. The cockpit was not the futuristic, next-generation command center he'd expected. Instead, Mriya's engineers had preserved much of the original design.

The chairs were upholstered in red and white. A desk of brown oak with black paneling stretched along the instrument wall. The clusters of instruments retained their bluish-green glow.

It was a cockpit born of another era: robust, functional, heavy with analog dials, gauges, and switches. The overhead panel bristled with controls for the electrical system, fuel pumps, engines, and more. Space had been designed for a six-member crew of two pilots, a navigator, two flight engineers, and a communications specialist.

Melnik gestured to the pilot seats, nudging Harvey and Webb forward.

Harvey slid into the left seat, his hand brushing the leather armrest as he took in the view. Webb settled into the right.

"I guess we're doing this," Webb muttered.

Harvey slipped into preflight mode, flipping switches and adjusting dials, his co-pilot mirroring the motions.

General Melnik stepped forward, resting a boot on the center pedestal between them.

"She may not be top of the line in every area, but her communications have been fully upgraded. She can link to both military and civilian satellites worldwide. We'll stay in contact with you the entire time," Melnik boasted.

"She's fueled, she's stocked, and she's yours ready to go once the president boards."

Just then, Pavlyuk's phone chimed with a text. He glanced at it, then out the window. At the same moment, Melnik's radio crackled. He lifted it to his mouth.

"Ya rozumiyu. Showtime, boys. The president and his family are accounted for. Good luck."

With that, Melnik exited the cockpit.

"Good luck," Harvey muttered, mocking his tone. "I can't believe this is happening."

Outside the main gate, three black SUVs with small Ukrainian flags fluttering on their hoods pushed through the restless crowd and rolled toward the airfield. Soldiers in full tactical gear manned the gates, snapping them shut the moment the convoy cleared the entrance.

Beyond the fence, the air vibrated with the low rumble of a mob an angry chorus swelling into a menacing roar. Sixty, maybe seventy people surged at the gates, their faces blurred in the fading light by desperation and rage.

An explosion rumbled in the distance, startling the crowd. Women screamed, children cried, and smoke curled upward in dark plumes. The chain-link fence, topped with barbed wire, was the first line of defense, but already it was buckling under the mob's assault. Hands wrapped in rags and gloves clawed at the steel, yanking and shaking with frantic unity. Their eyes were locked on Mriya.

Many carried backpacks or duffels. Some dragged children by the hand. All were determined to reach the tarmac.

Behind the gate, two soldiers and three security guards stood their ground, dwarfed by the sheer number of people pressing forward. Nearby, an abandoned patrol vehicle sat with its lights still flashing its red-and-blue glow pulsing eerily across the chaos.

Minutes later, the convoy of SUVs pulled into the hangar and stopped before the nose of the AN-225.

Special agents spilled from the lead vehicle and took positions by the aircraft's entrance as the massive plane prepared to taxi.

From the middle SUV, President Zelensky emerged, dressed head to toe in black: button-down shirt, military-style pants, and an all-weather jacket. His trademark smile was fixed in place, but his stomach churned beneath the façade.

On the far side, his wife Olena stepped out forty, composed, her beam poised and sophisticated. She took a few steps, then turned back, waiting for their daughter, Kassandra, eighteen and striking, who trailed behind. Close at her side came her best friend, Vira, twenty, who climbed out last.

"Come on, babe," Kassandra urged.

Olena extended a hand to her daughter. "I'm coming, Mom," Kassandra replied, tightening the straps on her backpack until they fit snugly, then slipping her hand into her mother's.

The doors of the third SUV burst open, and several aides emerged carrying briefcases and go-bags. Special agents flanked the exit as Zelensky approached the airstairs, his family and Kassandra's best friend, Vira, close behind.

He swept the horizon with one last look, then gave his security detail a firm nod before climbing the steps. The door clanged shut behind the final occupants of the convoy.

Upstairs in the cockpit, the crew was already braced to get moving. Captain Webb ran a hand across the control panel, as if psyching himself up. He studied the old-school simplicity of it.

"So we picked up a few strays … big deal," Webb muttered, fastening his harness. "I say we get the hell out of here before something else goes wrong. This'll be one hell of a war story … if we don't get shot down first."

The engines spooled harder, the turbines shrieking until the noise became deafening.

Harvey leaned toward his co-pilot. "You're right about one part, my friend … we need to get the hell out of here."

Then, without hesitation, the two men fell into rhythm executing the carefully orchestrated procedures they had drilled in simulation back in Qatar. They had studied the

Antonov's systems at least thirty-five times without ever sitting inside the real thing.

They cycled through preflight calculations, radio checks, and communications with air traffic control. Not a word was spoken about what they both knew: this was going to be the ride of their lives. It was, ironically, the only time they'd agreed on anything.

The Antonov was a marvel.

Webb double-checked the weather reports while Harvey confirmed the V1 and V2 speeds. Pavlyuk leaned forward, adjusting several dials until he was satisfied with their readings. The crew checked brakes, navigation, and fuel levels in quick succession.

"I'll be right back," Pavlyuk said, rising from the navigator's chair.

Both pilots glanced over their shoulders to find the seat still spinning.

"Where are you going?" Harvey asked.

Harvey asked again, but no response came. Pavlyuk was gone before he could answer.

"If I had to guess, he's stocking up on barf bags," Webb quipped.

The joke earned him half a grin from Harvey more than he usually got out of him in moments like this.

The panels glowed bright, and the engines roared, their whistles rising into a shrill scream.

"She's screaming now!" Webb laughed into his headset.

She is, Harvey thought. Now let's see how she flies.

"What do you think the odds are of getting court-martialed for this?" Harvey shouted over the din. "We came here to get a plane, and now we're leaving with unaccounted human cargo. I don't even know how many souls are on board."

"The odds are high enough that we should probably hide out in Egypt instead of going home," Webb fired back.

Harvey shoved the throttle forward. The Antonov rocked back, then began to roll.

"How the fuck are we supposed to hide this hunk of metal in the desert?"

"Hey don't talk about her like that. She's not a hunk of metal. She's beautiful."

Webb patted the panel, caressing it like a lover. "It's okay, Annie. Harvey didn't mean it," he whispered.

Then it came a muffled boom somewhere close. The shockwave rattled the aircraft, and the plane screeched to a halt. Both men froze, scanning the runway. No visible damage.

"What the hell was that?" Webb barked, more to the air than anyone in particular.

Harvey stood, craning his neck toward the rear compartment. Smoke billowed skyward, shouts carried on the wind closer now.

And then he saw it.

A mob, faces stricken with desperation, surging forward. Men, women, children all running, all gasping for air, all clawing for a chance to escape aboard the mothership before the war closed in on them.

"Oh, fuck," Harvey yelled. "There's been a breach at the gate!"

CHAPTER NINETEEN

(THE LONG WAY BACK)

THE TELEVISION OUTSIDE THE cockpit had once again become the center of attention.

"Russian forces launched more than one hundred ballistic and cruise missiles into Ukraine last night," the BBC reporter announced to millions of viewers worldwide, her tone flat and unsparing. The Antonov's flight crew gathered in the crew area, eyes fixed on the screen.

"The U.S. president says Russia has effectively declared war and that this aggression against Ukraine will cost Russia dearly, both economically and strategically. A senior defense official tells BBC News that the president is deploying an additional seven thousand U.S. troops to Germany to stand by and reassure NATO allies.

"The president is also meeting with his G7 counterparts to push forward a sweeping package of sanctions against the Russian Federation. Meanwhile, Russian troops part of the 150,000 massed on Ukraine's borders continue to advance from the east, from Belarus in the north, and from Crimea in the south.

"Ukrainian officials report that Russian forces have seized the entire exclusion zone around the Chernobyl nuclear power plant, including the facility itself. Troops have also captured an airport just twenty miles from Ukraine's capital, Kyiv.

"Tonight, many Ukrainian citizens are fleeing their homes, attempting to escape the country."

Master Sergeant Daniels lowered the volume on the TV as Captain Webb stepped into the seating area, where Daniels, Lt. Abrams, Lt. Goss, Staff Sergeant Knowles, and Staff Sergeant Cunningham sat glued to the news.

"Gentlemen, we are officially in the middle of a war zone," Daniels said flatly. Then he turned to Webb. "What's the holdup?"

"The Ukrainian president has opened the floodgates," Webb replied, "and we're taking on water."

Sergeant Cunningham frowned. "What does that mean, sir?"

Webb shot him a look. "It means we're taking in more strays."

He grabbed the remote and switched on the CCTV feed. One by one, civilians were shown boarding the Antonov.

"Zelensky says he feels guilty that his family is fleeing to safety while Ukrainians outside are begging for the same chance. He's decided this plane isn't leaving until he takes in as many people as possible."

Webb shook his head in disbelief. Unbelievable. "The man's got a bleeding heart and someday, it's gonna get him killed. The Major should be back any minute so we can get the fuck out of here."

Moments later, Harvey climbed up through the open hatch.

"All right, everyone Air Traffic Control just gave us the green light. Strap in. Let's get this bird in the air. We'll deal with the rest later."

And just like that, everyone moved to their assigned stations. Harvey and Webb settled into the pilot seats. Abrams and Goss manned the two flight engineer stations.

Cunningham and Knowles carried the large black hard-case into a secured closet, locked it, and took seats directly beside it. Both carried sidearms on their hips, while the rest of the crew wore shoulder holsters, each armed with standard-issue Beretta M9 pistols.

The behemoth rumbled backward, then taxied forward, aligning perfectly with the centerline.

"Antonov 225, cleared for takeoff," came the final call from Air Traffic Control.

The throttles eased forward, smoothly and continuously advancing to the calculated power setting. The six engines screamed at full thrust, propelling the monster forward, leaving behind the desperate crowd that hadn't made the cut. Their eyes followed the plane faces etched with disappointment as distance grew between them and the beast.

The Antonov towered above the airfield like a green giant over an anthill.

In the distance, rockets streaked across the sky, some arcing disturbingly close to the airport's perimeter. Still, Mriya did not falter.

The aircraft gathered speed, the pilots scanning instruments for any anomaly. Harvey pulled back gently on the yoke, and the nose lifted from the runway. The wings found their grip, and then the main gear broke free.

The giant was airborne.

The plane clawed upward, altitude building with every second. Harvey and Webb adjusted pitch for V2 speed. Once a positive rate of climb was confirmed, the Antonov's 32 wheels tucked neatly into its belly.

Following ATC instructions, they climbed steadily until reaching their assigned cruising altitude of thirty-two thousand feet.

At last, the immediate pressure lifted. The engineers and navigators unbuckled and stretched their legs.

That's when Lt. Abrams turned just in time to see Pavlyuk re-entering from the crew area.

But he wasn't alone.

"Gentlemen," Pavlyuk said smoothly, "this is Vira."

Pavlyuk stepped forward, introducing the young woman at his side. Webb glanced back, then shot Harvey a look his brows arching, then dropping. Only then did Harvey turn.

What he saw made him do a double take.

It clicked instantly. This was the girl from Potluck's photo, the one he kept so close, tucked away like a treasure.

"Vira is my daughter," Pavlyuk said, answering the unspoken question.

"His daughter. Well, alrighty then," Webb muttered with a snicker, eyes flicking to his copilot.

Harvey had known she was beautiful. Even in the small, worn photograph, her features stood out fair skin, blonde hair, pouty lips. Like Marilyn Monroe, but without the sorrow in her eyes. And now, in person, she was stunning every curve and angle heightened by the reality of her presence.

Too stunning, Harvey thought. Gorgeous enough to make him think dangerous thoughts about forever. He cursed himself silently. He barely knew her. And he wasn't about to repeat the mistake that had once driven a wedge between him and Captain Webb. The last time he'd let his guard down over a woman, Webb had been in the same room feeling the same feelings.

"Goddamn it, Potluck," Harvey snapped. "Where did she come from?"

"She is best friends with Kassandra Zelensky," Pavlyuk replied calmly.

Vira smiled sweetly and lifted a hand to wave when Webb greeted her.

But the levity evaporated as quickly as it came. The stakes had never been higher. They weren't clear yet. They were still flying over Ukrainian airspace, an airspace already compromised. And this was no place for such precious cargo.

"Was anyone screened before boarding?" Harvey asked, though he already knew the answer.

Pavlyuk shook his head. "No. I don't think so."

Pavlyuk replied evenly. "I'm sure the fine Ukrainian government took care of that right after the security gates were toppled."

Webb snorted. "Yeah, I'm sure." But Harvey wasn't laughing. Webb caught his co-pilot's expression and quickly stifled his grin.

"Should we be concerned?" Pavlyuk asked.

Webb locked eyes with Harvey. "We're definitely getting court-martialed for all the nonsense we could've prevented. Fort Leavenworth, here we come."

He added, "Probably Guantanamo, if we're lucky. This isn't protocol. This isn't how we do protocol."

Harvey ripped open his buckle and shot out of his seat. He'd had it with Pavlyuk's casual attitude. If the man hadn't been their Ukrainian ally and a valuable aviation expert who might prove useful before the journey was done Harvey would have gladly tossed him out the rear hatch and filed a missing person report when they got home.

"Potluck, you're up," Harvey said sharply, motioning toward the pilot's chair.

Vira, confused, looked at her father, but Pavlyuk avoided her gaze as he moved deliberately to the left side of the cockpit. He slid into position beside Webb, adjusting his harness with steady, precise movements. Muscle memory returned, and with it a quiet satisfaction every motion savoring the familiar rhythm.

Outside, the clouds gathered, inside, the Antonov continued to put distance between itself and the war unraveling below, a conflict expanding by the hour into full-scale chaos.

For a moment, in the skies, there was peace.

Harvey, restless, headed toward the rear of the plane. From one section to the next, he studied the Antonov's vast interior. He intended to make his way to the lower deck, to feel the ship beneath his boots and get a true sense of what the Mriya was made of.

Even amid crisis, the plane was magnificent. The cargo bay. The cavernous passenger deck. A marvel of steel and engineering.

In the galley, Harvey paused. He needed coffee, he'd been craving it since they landed in Kyiv hours earlier. Truthfully, he needed more than caffeine. But whiskey would have to wait. He promised himself things would run smooth from here on out. When this was over, he'd earn that drink.

He rifled through the overhead cabinet until he found a sleeve of paper cups. He pulled one free.

This'll do for now, he thought.

"Harvey, right?"

The voice startled him. He turned to see Vira standing by the coffee maker.

"Yeah …" was all he could manage as she smiled, brushing a curl of blonde hair from her eyes.

"My father talks about you a lot."

Her accent was thicker than her father's, but Harvey found it … alluring. Everything about her was beautiful in his eyes.

"Good things, I hope?" he said, grabbing a K-Cup marked House Blend. He slid it into the machine, pressed the handle, and hit the button. Nothing happened.

"The fuck is this contraption? Why don't they just have a regular coffee pot?"

"You have to pick a size." Vira leaned closer, pointing with a delicate finger.

Harvey froze, the scent of orange blossom rolling off her so close it filled his senses.

"See here? You choose how much you want."

"I want all of it," he blurted without thinking. That sounded sexual, he thought.

She laughed, the sound sending a swarm of butterflies through his chest.

"So … how big is it?" she teased.

He opened his mouth but couldn't form a word.

"Twelve ounces, yes?" she asked, pressing the button simultaneously. The machine sputtered awake, grumbling and steaming until coffee began to drip "Oh, shit."

Harvey hadn't set a cup down. He scrambled, knocking over the stack in his haste.

Vira snatched one mid-fall and slid it under the stream before a drop was wasted all in one smooth motion. Then she turned to him, smiling.

"I hope you fly planes better than you work coffee makers."

"I hope so, too," he admitted with a sheepish grin.

He replied, though who was he kidding? He had no idea how to navigate anything right now.

"Excuse me, I'll be right back," Harvey muttered, lifting his coffee before heading deeper into the plane. He shook his head and let out a weary sigh. Dumbass, he thought.

With what felt like the weight of the world on his shoulders, Harvey strolled section by section, feigning calm. He waved halfheartedly, offered haphazard handshakes and nods, and dodged conversation whenever possible.

The passenger seating was packed, every chair filled with would-be refugees. In the cargo bay, people huddled in clusters, some stretched out on the floor, others slumped against crates. Harvey stepped carefully, weaving through the crowd. His mind ticked like an inventory list: No background checks. No screenings. Hell, no one's even been patted down. For all I know, some of them are armed.

The faces told their own stories. Hardened men sat with eyes hollowed by years of survival, some asleep, others staring into nothing. Women clutched children, rocking them gently, whispering comfort over the drone of the engines. The sight tugged hard at Harvey's chest. These people just wanted out. This wasn't the right way but who could blame them, desperate times called for desperate measures.

And then two hard stares stopped him cold.

At the rear sat two men: Nikolai Petrov and Yulian Aleksandr.

Petrov was burly, mid-forties, with a round face, a close-trimmed goatee, and a cropped haircut to match. Yulian was slimmer, with wavy hair, bushy brows, and wire-framed glasses that gave him a deceptively soft look. But there was nothing soft about his eyes.

Yulian had a red backpack resting on his lap, fingers idly working the zippers, while Petrov kept a black leather pack by his boot. Both men looked up as Harvey drew near, their gazes sharp, cold, and utterly void of emotion.

Yulian leaned toward Petrov, his voice low but deliberate, his eyes never leaving Harvey.

"Кто этот идиот?"

(Who is this idiot?)

Both men stared silently as Harvey passed, coffee cradled carefully in both hands. The hair on the back of his neck prickled. Something about them didn't sit right, but this wasn't the time for profiling. These people needed help, and help was what he was here to provide.

Still their eyes burned into his back as he walked away, sharp and unrelenting.

"Ladies and gentlemen..."

Captain Webb's voice came over the PA, startling a few passengers who had already begun to drift off.

"We've now turned off the seatbelt sign. Please feel free to use the restroom at this time, but don't wander far from your seat. We may experience turbulence without warning. Use the restroom and return promptly.

"We have three hours and forty-five minutes until we reach Doha, Qatar. Sit back and enjoy the ride."

Petrov glanced at Yulian and gave a subtle nod. Then he checked his watch.

8:45 p.m.

CHAPTER TWENTY

(THIS MEANS WAR)

Higby sat at his desk as the duty day wound down. The clock read half past five. Another late night in the office despite his day having started at zero six hundred. He knew he should be leaving right now, taking his own advice about rest and balance, the same advice he gave to his junior officers. But he never practiced what he preached. He was terrible at it. That was military life: you sign a paper, and in return, you sign your life away.

He took a sip of black coffee and braced himself for the evening. He could have headed home, but the breaking news on his television held him captive.

"Russian warplanes crossed deep into Ukrainian territory last night . . ."

A U.S. Air Force spokesperson delivered the update the latest in a series of aggressions against the sovereign nation.

"... The operation, which began Wednesday night, continued into Friday. Russian armored units, ground forces from the east and south, and several MiG-29s carried out coordinated strikes. The MiGs targeted power plants and other key infrastructure. This mission, in particular, focused on Hostomel Airport, where the world's largest cargo plane is believed to be housed."

The spokesperson's words hung in the air when a sharp rap sounded on the door.

"Sir!"

A lieutenant burst inside, startling Higby so badly he spilled steaming coffee down the front of his uniform.

"Goddamnit, don't you know how to knock, lieutenant?" Higby roared, but the junior officer didn't flinch. The news he carried clearly justified barging into any commander's office.

"I'm sorry, sir, but you're going to want to see this."

Higby wiped himself off with a napkin, wondering what could be so urgent that a junior officer would barge in unannounced. He froze when a stack of papers landed on his desk.

He studied the images the lieutenant carefully spread across the table, then reached for the first sheet.

"What the bloody hell is this?"

"Satellite images, sir. Of the Hostomel Airfield hangar."

General Higby narrowed his eyes at the grainy photos.

"That right there..." the lieutenant said, pointing to the center of the page, "...is the site of the largest single hangar in the world."

Higby pressed his palm over his mouth, fingers against his lips.

"And the Antonov?" he asked, the question the lieutenant had been waiting for.

"They took off an hour before the bombing started. Just missed it. But that's not all, sir."

"Spill it."

"President Zelensky and his family are on board."

"Why the hell is he on the Antonov?"

The lieutenant had no answer. Higby turned to the next photo, more shocking than the first.

"And who are all these people?"

"Refugees, sir."

The lieutenant stumbled over the word, bracing himself as though the messenger might be shot along with the message.

"How did they get through security?"

The lieutenant shuffled through the stack and pointed to the top corner of a photo.

"By breaching this gate, sir."

Mouth still agape, Higby pieced it together. The lieutenant shifted into parade rest, hands clasped behind his back.

"And you're telling me the Antonov is airborne right now with all these people aboard?"

It came out more as a statement than a question. But when a commander spoke, you answered. That was the military way.

"Yes, sir."

"Including the President of Ukraine?"

"And his family, yes, sir."

"Jesus fucking Christ."

Higby exhaled hard, rubbing his forehead. "Anything else?"

"We have reason to believe the president's personal aircraft is also in the Antonov's cargo bay."

Higby dropped into his chair, dragging a hand over his face.

"Get the Secretary on the horn. Now."

"Yes, sir."

The lieutenant snapped to attention and hurried out. Higby, alone again, wondered what in the hell his elite aviators were doing at that very moment.

Deep inside the belly of the beast, Harvey stood before the Z-plane. The luxury superjet gleamed with a two-tone black-and-gray finish, accented by a yellow wraparound stripe. Its front wheel was down and chocked, the airstairs extended to the Antonov's deck. The cabin door stood wide open. The plane was held down with reinforced steel webbing at various points.

Harvey gripped the polished handrail and climbed with deliberate precision, his movements smooth and practiced.

Years of hard work had left his hands calloused yet now they were the only specialized tools he needed. The faint vibration of the Antonov's engines pulsed through the air as he ascended the gulfstream.

Inside the President's aircraft, two guards flanked the entry. Harvey nodded a greeting, and they directed him toward the stateroom in the rear.

Stateroom, he thought with a wry smirk, pushing forward.

The plane's interior radiated opulence. Crème leather seats trimmed in brown lined the cabin. As Harvey neared the back, the door flew open. A man in a black blazer stepped through, a white coiled earpiece trailing from his jacket. Professional bodyguard, Harvey assumed. Another similarly dressed man sat inside, and Harvey had no doubt both were armed to the teeth.

In the stateroom, Olena and Kassandra sat together. A massive television on the wall replayed a re-run of a FIBA international game. Four soldiers in camouflage leaned forward, fixated on the action. Beside the TV, a sophisticated communications array dominated the table and stretched up the wall: a satellite phone receiver, a high-end computer, and a tangle of wires feeding into a metal box.

After brief pleasantries, Harvey learned the most critical detail of all, President Zelensky was not aboard.

That was news to Harvey.

"So, where is your...?"

He didn't have to finish the question she already knew. Olena held his gaze, her eyes steady yet full of regret.

"During the commotion, my husband slipped off the plane," she confessed. "It was the plan all along. He had no intention of fleeing his nation not now, not in a time like this."

Her voice hardened with conviction. "My husband is a fighter. He would never abandon his people."

Harvey stood there, stunned. Part of him admired the man for refusing to run, proving he wasn't the coward Harvey and his crew had suspected. But the other part reminded him of the reality: he was still responsible for the First Family, and their lives now rested squarely in his hands.

"I know we have caused quite the stir…"

Olena offered a faint smile, placing her hand on Kassandra's shoulder and pulling her daughter closer.

"I am sure the President of the United States understands the danger my family and my people are in."

Harvey weighed her words. "I'm not so sure I agree with that. But here we are."

He spoke evenly, hiding the anxiety churning beneath the surface. The truth was, he couldn't vouch for everyone aboard, and that unsettled him.

Olena seemed to sense it. "May I introduce you to my family?" she asked. Before Harvey could answer, she was already gesturing.

"This is my daughter, Kassandra. You've already met my husband, I suppose. Look I am sorry for the trouble."

Her English was broken but heartfelt, her meaning carried as much by gestures as by words. Each sentence came with weight. Now and then, a weary sigh escaped, as though she were admitting just how much effort it took to convey herself in a foreign tongue.

"Are you, though?" Harvey asked quietly.

Kassandra plucked her phone from her pocket and spoke with a sneer.

"Povodytysya."

Olena shot her daughter a sharp look, returning the glare with equal fire. Forcing a thin smile to cover her embarrassment, she scolded her again.

"Why? It's obvious we are a problem," Kassandra snapped, her voice rising.

Unlike her mother, Kassandra's English was nearly flawless, polished by years of study abroad and frequent trips to the United States and Britain.

"You must excuse my daughter," Olena said as the two slipped back into a heated exchange in a language Harvey couldn't follow. Still, he had little doubt their words weren't kind.

"She's just a little … how do you say?"

"Afraid?" Harvey offered, seeing her struggle.

"Yes. Afraid. Children they don't always understand safety."

Suddenly, the man in black at the comms table straightened. Two lights blinked on the equipment.

"Ma'am, the Americans are on the line."

Harvey's head snapped up. The guard's English was crisp. So Washington knew. Of course they did. And if he had to bet, someone high up was furious. Furious at him. Harvey braced himself for the earful on national security he knew was coming.

As Olena turned her back to the door, Harvey caught sight of Kassandra slipping out, unnoticed by her mother. Artem, the bodyguard near the door, gave a subtle nod. The four camouflaged men rose silently and followed after the girl.

"My husband arranged this call before he left. Please join us."

Olena gestured to the guards. "That is Artem. That is Roman," she said, pointing to the man at the door and the one seated at the comms. Then she turned, intending to speak with her daughter only to realize Kassandra was gone.

Olena's eyes flashed, but Roman simply shrugged. His expression said: kids will be kids. Don't worry.

Artem motioned Harvey toward the satellite phone, then clicked a black remote. The basketball game froze on-screen, paused near the end.

Harvey shook his head inwardly. The lack of protocol in all of this was staggering. But now wasn't the time.

"Hello, sir," Artem said into the mic.

Harvey instantly recognized the voice on the other end: General Thomas Higby.

"President Zelensky, this is General Higby, U.S. Central Command. It's come to our attention that you and your family have breached our mission and hitched a ride on the Antonov. Is that correct?"

Olena cleared her throat but held back, letting her security detail respond.

"Excuse me, General," Artem said, his tone controlled. Harvey stepped in closer, ready to take over when needed.

"My name is Artem Kovalenko, special envoy and chief of security to the First Lady and her daughter. The President is not aboard. But I do have sixty of my people with me most will be classified as refugees when this plane lands."

"Refugees?" Higby's voice cracked through the speaker.

"Yes, sir. Victims of the war, Russia's war. And with us is Major Harvey."

Higby didn't waste time. "Were any of them screened or vetted before boarding?"

"No, sir," Harvey cut in before Artem could answer.

The line went quiet. Harvey could almost see Higby on the other end, hurling staplers and paperclips against the wall.

Finally, Higby spoke. "All right. We need to focus on the safest route of passage now. With these developments, most of our allies will need time to process. This mission is already too risky."

His tone hardened. "Qatar is officially off the table. You are being rerouted to Ramstein Air Base. Upon arrival, all civilians anyone without security clearance will deplane. Understood?"

Olena leaned toward the mic. "Thank you. My family and my people thank you."

"That was the First Lady, Olena Zelensky," Artem clarified.

"Roger that," Higby replied. "Stand by for further instructions."

"Copy, sir. Standing by," Artem confirmed.

"Hey, Major."

"Yes, sir."

"Godspeed."

"Thank you, sir."

The line went dead. Olena turned to Harvey with a soft smile. He returned it with a quick grin before addressing the cabin.

"Ladies and gentlemen we're going to Germany."

CHAPTER TWENTY-ONE

(HIJACKED)

"It's time," Yulian whispered to Nikolai Petrov. They had been up in the air for about thirty minutes, just enough time to set their plan in motion.

Petrov glanced at his watch. 9:15 p.m.

Until now, they had blended seamlessly into the cabin, but whatever they were planning was about to turn everyone's world upside down.

"You have the green light," he said in a thick Slavic accent.

Petrov was soft-spoken but direct. His voice carried a nasal quality more a result of substituting native Russian for English than any physical defect.

In one smooth, choreographed motion, Petrov and Yulian stood. Yulian held a red backpack, while Petrov reached down by his leg to pick up a black leather bag. With purpose and intense focus, they advanced toward the front of the plane.

As they approached the lavatory, they paused and glanced around. No one was paying them any attention. This is all going to change. Petrov thought.

Yulian grabbed the door handle and popped it open with a firm push. It swung inward. Yulian stepped into the tight space, and Petrov followed, closing the door behind them.

The lavatory was designed for a single user, but they weren't in there to relieve themselves.

With the door locked, Yulian unzipped the red backpack and pulled out a roll of plastic zip ties and a block of C-4 explosive. While Petrov leaned his weight against the door, he opened the leather bag and retrieved a small arsenal of short-barreled machine guns.

He began assembling the weapons, attaching components that had been intentionally left detached.

Once Yulian was finished prepping the explosive and zip ties, he joined Petrov.

Suddenly, there was a knock at the door.

Yulian froze and looked at Petrov, who raised a hand signaling him to stay silent. He held it aloft for a few seconds until the knocking stopped. Then, with a subtle circular motion, he instructed Yulian to continue.

It was clear Petrov was in charge, judging by how the two men deferred to one another.

They returned to work assembling MP5s, Uzis, and handguns with practiced efficiency.

After a short while, Petrov and Yulian emerged from the lavatory wearing bulletproof vests, their weapons slung behind their backs. Yulian still carried the red backpack.

Petrov came face-to-face with the man who had knocked on the lavatory door. The stranger's jaw was tight, anger flashing in his eyes. He opened his mouth to speak, but before he could utter a word, Petrov raised a silenced pistol and aimed it between the man's eyes.

The man froze and was dead before his body hit the floor.

A single suppressed shot had bored a clean hole in his skull. Blood spilled out in a slow, deliberate pour, pooling beneath him as his cold, lifeless eyes stared into the void. Petrov stepped over the body and moved forward toward the other passengers.

When they reached the main cabin, where most passengers were seated, Yulian exchanged quick glances with four men and a woman wearing a hijab. The rest of the cabin appeared to be asleep, blissfully unaware of the nightmare about to unfold.

As if rehearsed, each man caught a weapon tossed midair and began examining it with seasoned precision. The first checked his magazine and slammed the bolt forward with a metallic snap. Yulian handed the woman an Uzi. She examined it, her movements confident and mechanical. She held it like a pro.

Boris Simeon, tall and athletic, with a pointy nose and hair tied back in a ponytail received an MP5. He swiftly serviced the weapon, adjusted the buttstock to a compact setting, and tucked it into the crease of his right shoulder. He peered through the sight, crosshairs resting casually on the overhead compartment.

The Volkov brothers Drago, 35, and Svingei, 27 each received a machine gun and a sidearm. Both wore Adidas tracksuits: Ivan in black, Svingei in blue, with signature white stripes. Ivan took an MP5; Svingei an Uzi.

Viktor Bogomolovitch, the youngest of the crew at 22, stood six feet tall. Neck tattoos peeked above his navy blue turtleneck, and a cigarette was tucked behind one ear. His bleached-blond hair was slicked back, his face unfriendly.

Svingei licked his palm and smoothed his hair before adjusting his Jeffrey Dahmer-style glasses. He caught a few stares but remained unfazed.

When Sasha, the lone woman in the crew finished servicing her weapon, Petrov gave the order with a single nod. The group began moving silently down the cabin, scanning sleeping heads like predators in a herd.

"Sasha, stay close to me," Petrov called out.

Yulian led the way, but suddenly, two men in camouflage appeared across the aisle. Yulian raised his weapon and opened fire.

The two men tried reaching for their weapons but were caught mid-motion. Panic flickered in their eyes just before Yulian emptied several rounds into them. Blood exploded across seatbacks and carpet as their bodies collapsed backward.

The sudden gunfire and chaos jolted passengers awake. Screams pierced the air.

Sasha and Svingei pointed their guns at the panicked crowd and barked commands.

"Get up. Get up now!"

Sasha shouted as she and Svingei grabbed anyone they could reach, barking orders while jabbing the barrels of their weapons into terrified backs.

"Walk in front of us! Do it go! Go!"

The chaos stirred more passengers awake. Amid the rising panic, another man in camouflage burst through the cabin door with his weapon drawn. He tried to take aim, but the terrorists had already positioned a dozen hostages as human shields.

Before he could fully assess the situation, Petrov emerged from the crowd and dropped him with a series of well-placed shots. The man crumpled instantly. Screams erupted louder than before as blood pooled in the aisle.

Sasha and Svingei shoved the herd of hostages into the next cabin, where another soldier in camouflage lay in a prone position, a handgun aimed at the door.

As it opened, he fired a single shot then paused.

Five tense seconds passed before an Uzi peeked through the opening and unleashed a spray of bullets into the room.

The soldier immediately reached for his radio, mashed the talk button, and screamed, "Shots fired! Shots fired!"

Panicking, he fumbled for the secondary radio clipped to his utility belt but missed. It clattered to the floor with a sharp crack. He fired two rounds in the terrorists' direction to suppress their advance, then snatched the radio and fled through a rear hatch.

Seeing this, Petrov turned to Yulian. "Go after him."

"Yes, boss," Yulian replied and sprinted after the fleeing man toward the rear of the plane.

He raised his weapon, took aim and missed. A moment later, he heard the man shouting into the radio:

"Code red! We have active shooters in the upper cabin!"

The camouflage-clad soldier reached a box labeled ALERT SYSTEM. Just as he began to pull the lever, Yulian fired again three sharp cracks. All three rounds hit their mark, severing the man's spine. He collapsed instantly.

A few minutes later, Yulian returned with the dead man's radio. The hostages, scattered between kneeling and seated positions, panicked when he appeared around the corner.

Screams echoed, but Sasha raised her weapon overhead and swept the barrel in an arc, asserting control.

"Zatknis'!" she barked.

She waved the muzzle over the group like a warning.

"Vstavay zaraz! Get up now!"

Harvey stood across from Olena in the 747 jet, completely oblivious to the mayhem unfolding in the cargo plane below. It was understandable after all, they were sealed inside an aircraft that sat in the belly of another plane, with stateroom door and all windows closed.

They appeared to be deep in conversation, but Harvey had zoned out, despite looking engaged. He saw her lips moving, but all he could think about was the striking resemblance Vira bore to the woman standing before him.

He'd noticed Olena's beauty the moment they met. Whether it was appropriate to say so was another matter entirely. Complimenting the wife of another man especially the wife of a foreign president was dangerous territory. Powerful men had ways of making people pay for that kind of misstep.

He'd tried to talk, but stumbled over his words. Beautiful women sometimes had this kind of effect on him. Even if Vira wasn't his "special someone," he liked knowing he could make her smile even if it was at his own expense, for being a little silly.

"You seemed lost in there. You didn't answer my question," Olena said, pulling Harvey back into the moment.

Only then did he realize he'd been staring with a dopey smirk tugging at the corner of his mouth.

"Is there a special someone?" she added. It was meant as a statement, but it landed like a question.

Harvey opened his mouth to respond but before he could, the meeting room door to the 747 burst open.

A soldier in camouflage stumbled into the room, a radio in one hand and a pistol in the other. He was drenched in sweat, his breathing ragged, fear carved into his expression.

"Shots … fired …" he gasped.

Everyone shot to their feet. Artem rushed to Olena, positioning himself between her and the door. He drew his Glock and held it in a ready stance.

"Where?" Harvey barked.

"Upstairs," the soldier managed to say before collapsing. Blood pooled rapidly beneath him, soaking through his clothes and spreading across the floor.

"How did this happen?" Olena asked, her voice tight with disbelief.

"Unvetted passengers," Harvey answered grimly.

Olena's eyes widened, darting around as though searching desperately for the right word. Panic gripped her features. The color drained from her face, leaving her pale and breathless.

"Kassandra!" she cried.

She screamed, and the corners of her mouth trembled.

The cry that tore from Olena's throat was raw and animalistic, one Harvey couldn't bear to hear. It dragged him back to a place he never wanted to revisit. He had heard that scream too many times before when service members returned home in flag-draped coffins. There was something about a transfer case or a casket that made a mother's heart stop for just a moment as she searched, in vain, for the right words.

"Kassandra is out there!" Olena cried again, pointing a trembling finger toward the ceiling of the 747.

Harvey understood instantly. His mission had just changed again and, once again, he had no say in the matter.

He knew what had to be done. But acting as glorified security detail for a First Lady he had only just met wasn't supposed to be part of the plan.

He was a Major in the United States Air Force, and nothing he had done over the past several hours appeared anywhere in his job description.

Yet here he was.

Harvey unholstered his standard-issue SIG Sauer handgun, checked the chamber, and flipped off the safety.

He placed his left hand gently on Olena's right shoulder.

"Ma'am, I'm going to find your daughter," he said, calmly but firmly. "But I need you to stay in here. You and you."

He pointed to Artem and Roman.

"Stay here and keep her safe. Lock the doors. Don't open them for anyone."

Roman nodded, then glanced at Artem. Artem responded with a nod of his own.

Satisfied, Harvey turned and bolted out the door, slamming it shut behind him.

Upstairs, in the upper cabin of Mriya, the hijackers faces grim and resolute were herding terrified hostages like cattle on the way to the slaughterhouse. Their goal: get everyone into a single location at the rear of the aircraft.

Thick smoke billowed from a device on the floor, likely a smoke incendiary canister. Chaos reigned. Hostages stumbled into one another amid frantic pushing and shoving. Some tripped, others were trampled as they scrambled under shouted commands. Coughs racked many of them, the rising smoke choking the air.

A palpable dread hung in the cabin. Some passengers wept openly; others moved in stunned silence, their bodies shuffling down the narrow aisle. The metallic scent of fear clung to everything. Each step was more terrifying than the last, every footfall a surrender of hope lingering near the exits.

At thirty thousand feet, there was no escape from this airborne nightmare.

Sasha used her hijab to cover her nose and mouth as she pushed through the smoke. Among the hostages near the front was Kassandra. She hit the floor hard after being shoved by a fellow passenger in the confusion. Gasping, she clutched her chest, short of breath.

She rubbed her eyes, but the irritation only worsened. Then a sharp crack. The cold pain of metal slammed into the back of her head. The butt of the hijacker's Uzi.

Instinctively, she reached back and felt blood.

"Vstavay, suka!" the woman spat, then barked in English, "Get up, bitch."

Kassandra lifted herself carefully from the ground only to be shoved back into the moving herd.

From the rear of the crowd came three sharp bangs, followed by shrill screams.

Kassandra wanted to scream too.

But fear locked her in place. One wrong move could be fatal.

Tears traced down her cheek.

The captors' rushed commands, punctuated by erratic cries echoed through the plane as the hostages were herded into a confined space at the tail end of the fuselage.

CHAPTER TWENTY-TWO

(THE RUSSIAN PILOT)

In the cockpit, Pavlyuk sat hunched over, breathing heavily into a brown emesis bag. The barf bag was clutched tightly around his mouth as he shot a horrified glance toward the cockpit door.

Muted gunfire echoed from the other side.

"Did you hear that?" he asked Webb.

Webb was on the handheld radio, trying to reach his co-pilot, who he believed was somewhere roaming the cargo hold.

"Harvey? Harv come in!" he shouted into the radio.

No response.

He had no idea where Harvey was or what exactly was happening. He knew this was a military operation, and there were weapons onboard including the one in his shoulder holster. But the sounds outside weren't routine. That was automatic gunfire.

He listened closely.

More shots. Screams or what sounded like them.

Then, more gunfire.

The cockpit door remained closed and locked, a security protocol activated by Staff Sergeants Knowles and Cunningham.

A large black case lay open on the floor, its contents, long rifles and handguns now distributed among everyone in the cockpit, including Pavlyuk, who had needed instructions just to handle a handgun. He seemed petrified by the piece of metal as if holding a gun for the first time.

Master Sergeant Daniels pressed his ear to the door. He heard a muffled thud, then a vibration underfoot.

Webb and Pavlyuk, both seasoned pilots, felt the subtle tremor but dismissed it until another came. Sharper. Closer.

Unmistakable.

Gunshots.

Not the distant pop of Fourth of July firecrackers, but the chilling, resonant crack of a firearm. Close.

Just outside the cockpit.

Both pilots exchanged a wide-eyed glance as the comfortable hum of the turbo engines swelled, momentarily drowning out the chaos beyond.

They knew what those sounds meant.

The sterile calm of the flight deck was gone replaced by a cold dread that gripped them both. Their hands hovered over the controls. Their eyes flicked anxiously toward the locked door.

At 30,000 feet, the outside environment was stark and unforgiving. Below the giant aircraft, clouds stretched like a vast, undulating blanket, obscuring the deep dark Black Sea still presumed to lie beneath the atmosphere.

The Antonov sliced through inky blackness, the kind of darkness found only far above Earth's scattered lights. At this altitude, over expansive bodies of water like the Gulf or the Black Sea, there were no lights in sight. Only the red, pulsating beacon beneath the aircraft broke the void.

The air outside was unimaginably thin and frigid a biting vacuum that would instantly freeze any exposed moisture. There was no wind to feel, only the faint hum of the engines and the eerily smooth, almost imperceptible forward surge as the massive aircraft pushed through the atmosphere.

Inside the cockpit, Webb was frantically trying to establish communication with the U.S. military base in Germany. He toggled his headset until he found a secure line.

"Ramstein, this is AN225. We have a code red, multiple shots fired onboard. Active shooter protocol in effect. Requesting priority clearance for any available runway. Do you copy? We are approximately forty-five miles out. I repeat… multiple shots fired. Do you copy?"

There was a five-second pause.

Then a response crackled over the comm system. The air traffic controller's voice usually calm, measured, and precise now carried a subtle edge. Still, he kept control as he relayed critical instructions to the inbound aircraft.

"Copy that, 225. This is Master Sergeant Elliot. You are cleared for emergency landing. Wind is ten knots from the east. Contingency is in place. You are clear… I repeat, you're clear. Please provide your fuel state."

Elliot and another airman were hunched over a control terminal, tracking AN-225's radar signature.

"We're okay on fuel. Requesting military and medical standby," Webb added.

"How many wounded?" Elliot asked.

"Unknown. They're still shooting out there," Webb replied, voice breaking.

After a tense ten seconds, Elliot added something Webb hadn't yet considered, a detail that revealed the man on the other end had seen, or at least studied in a situation like this before.

"225… make sure you're subtle about the drop in altitude, don't spook the hijackers."

Elliot continued to guide the distressed pilots. His voice remained remarkably steady, despite the severity of the moment. A silent prayer echoed in his heart for everyone aboard the cargo plane.

He pressed a large red button on the console, and klaxons immediately began wailing across the base.

"Roger that. Dropping to twenty-five thousand feet … and doing it gradually," Webb replied. He reached for the dials and made some adjustments. Pavlyuk mirrored his actions.

"Dropping to twenty-five thousand feet," he confirmed.

On the radar board, Master Sergeant Elliot and Staff Sergeant Kristi Boyd watched the tiny green blip representing the Antonov slowly bleed altitude.

They stepped toward the glass enclosure overlooking the runway, confirming that the airbase was moving exactly as promised for the incoming aircraft in distress.

If any base could handle a beast like the Antonov, it was Ramstein Air Base a United States Air Force installation in Rhineland-Palatinate, southwestern Germany. It served as the headquarters for U.S. military operations in Europe, Africa, and NATO Allied Command.

The control tower stood nearly ten stories tall, its panoramic windows offering a stark view of the runway lights slicing through the inky blackness.

Below, the tarmac alarm blared. Military rescue vehicles rolled into position with practiced precision, preparing for a once-in-a-lifetime emergency.

The night sky was studded with stars and dominated by a blood moon looming over the exosphere.

Sirens wailed from security and fire-rescue units. Uniformed personnel in reflective vests moved swiftly under the floodlights. Foam trucks gleamed in the dark. Ambulances idled, their crews at the ready. Other vehicles maneuvered into precisely predetermined positions.

Everyone moved with purpose. The message was clear.

Two large fire engines formed a barricade at the tarmac's entrance.

Back at the radar screen, the green blip of the Antonov continued its slow descent.

"Come on … you can do it," Elliot whispered.

"Is that really the legendary Antonov-225?" someone asked, eyes fixed on the screen.

Staff Sergeant Boyd turned to her supervisor, her eyes fixed on the glowing radar screen.

"The one and only?" she asked.

"The one and only," Master Sergeant Elliot replied, his voice filled with reverence.

Boyd turned her gaze toward the night sky, scanning for any twinkling lights from the east.

Back in the cockpit, Webb updated the others on the emergency preparations awaiting them at Ramstein Air Force Base. Then he glanced at Pavlyuk who was reading something on his phone.

Webb snapped.

"Put that thing …"

He didn't finish his sentence.

A sudden burst of gunfire rattled against the cockpit door.

Webb and Pavlyuk locked eyes, then quickly redirected their attention to the dark sky ahead.

Pavlyuk gripped the yoke tightly, his knuckles pale, hands trembling. Webb wasn't much better. A cold bead of sweat traced down his temple, but his eyes burned with focused determination. He stayed locked on the instruments, monitoring the fuel gauges closely.

They needed to make it to Ramstein. He silently prayed the hijackers hadn't tampered with the fuel system.

After a few seconds, Pavlyuk finally spoke.

"We need to do something about that," he said, nodding toward the door.

"Pavlyuk, under no circumstances do we open that door."

"But my daughter is out there …"

Pavlyuk's voice cracked, and worry carved deep lines across his face. He hesitated, as if about to speak again.

Webb cut him off before the words could come.

"If they get in here, we're all going to die. Do you understand me?!"

Webb spoke with sharper authority, as if addressing a child, making sure Potluck didn't get any funny ideas. He was acutely aware that every soul aboard this leviathan rested in his hands. He was now the man in charge. "The door stays locked. We don't open it for anyone!" Pavlyuk nodded reluctantly, his face taut with immense stress.

Kassandra knew she should stay in line. But she had to find her father. She wasn't sure if the hijackers knew who she was, but she knew they were Russian and that was enough to explain why they were here. Contrary to what most people believed, she wasn't just a pretty face. She was smart, educated, and well-informed on global affairs. She knew about the mighty AN-225 and why the Americans were so interested in it.

In her mind, she'd already concluded: if someone had to take control of the aircraft, better the Americans than what remained of the USSR. If Russia got its hands on it, a lot of people would suffer. The Russian President and his henchmen would undoubtedly use it for darker purposes. Above all, she was convinced the hijacking was a Russian attempt to literally kill two birds with one stone, or maybe even three if Ukraine surrendered to Russian ground forces.

Come on, Dad, what were you thinking letting these people on board? It wasn't smart. No, it really wasn't. But that's the kind of man her father was he'd give the shirt off his back to a stranger. She loved him for it, but she also knew that kind of generosity and naiveté could backfire.

He was a great leader, but a poor protector.

And today, it had backfired.

She edged toward the front of the line, eyes scanning the crowd for a familiar face. She didn't want to draw the attention of the gunmen. One wrong move and she could become the primary hostage. Up to now, she'd been content to keep a low profile.

But the butterfly clip in the jet-black hair three people ahead gave it away.

I've got to get to Vira, she thought.

Picking up speed, she weaved her way to the front, pushing forward under shouts and pressure from the hijackers.

"I need to find my father."

Vira gasped when she turned and saw Kassandra. She looked flustered, on the verge of a panic attack, sweating, her face pale with dizziness. "My father," Vira whispered.

"Where is he?" Kassandra asked urgently.

"He was in the cockpit the last place I saw him."

Vira slowed and subtly gestured toward the front of the aircraft, careful not to draw attention from their captors. Behind them, people began bumping into each other as the line stalled.

"The cockpit should be safe if the plane's still on course," Kassandra murmured.

But her words were cut short by the cold press of a gun barrel against her cheek.

Thwack! Svengei struck her with brutal precision, knocking her off balance. Kassandra stumbled and crashed to the floor coming face to face with a dead man. She screamed. The corpse just stared back at her, eyes wide, empty.

Vira dropped to one knee and tried to help her friend. But just as they were getting up, she felt the chilling press of a gun muzzle against the back of her head. Her eyes clenched shut. Tears streamed down her already terrified face.

"Perestaty rukhatysya," Svengei commanded coldly his eyes void of emotion.

"Stop playing games," he snarled, switching to English, "or I'll blow those pretty little heads off. Got it?"

They both nodded quickly.

As the group neared the rear galley, the hijackers chose to settle the captives in the open cabin area at the back of the plane. The doorway was narrow, but there was enough legroom for a tight grouping. Some passengers were shoved violently to the floor, while others lowered themselves voluntarily, awaiting further instruction.

The remaining stragglers were herded into the space and forced to join the rest of the crew. A small child cried out for his mother.

Then came a new sound muffled thuds echoed through the cabin as overhead bins were flung open one by one. The noise punctuated the sudden presence of Nikolai Petrov in the entryway.

Stroking his goatee, he spoke in Russian. "Any word on the President's capture?"

"Not yet, Petrov," one of the guards responded. "We've been guarding these two little birds and the rest of the cattle."

Svengei responded to Petrov in Russian, hoping no one else would understand their plan.

But Vira swallowed hard and looked over at Kassandra because she did understand. Every word.

Fluent in Russian, just like her father, Peter Pavlyuk, Kassandra was piecing it all together. Vira now faced a critical challenge: how to tell her friend that her family was the prime target, without putting her in even more danger.

She leaned back, thinking hard, trying to figure out how to deliver that message discreetly. So far, it seemed the hijackers hadn't singled Kassandra out which meant they probably didn't know who she really was.

The girls watched silently as Petrov's eyes scanned the line of hostages.

He glanced at his watch. It was 11 p.m. He set a timer for one hour.

Suddenly, Drago and Viktor burst into the rear cabin.

"Hey, boss!" Drago called out.

"Where is he?" Petrov asked, voice tight.

Viktor responded in Russian, "Boss, he's not here."

"What do you mean, he's not here?" Petrov shouted, his patience snapping.

"We searched the whole plane. Maybe he jumped," Viktor said, idly tapping the butt of his MP5 with his fingernails.

Petrov raised his pistol and leveled it at Viktor's head. Viktor didn't flinch.

"I have no time for games. Bring me Zelensky!"

At the name Zelensky, Kassandra jolted, panic seizing her spine. She quickly turned her head to hide the flash of emotion.

Vira placed a steadying hand on her shoulder.

"He was last seen in the lower deck," Drago offered quickly, trying to calm his superior. "With his wife and another man. But they're gone. All of them."

"We should go check the plane downstairs," Drago added.

Petrov narrowed his eyes.

"What plane?"

Petrov's face twisted in confusion. This was a valuable piece of intel, one that had never been reported over the radio, despite the back and forth transmissions. His expression darkened. Rage flooded in, turning his face a deep red.

"There's a Gulfstream in the cargo hold. Maybe someone brought it for repairs or something. I don't know," Drago said, smirking, proud of his English delivery.

The grin faded fast when he realized no one else found it funny.

Petrov slowly lowered the gun from Viktor's face. The younger man exhaled in quiet relief.

"Well then, fuckin' find them!" Petrov roared.

"Yes, sir," Drago replied quickly.

He and Viktor turned and rushed out of the hostage area.

"Wait," Petrov called after them. "What man was with them?"

"I'm not a hundred percent sure, sir. But we think it might have been one of the pilots," Boris added, tone matter-of-fact.

Petrov clenched his jaw, a flicker of fire igniting behind his eyes. He checked his watch twenty-five minutes had already passed.

He turned sharply to Yulian and Boris.

"Get back to the cockpit. Now."

Viktor grabbed the red backpack filled with explosives. Without wasting a second, he and Drago sprinted toward the front of the plane.

CHAPTER TWENTY-THREE

(ROAD TO GERMANY)

WITH A DISTINCTIVE WHIRRING crescendo, Marine One a towering Sikorsky VH-3D Sea King, also known as the White House helicopter descended gracefully onto the South Lawn of the White House. Its powerful rotors kicked up a swirling vortex of wind, flattening the meticulously manicured grass as it made its final approach. The Presidential Seal of the United States, emblazoned on its side, caught the morning sunlight.

As the landing gear gently touched down, a phalanx of Secret Service agents ever poised and vigilant moved into position, ready to secure the perimeter and escort the President across the lawn with an impressive display of precision and control.

Almost before the rotors had fully spun down, the cabin door slid open, and President Maurene Markle stepped out. She greeted several servicemen before the White House advisor joined her, and together they walked toward the iconic building.

"Who else knows about this?" Markle asked the man walking beside her.

"CENTCOM, ma'am. The commanders in the region are supposedly keeping a tight lid on this one."

"I can see why … but it seems the whole thing is blowing up in our faces. I need a secure line to that plane ASAP."

"Yes, ma'am. I'm on it," the advisor replied.

Moments later, they disappeared into the White House.

Deep in the night sky, at 22,000 feet above sea level, the behemoth streaked through moonlight, soaring through thick clouds as it began a gradual descent. Its powerful turbo engines still worked their magic, keeping the massive metal tube airborne. Navigation lights, like tiny winking stars, traced its path across the sky.

Far below, the world was a tapestry of scattered lights a faint glow hinting at human presence. The air outside remained frigid, a stark contrast to the warm, pressurized cabin being used to hold the hostages. Some of them were already sweating from a mix of heat and stress.

Petrov walked toward a small built-in table. He perched on it, one buttock resting on the edge while the other hung off the side, one foot barely touching the floor, the other planted firmly. He tapped the silencer of his pistol against his right leg, then glanced at his watch. When he looked up again, Kassandra saw desperation mixed with determination in his cold, hard stare.

A sudden vibration underfoot and a sharp chirping from the handheld radio made Petrov lift it to his mouth.

"What's happening?" he asked.

A moment later, Yulian's voice crackled through at a high pitch.

"Boss, we're losing altitude. I think they're preparing to land."

Petrov stood up, incensed. He tapped the antenna of the radio repeatedly against his thigh as he thought through their next move.

"Breach. Use the explosives if you have to." He then shouted something in Russian.

The custom 747 had remained untouched until now. Though the cabin entry door had been lowered to the floor, the interior doors remained locked. Artem and Roman were hunkered down in the jet's rear cabin, pistols at the ready. Olena sat in an armchair tucked in the corner, wrapped in what appeared to be a man's oversized coat. She rocked slowly, back and forth, in a soothing rhythm.

"Madame First Lady," Artem said, turning to the sobbing woman. "I know your daughter is out there, but I need you to focus. I need you to think. Is there any reason to believe your people would want to harm you?"

"No," Olena replied, shaking her head side to side. Her eyes were red and burning. "Of course not. This has Kremlin written all over it. My people are innocent. They would never do this."

She turned her attention from Artem to Roman.

"Where are my husband's papers?"

"In the safe," he replied.

"If I'm captured … or killed … shred it. All of it."

She held his gaze for a few seconds to ensure he understood how serious she was. Roman and Artem felt the weight of the favor she was asking. If she were captured or killed, chances were they'd be in danger too. She was asking them to carry out one final patriotic duty: to destroy all classified documents once the 747 was completely breached by the men outside with machine guns.

"Don't worry. You're safe in here with us."

Artem tried to reassure Olena, but she was too far gone to believe it. There was too much chaos, and both Artem and Roman were out of their element. For once, they didn't have the upper hand and Olena saw no way this could end well. Not for herself. Not for her daughter. Not for the innocent people on board. Not for the American pilots trying to help. And not for the Antonov.

Meanwhile, of all the things Webb thought he might have to do on this mission, being taken hostage wasn't one of them. Now, he had to land this beast without his wingman.

He had trained for moments like this, but never imagined not in a million years that he'd have to land under these conditions. The Antonov-225 was a true monster. It was three times the size of anything he'd ever brought down solo. He was thanking his lucky stars he had Potluck beside him at a time like this.

With a distress signal already sent, he expected full military response once they touched down in Germany. He knew Ramstein was on high alert and prepared for whatever might unfold on the ground. The mission had changed: now it was about saving lives and protecting the plane. Letting the hijackers gain access to the cockpit was out of the question.

The cockpit door would remain sealed no matter who showed up on the other side.

He'd already given strict orders: even if Harvey appeared and knocked, they weren't to open that door. Not for anyone. They couldn't risk falling for another enemy trick.

"Focus."

Webb's voice cut through the room. He had to shout to snap Pavlyuk out of it. Pavlyuk had been staring at the cockpit door like he was expecting the pizza delivery guy to walk through at any moment. He was sweating profusely and visibly anxious. Webb held back from mocking the old man. He gave him a pass and didn't say the off-color comment he'd been rehearsing in his head.

With both hands on the controls, Webb and Pavlyuk eased the plane out of the clouds. They adjusted their gauge clusters, eyes forward.

"Easy, Potluck. Eassssyyyy…"

With Pavlyuk looking like a nervous wreck, Webb actually found himself missing Harvey.

Then rattling at the door lock.

The cockpit went dead silent. The rattling stopped.

"You see, Potluck? That's why the door stays locked."

Suddenly, something slammed into the door. WHAM! WHAM! It hit hard, over and over. It sounded like the butt of a machine gun or some heavy metal object trying to break through.

Pavlyuk jumped with every blow. Shaking, he pulled a photo of Vira from his pocket, gripped it tightly, and kissed it. Then silence.

With a click and a pop, Harvey opened the hatch leading to the upper rear cabin. First came his gun, then his head, and the rest of his body followed. He looked around. Quiet. Too quiet.

He stepped to the side but accidentally bumped the hatch cover. The metal lid slammed shut CLANG! Harvey flinched, panicked, and ducked behind a wall panel. Pressed flat against the edge, he peered around the corner.

The moment his head was fully visible, his eyes locked with two of the hijackers, Drago and Viktor.

Harvey ducked and weaved into the fray, nearly mowed down by automatic fire. He returned fire, bullets sparking off metal around the hijackers. Once he'd suppressed their attack, he bolted back to the hatch. He flung the lid up and jumped down just in time to avoid a hail of hot lead that hammered the steel cover.

Drago and Viktor looked at each other, then crept forward. Using the barrels of their rifles, they peered into the open hatch but saw nothing.

Meanwhile, in the cockpit, Webb strained to see out the windows. He looked left, then right, then straight ahead and spotted what looked like a faint, twinkling light in the distance.

"It seems they've given up," Pavlyuk whispered.

Webb didn't respond.

"Are they gone?" Pavlyuk asked, more to the air than to anyone specific.

A moment passed.

Then RATATATATAT!

A dozen rounds slammed into the far side of the cockpit door. The bullets didn't penetrate, but they left nickel-sized dents clearly visible from where they sat.

"Are they going to get in?" Pavlyuk asked.

"I don't know," Webb replied.

Webb responded by grabbing his pistol from the shoulder holster. He ejected the magazine, checked the rounds, then slammed it back into place and gave the weapon a once-over.

Pavlyuk stole a quick glance at Webb, then returned his eyes to the instrument cluster.

"Potluck, have you ever seen a man die before?" Webb asked, trying to keep his copilot's mind off that damn door. It was a distraction tactic one he hoped would help Pavlyuk focus on surviving this hell.

"Of course," Pavlyuk replied, as if the question itself was absurd. Out of line.

"Well, get ready then. Because if anyone comes through that door, I don't give a flying fuck who it is, they're going down."

He turned his attention back to landing the plane.

"I mean … they've tried guns already. What else could they be"

"Bombs," Webb cut in, finishing the thought before Pavlyuk could.

"These men have explosives. That's standard terrorist backup protocol. There's no way they didn't bring bombs on this plane."

That little detail didn't sit well with Pavlyuk.

"Bombs?!" he blurted. "The whole plane would blow up! We should just open the door … we can shoot them."

Webb slowly turned to face him, eyebrows raised, voice dry with sarcasm.

"Right. And I'll John Wayne my way through God knows how many gunmen with automatic rifles."

Pavlyuk blinked, visibly puzzled.

"Who is John Wayne?" he asked.

"Never mind . . . Potluck! We are not opening that door. Daniels, Cunningham, Goss, Abrams make sure you're prepared to shoot anything that walks through it."

Pavlyuk wiped the beaded sweat from his forehead and down both sides of his face with the back of his hand.

"I don't want to die," he whimpered.

Webb couldn't tell if the man was genuinely losing it or putting on an act. Even with everything going on out there, they were locked inside the cockpit with trained military men who knew how to defend themselves. So why was he unraveling now, just as they were preparing to land? It would all be over soon.

Sergeants Cunningham and Knowles stood at the ready, weapons in hand. Daniels, Abrams, and Goss were locked and loaded, prepared for a firefight if things went sideways.

"I don't want Vira to die," Pavlyuk cried out.

Webb eased up slightly on the stick, then shifted his attention toward him.

"Dammit, Potluck! Right now, you and I are the two most valuable people on this aircraft. I need you to stay focused. Do you understand me?"

Pavlyuk nodded, then turned back to his controls, helping guide the world's largest aircraft toward what had become the world's most heavily guarded runway.

Webb figured they had maybe twenty-five minutes of flight time left at low altitude if he kept the plane steady at maximum conservation power. He just needed to hold out a little longer. This would all be over in minutes.

But he also knew the hijackers might breach the cockpit in less than fifteen.

Whether they realized it or not, their lives now depended on holding that door. No amount of assault rifles would save the hijackers once the strike team waiting below stormed the aircraft.

The AN-225 banked into a curve, descending through broken clouds to reveal millions of floodlights ready and waiting.

CHAPTER TWENTY-FOUR

(GERMANY, THE PIT STOP)

THE PLANE DIPPED WITH a hard jolt, then leveled out, lining up with a runway lit by glowing amber lights below. They had been in the air for over four hours, and Webb wanted nothing more than to bring the beast to its knees and let the storm troopers rush in and kill the bastards who had made his life a living hell.

Webb pressed the radio transmitter button and brought the receiver to his lips.

"Ramstein, we are approaching Runway Two. We are coming in hot. I repeat … coming in hot at full throttle. ETA seven minutes."

Elliot's voice crackled back over the comm a familiar voice, Webb thought.

"We copy, 225," came the calm reply. Their composure was almost patronizing. "We're aware of the situation and prepared to intervene."

The radio cut out. The runway grew larger in the window. Time was running out.

"Oh no, no, no. This is not good."

Pavlyuk's panicked voice already grating on Webb's nerves. He was too focused on touching down to deal with another outburst.

Bombs. They have a bomb. We just need to open the door…

Why would Potluck suggest something so foolish? A trained aviator? Webb couldn't understand it and couldn't worry about it now. He'd deal with Pavlyuk later. For now, he had to focus on landing the equivalent of a bowling ball on a chessboard.

Through the cockpit window, the glowing grid of Ramstein Air Base came into view. Below them, a small German town and open fields drifted by.

"Ramstein, we're ten miles out final approach," Webb called into the headset.

"Copy that, 225. Tactical and emergency measures are in position. Prepare for intercept," Elliot replied.

More banging on the cockpit door. Then suddenly it stopped.

Sergeant Cunningham crouch-walked to the door. He pressed his face against it, holding still for ten long seconds. When his suspicion was confirmed, he pulled back quickly.

On the other side of the door, Boris unzipped the red backpack and pulled something out with glee like a kid shaping clay in a pottery class. When satisfied, he rolled the C4 into form and pressed it carefully along the seal of the door.

"Sir! Sir… they've attached some kind of explosive! They're going to blow the damn thing open!"

Cunningham shouted toward Captain Webb but loud enough for everyone to hear. There was panic and urgency in his voice.

Webb reached for the transmitter again, this time his tone urgent.

"Tower… Tower, come in," he called.

"We have a breach in progress, stand by for immediate emergency intervention."

"225, I'm still here. We're all still here," Master Sergeant Elliot reassured the captain. But what he heard next left him speechless. A bomb. He paused for a few seconds, then came back with new instructions for the aircraft.

"I need to go over an emergency checklist with you. Do you have any munitions onboard that could increase the blast radius?"

Webb denied having any warfare ordnance aboard.

"That's good," Elliot replied. "I need you to proceed to heading 2-1-2 and stay the course. Let me know when that's done."

Elliot watched as the plane veered slightly left just as he'd directed. Good pilot, he thought.

"You're doing well, 225. How's your fuel status?"

"Fuel state excellent," Webb responded.

"Copy. Stand by for further instructions."

Elliot turned to Boyd. "Go get Colonel Bailey. Now."

She was gone less than a minute and returned with the commander at her side.

Colonel Jack Bailey entered the tower like a storm. He was tall, gray-haired, and had a youthful sharpness in his eyes. You could hear him before you saw him.

"What?"

Bailey barked as he strode into the room and headed toward Elliot.

From the urgency in his voice, Elliot was sure Boyd had already briefed him about the situation. Bailey read the tension in the room immediately and saw the haunted look on Elliot's face. He didn't need to be told twice.

"A bomb?" Bailey asked. "What kind?"

"225 has confirmed there's an explosive onboard. We believe it's a homemade C4 device."

Bailey looked toward the radar screen, watching the blinking light descending now just five miles out.

"Who's flying that plane, again?"

"Major Arnott and Captain Webb, sir. Out of Travis Air Force Base. They're on some kind of special mission," the Master Sergeant reported crisply.

Boyd tapped a nearby keyboard and waited. When the monitor flickered to life, she punched a few keys, then paused as images of both Arnott and Webb appeared on the screen. She pointed, and Colonel Bailey followed the direction of her finger.

He didn't recognize the two Air Force pilots.

Bailey's mind kicked into analysis mode. These kinds of situations, though rare, often spiraled into national disasters. This will land front and center on every major news outlet in Germany and back home in the States. For this, he was sure.

He wasn't familiar with the pilots. Or their flight crew.

Hell, up until three hours ago, he had no idea the mighty Antonov-225 was even headed into his backyard.

The commander turned back to the screen for one final look before giving the order.

"Code Red."

With that, Elliot crossed to the controller station, picked up the red phone, and dialed. The call connected after a single ring.

"Tower Control with CC update. Initiate Code Red for incoming aircraft."

Elliot hung up and turned back toward Colonel Bailey.

"Are you ready for this?" the colonel asked.

It was meant to be a statement but came out as a question. Elliot already knew the answer. It was always yes when the boss asked something like that.

Bailey decided to remain in the tower to watch things unfold.

Seconds later, a voice echoed across the flight line, loud and clear over the PA system:

"Code Red! Code Red!"

The loudspeaker repeated the command twice more before falling silent. Boyd looked at the commander, then at her supervisor both still stunned by the news, half-expecting that hunk of metal to explode right before their eyes.

Down below, Code Red protocol was already underway. Huge blast walls were being erected around key buildings. Non-essential vehicles were moving off the concrete, some diverting to the grass to minimize potential damage from a plane detonation. Evacuations were in progress.

With the ground racing up fast, Webb whispered to himself, "Here we go." Shaking, he still couldn't believe this was real. He reached up to rub the tension from his neck. Pain shot through him. He winced and gripped the controls until his knuckles turned white.

A good distance away from the cockpit door and the C4 Boris raised his pistol, took aim, and fired.

BAM!

The plane jolted violently, but this time it wasn't turbulence. A thunderous BANG echoed through the cockpit, followed by a flash of blinding light and a shockwave that slammed into Webb like a punch to the chest. He crashed forward into the flight board. Through the haze of pain, he was pretty sure he'd snapped a couple ribs.

Ouch. That hurts.

The blast had ripped the cockpit door off its bottom hinge and shoved it sideways. Smoke flooded the confined space.

All be damned, Webb thought. A bomb. A goddamn bomb.

The detonation had done its job. The cockpit was now exposed to massive overpressurization, but its structural integrity held. Damage was minimal, thanks to the limited payload of the homemade C4. The bomb hadn't been designed to destroy the plane only to breach the door.

After a semi-conscious moment of disorientation, Captain Webb groaned and pulled himself back into control just as the aircraft dipped and swerved toward the earth.

The hulking mass of steel plunged downward. Moonlight glinted off its frame, catching streaks of silver as it fell. Below, the runway lights twinkled like scattered strands of pearls. The engines whined softly as the flaps slid in and out, adjusting to regulate speed.

The hijackers burst into the cockpit, rifles raised, barking orders. The no-nonsense ends of their weapons were leveled at both the airmen and the pilots.

Sergeant Knowles rolled into a firing position and aimed toward the doorway but before he could line up a shot, Yulian fired. A single round struck Knowles in the head, killing him instantly.

Not to be outdone, Boris fired two rapid shots into Sergeant Cunningham, who collapsed onto his fallen comrade.

Seeing this, Lieutenants Goss and Abrams dropped their weapons and raised their hands. Master Sergeant Daniels followed suit.

Boris secured their weapons and began restraining them with their hands behind their backs, binding wrists tightly with zip ties. He used the remaining ties to immobilize their feet.

The hijackers moved through the cockpit with swift, brutal precision.

Webb considered reaching for his gun but if they saw it, he wouldn't even have a second to react. They'd shoot. He'd die. And the plane would go down.

He let it go.

The chilling silence had shattered. Any hint of resistance was met with sharp shoves or barked orders intimidation backed by the looming threat of violence.

"Ne sazhat' samolet!"

The shout came from the hijacker pressing a rifle barrel into the back of Webb's head.

"Do not land the plane!"

This time, Yulian issued the command in English. He drove the barrel harder into Webb's skull.

"If I pull up now, we're going to crash!" Webb snapped. "It's too late, look!"

He pointed ahead.

Yulian leaned in, eyes wide as a blur of asphalt and concrete surged toward them through the windshield. He braced himself. The Antonov slammed into the runway hard, jarring them all. For a second, the front tires lifted before crashing back to the ground.

"Do not slow down!" Yulian shouted.

"We don't plan to," Pavlyuk said, coolly.

Remarkably, there was no hint of a Ukrainian accent, he sounded like a New Yorker.

Webb met his eyes. For a second, he saw someone else in the man's expression. Something colder. More controlled.

"Get up. Now."

Boris yanked Webb by the collar, hauled him from his seat, and shoved him straight into Pavlyuk who expertly disarmed him and tossed the gun aside. Without missing a beat, Yulian slid into the pilot's seat, both hands fumbling over the controls, trying to stabilize the aircraft.

Webb shared the fate of his still-breathing crewmates. His hands were tied behind his back, his ankles bound tight. Curled on the floor in the fetal position, he felt the vibrations of the plane beneath him as it continued taxiing fast.

The Antonov veered left, skimming dangerously close to smaller towers and hangars. Emergency vehicles gave chase, but they were no match for the massive transport.

Even with his hands bound, Master Sergeant Daniels managed to reach for a small blade tucked in his lower pocket. He gripped it, drew it out

The glint of the blade caught Boris's eye.

BANG. Boris fired, nearly point-blank.

Daniels slumped, dead.

Pavlyuk glanced back, saw the fallen sergeant, and shook his head.

"Keep moving. We're almost there."

Yulian shouted to Pavlyuk as he slammed the throttle forward.

From inside the cockpit, sirens and spotlights swirled outside the windows but the pilots had no intention of slowing down.

Outside, the engines strained toward full power, roaring like a beasts.

Inside, Webb watched Pavlyuk closely, trying to make sense of it all. Pavlyuk was untouched, unharmed and working alongside the hijackers like he belonged there. And he looked … calm.

Too calm.

It didn't make sense. The man had always projected weakness, timid, deferential. Now here he was, steady-handed beside the attackers.

Webb's gut twisted.

Something's not right.

"Aw fuck, fuck, fuck. We're losing it!" Yulian shouted, his voice cracking.

"225, decrease speed immediately."

The tower's voice broke into the cockpit by Master Sergeant Elliot.

"225, do you copy?"

No reply.

Elliot stood frozen as the Antonov hurtled down the runway, picking up even more speed.

Yulian made quick adjustments to the cluster controls and eased back on the stick. The aircraft responded, massive, obedient and picking up speed.

Beside him, Pavlyuk adjusted the flaps. The plane had reached maximum velocity and was running out of real estate.

The Antonov rumbled with brute force. The engines howled, their thunder shaking the ground. The runway markers blurred into a single white line as the world outside shrank in comparison.

Together, Yulian and Pavlyuk pulled back on the sticks and the bird answered.

The nose pitched skyward. The intricate web of landing gear groaned and retracted. For a heartbeat, the Antonov hung between earth and sky, then, impossibly, it lifted.

The emergency crews below, sharpshooters posted on rooftops, and all essential personnel could only watch as the giant aircraft clawed its way back into the night sky.

In the tower, Bailey, Elliot, Boyd, and the others watched in stunned disbelief as the Antonov climbed higher.

"We did not plan on stopping here, Captain Webber."

Pavlyuk's voice made Webb sick to his stomach.

He called me Webber. What an asshole, Webb thought.

It didn't register yet he was getting a taste of his own medicine.

"Fuck you."

Webb clenched his jaw but kept his face impassive.

Pavlyuk gave Boris a subtle nod. The message was clear it was time to shut the captain up.

Boris drove his right boot into Webb's abdomen. Webb screamed.

Still gasping, Webb was coughing when Boris planted the same boot against his head.

Webb's mind raced.

All this time … Pavlyuk had been working with them. He remembered the constant texting, the stolen glances at his phone always distracted when he should've been focused on the mission.

"Are you going to kill us all?" Webb asked.

He regretted it immediately. If they hadn't been planning on it, why put the thought in their heads?

"Not yet. Soon enough."

Pavlyuk turned and flashed a devilish grin at Webb and the others.

By now, Webb was sure the hijackers were Russian. And they were taking this plane to Moscow.

Who else could be behind this?

His thoughts jumped to the most powerful man in Russia.

Oh shit.

"Poydem domoy," Pavlyuk said to Yulian and slapped him a high-five.

Webb nearly gagged.

"You'll pay for this," he growled, spitting blood-flecked saliva onto the floor.

"I don't think so," Pavlyuk replied, eyes on the instruments.

The altimeter ticked upward 20,000 feet … 25,000 … 30,000.

Once they reached cruising altitude, Pavlyuk banked the plane smoothly into a curve. When the aircraft leveled off, he activated autopilot, then spun his seat to face Webb.

"A few hours ago, an email was sent to Moscow," he said calmly, "confirming the VIP guests aboard the Gulfstream we have downstairs. How did we know this? All thanks to a stupid social media post from some teenage girl. They're all idiots."

He spoke with venom.

"And in a few hours," he continued, "Zelensky and his family will be sitting in a Russian prison. Then Zelensky will go on record, resigning for the whole world to hear.

An hour after that, the Russian President will be on every TV and radio station in the country, accepting the resignation."

Oh my god, Webb thought. This goes deeper than I imagined.

CHAPTER TWENTY-FIVE

(FROM RUSSIA, WITH LOVE)

WHEN THE PLANE TOUCHED down at Ramstein Air Base, chaos erupted aboard the AN-225. Some passengers celebrated, while others like Petrov and his compadres seethed with rage. Olena was relieved; the landing meant she and her family might escape a terrible fate. In the upper cabin, the hostages cheered too, but their joy was fleeting. Without warning, the plane began to climb again. A strange, sickening sensation sank in. Hope evaporated in an instant.

Petrov, receiving an update over his radio, suddenly heard only static. Frustrated, he stepped outside to get a better signal.

As soon as he left the room, Svingei took his chance to say something he'd been holding in for a while.

"You are pretty."

Svingei's thick accent scraped all the charm from the gritty compliment he offered Kassandra. He'd noticed something different about her while shoving her around with the other hostages, though he couldn't quite place it. Sasha gave him a look that said, Keep it in your pants.

Aside from Vira, Svingei thought Kassandra was the most attractive woman on the plane. Sasha, of course, was a bombshell but she was sleeping with the boss, which made her off-limits. Still, something about Kassandra's face nagged at him. It looked familiar.

He pulled a cell phone from his pocket and tapped the screen a few times. Kassandra stiffened. Her heart pounded. She feared he was about to uncover her identity that she was the most valuable hostage of them all.

Svingei scrolled through photos until he found the one he'd been studying. Then he walked over to Kassandra, knelt beside her, and held the screen next to her face. It was a perfect match. The girl in the photo was unmistakably the one sitting before him. He swiped again to a family portrait of the Zelenskys.

He smiled.

She knew immediately: her cover was blown.

Sasha, watching closely, understood what was happening. When Svingei turned the phone toward her, she saw it too.

"It would be such a shame to put a bullet in that lovely little face of yours," the hijacker said to Kassandra, now that he knew who she was.

"You won't get away with this. None of you will," she said.

Kassandra shouted, then spat at Svingei. The saliva splattered across his shirt. He glanced down at the stain, his jaw tightening. For a brief moment, he considered striking her with the butt of his Uzi but decided against it.

Petrov reentered the room and immediately noticed the broad grins on both Sasha and Svingei.

"What?"

Svingei walked over and handed him the phone. Petrov studied the photo for a few seconds, then turned to stare at Kassandra. He gave Svingei a nod a silent congratulations for a job well done. Then he raised his handheld radio to his lips.

"Drago! Viktor! Come in."

A moment later, the radio crackled to life with Drago's voice.

"Boss … we"

POP! POP! POP! A burst of automatic gunfire echoed through the transmission.

"Drago, what's happening?"

There was a pause, then Drago's voice returned, breathless.

"Boss, we have him trapped!"

Another barrage of gunfire roared through the radio. Now clearly concerned, Petrov looked at Svingei, then at Sasha, and back at Svingei before pointing.

"You. Go down there and see."

Below, in the lower deck gangway near the baggage hold, Harvey was pinned down, bullets zipping past him on both sides. Pressed against a large metal crate, he took a deep breath and examined his weapon. He removed the magazine, checked it, then slammed it back in.

As he tried to move, a sharp pain ripped through his arm. He glanced down and blood had soaked his uniform around the bicep area. He touched the wound and winced. It hurt like hell.

He sat still, listening. Everything was quiet except the distant whine of the engines outside the fuselage. Harvey's eyes darted, scanning for options. He heard footsteps approaching from behind.

They're relentless, he thought.

In a last-ditch effort, Harvey raised his weapon over the crate and fired blindly. The two hijackers dove behind a nearby equipment cart. Seizing the opportunity, Harvey sprang to his feet, sprinted past them, and climbed down a metal ladder, landing in the 747's cargo bay behind a stack of containers.

Back in the upper deck's rear cabin, Petrov watched over the hostages packed in tightly. Sasha kept her weapon trained on them. Vira wrapped a comforting arm around Kassandra, trying to keep her calm.

"Anyone who does something foolish will die. Don't be a hero," Petrov warned the frightened group on the floor.

"What do you want with us?" Vira asked, her voice trembling.

"Just your cooperation. That's all. If you run, you die."

The hostages glanced around at one another, searching for a silver lining but there was none. If they remained on the plane and it landed in Russia, which they had all figured out by now, they were either going to be killed or face an even worse fate in a Russian prison.

So far, only a handful of hostages had been killed because they failed to follow commands or appeared to be a threat. Some were bloodied and bruised; others, untouched. Hushed conversations continued whenever the captors weren't paying attention.

Meanwhile, Viktor and Drago were still hunting the elusive American.

When they reached the bottom of the metal ladder Harvey had descended earlier, they paused to scan the area. In front of them sat a modified 747, wingless, but otherwise fully intact. With their eyes locked on the aircraft, the two men advanced with deliberate precision. The looming body of the plane cast heavy shadows in the dim light.

Every step was calculated. Every glance sharp. They scanned the dark underbelly and surrounding crates for any hint of danger.

Harvey was pressed flat against a web of nylon netting that perfectly blended with his uniform. The hijackers passed within feet of him. He could hear their whispers as they moved toward the slaller aircraft's door.

They examined the cabin entryway, which was lowered. Drago and Viktor wore grim expressions, etched with cold determination. One after the other, they ascended the stairs into the sleek jet. The polished metal glinted faintly. A low hum vibrated from deep within the aircraft.

Weapons drawn, they swept the front galley but found nothing. It was too quiet. Yet both men could feel it: Mriya was moving fast.

Shoulder to shoulder, they moved toward the back of the 747, breathing in sync, every motion deliberate. They used seatbacks and overhead bins for balance as the jet subtly shifted.

Finally, they reached a three-inch-thick fireproof door leading to the aft compartment.

Drago signaled Viktor.

Viktor yanked on the handle. Locked.

Drago gave another signal. The two men stepped back several paces, raised their weapons, and aimed at the door.

"Come out now with your hands up!"

Drago barked the command loud and clear. The hijackers waited a minute, but no one emerged from the room.

"I repeat come out now and you won't get hurt!"

Still no response. Time to back up threats with action. Drago motioned to move in but paused, he had one more trick up his sleeve.

"Mr. President, we have your daughter. Come out with your hands up, and she won't be harmed."

He and Viktor exchanged a quick glance and a grin, hoping the deception would work. They waited a few seconds. Then Drago tried again.

"Mr. President, if you want to see your daughter alive again, I suggest you come out immediately with your hands up."

Drago listened intently. A sound muffled sobbing. A woman's voice. It was faint but enough to confirm someone was behind that door.

"I'm going to count to three," Drago growled, "and you're going to come out or I'm going to put a shiny bullet in her pretty little head. One!"

He glanced at Viktor to make sure his partner was ready.

"Two!"

Both men racked their weapons, the bolts slamming forward with a menacing clack a sound meant to carry through the fire door. Suddenly, Viktor felt something behind him. He turned slowly. Nothing.

He let out a nervous chuckle, brushing it off. Just nerves. Still in control.

He turned back toward the rear cabin door and slipped his finger into the trigger well.

Then POP!

Viktor jerked forward. Blood gushed from his chest and neck. Drago dove behind a high-backed seat as Viktor's body hit the floor.

Eyes wide and glassy, Viktor stared at Drago in frozen disappointment.

Back to the rear cabin, Drago fired a tight three-round burst from his MP5 toward the front of the plane.

He waited.

Peered slowly from behind the seat.

Nothing.

Still no sign of the shooter.

He scanned the cabin still nothing. He grabbed his radio and pressed the talk button.

"Petrov, we've lost Viktor."

A second later, Petrov's voice crackled through Drago's radio.

"Repeat last traffic."

Drago raised the radio to his lips, just about to respond when Artem suddenly popped open the cabin door from behind. Drago panicked, spinning with his gun but Artem already had the drop on him.

Too late.

POP! POP! POP!

Three clean rounds dropped the hijacker mid-transmission.

Harvey stepped into view and gave Artem a quick nod. Artem nodded back, then vanished into the room, shutting the door once again.

Harvey waited for the satisfying click of the lock before finally turning to his wound. He scanned the room, frantically looking for something, anything for first aid. He'd trained for this. But not like this.

He spotted a stainless steel cabinet, popped it open, and found a fully stocked med kit. He grabbed the first aid pack and opened it, pulling out a roll of white linen and a ball of gauze.

"Freeze! Get on the floor now!"

The voice was so close, the hairs on Harvey's neck stood on end.

Think fast.

He hurled the first aid kit over his shoulder, momentarily distracting the hijacker. Spinning on his heel, Harvey slammed the butt of his rifle into Svingei's jaw, knocking him back. The hijacker dropped his Uzi and grabbed for Harvey's rifle as he fell. The motion was a blur as both men tumbled to the floor.

The rifle clattered a few feet away.

Harvey drove his elbow hard into Svingei's kidney. The hijacker grunted, low and guttural. Harvey jumped to his feet and spotted his weapon.

He lunged for it.

But when he turned back, Svingei was already up. He charged with a bull-like rush straight into Harvey's solar plexus.

The momentum carried them through the open hatch and down the narrow stairs, crashing onto the Antonov floor beneath the smaller 747.

Both men staggered to their feet, squaring off in fighting stances.

Svingei jabbed.

Harvey ducked the punch barely missed, ruffling his hair.

He countered with a knee strike.

Svingei blocked it with his forearm.

The fight settled into a brutal rhythm flesh against flesh, breath against breath.

Harvey, the slightly bigger man, relied on brute strength and heavy blows, pushing Svingei backward until he was trapped against the nylon webbing lining AN-225's cargo hold.

Harvey saw an opening and darted in, closing the distance. His movements were fluid, economical. A swift kick to the hijacker's knee buckled the leg with a sickening pop.

Before Svingei could recover, Harvey unleashed a flurry of strikes, rapid-fire punches to the ribs, each impact echoing through the cavernous hold.

Svingei wheezed and pitched forward.

Harvey drove an upward elbow directly under the chin. Crack.

Svingei's head snapped back. His eyes rolled. He collapsed.

Harvey stood over the lifeless body, chest heaving.

"Ouch," he muttered, rubbing his left bicep.

Then he looked up the steps of the 747 and saw the first-aid kit still lying in the doorway.

CHAPTER TWENTY-SIX

(AN OVAL SITUATION)

UNBEKNOWNST TO EVERYONE ON the aircraft, a powerful ally had been keeping a close watch on the unfolding situation quietly coordinating with U.S. and international agencies to ensure the hostages' safety.

In the Oval Office, a select group of military brass stood clustered around a large screen, carefully monitoring a radar display. White dots traced the Antonov 225's flight path from Kyiv, Ukraine, west to Ramstein Air Base in Germany, and now looping back northeast over the Black Sea, heading toward Belarus.

"Has that last update been verified?" the President asked, her tone sharp.

"Yes, ma'am. It's confirmed Zelensky did not board the plane. However, we've verified that his family is onboard. The hijackers likely took control just before landing at Ramstein," the White House Advisor replied.

"This sure is a clusterfuck," President Markle murmured.

"How did the Russians learn about this mission?"

"It seems they were tipped off by a tweet. Their eighteen-year-old daughter posted it hours before our C-5 landed."

President Markle shook her head. Damn teenagers.

"What are the terrorists' demands?" she asked.

"They haven't made any yet," the Advisor responded.

"What are they waiting for? Everyone has a price. Find out what they want … and get me everything you have on the Major and the Captain."

Then she turned to a nearby White House aide.

"Get the Joint Chiefs on a secure line in the Situation Room. I want full intel on our airmen onboard and everything there is to know about that damn plane."

"I'm on it, ma'am." The White House aide hurried out of the room.

It wasn't long before the crew had reassembled in the Situation Room and were closely monitoring the Antonov's flight path on one of the radar screens. High-tech maps and communications systems lined the walls, encircling an austere conference table equipped with laptops, tablets, and secure phones at every seat.

President Markle studied the projected course of AN-225 on the tactical display.

"This is what we're dealing with … the Antonov-225, nicknamed Mriya," General Pope said as a new image of the aircraft appeared on a separate jumbo screen.

He continued, "Her first flight was in December 1988, developed under the USSR's space program. Gorbachev himself took part in the original design. She's the real deal, folks."

Another image popped up, displaying the aircraft's cavernous cargo hold and enormous fuselage capacity.

"It started as a Soviet asset," Pope went on, "but was eventually transferred to the Ukrainian government as part of the disarmament deal. I think our soviet friends are having second thoughts."

The President leaned back in her chair, finger to her lips, deep in thought. When the general paused, she asked, "So our intel is solid this is Russia's doing?"

"It's the only thing that makes sense," the general replied. He added, "In an hour, they'll be flying over parts of the Black Sea patrolled by Russian naval forces. That means in two hours, they'll be inside Russian airspace. Once they cross that line it's game over."

The White House Advisor, who had been leaning back in his seat, straightened up to address the room.

"The United States has a vested interest in that aircraft. That's why we can't let it fall into Russian hands."

"And if it does?" Markle asked.

"We go from hostages to assassinations on Russian propaganda TV. And if you're wondering whether we can blow it out of the sky…"

"The answer is no," General Pope interjected firmly.

Destroying the plane wasn't an option not with U.S. airmen still believed to be alive onboard.

President Markle took a deep breath and voiced the question on everyone's mind.

"What assets do we have in the region for a quick response, if needed?"

General Pope was already ahead of her. He pressed a button on a clicker, and the jumbo screen shifted to display the USS Midway.

"The carrier is en route to the Korean Peninsula. She's locked and loaded with Marine, Navy, and Air Force fighter jets. They can provide escort in under thirty minutes."

"Oh no, what is that?"

Markle pointed to a secondary monitor at the back of the room, which immediately drew everyone's attention.

The screen showed a CNN broadcaster reporting live from Ramstein Air Base.

"The aircraft was traveling from Ukraine to Germany when hijackers took control," the reporter said. "This is highly unusual…most hijackings involve passenger planes.

I've never seen anything like this. The Antonov aborted its landing here at Ramstein and has lost communication since. U.S. service members are believed to be onboard."

The room fell silent.

In the charged quiet of the Situation Room, the President watched intently. The glow from the screen cast long shadows across the faces of her advisors. After a final, grim pause, she leaned forward, eyes fixed on the real-time footage and tactical maps. The weight of her decision hung heavy in the air.

With a clear and resolute voice, she gave the order.

"Make the call. And get me the Press Secretary now."

General Pope picked up one of the secure phones and issued the order: launch the jets now. Their mission was to protect the aircraft from any hostile planes.

After he hung up, President Markle turned to him. "Keep me abreast of all developments."

Within minutes, the Midway was scrambling fighters in response to the President's command. Jets thundered down the flight deck, afterburners glowing a brilliant orange against the dark sheen of the East China Sea. Steam billowed from the catapults as F-15s, F-16s, an F-22 Raptor, and two F/A-18 Hornets launched with explosive force, disappearing as specks into the vast sky.

Below, the aircraft carrier sliced through the water a floating fortress of steel and power.

Leading the response team was Captain Theodore Meczoire, callsign "Teddy Bear," piloting an Air Force F-22 Raptor. Teddy banked hard to the left, his afterburner trailing a streak of fire across the night sky.

"Teddy Bear, airborne," came his calm, professional voice over comms.

One by one, the others followed suit, engines roaring as they took to the sky.

"Money Bag, airborne," Lieutenant Grant reported. "Whiskey One, airborne," came Lieutenant Jamison's voice. "Rocky, airborne," said Captain Fingerle. "Hollywood, airborne," added Abby.

The last two to check in were a Navy F-14 Tomcat and a Marine-piloted F/A-18 Hornet.

Once all pilots were airborne, Teddy Bear checked his watch. 0100 hours.

Harvey was back on his feet, sprinting through the corridor on the mid-level of the cargo plane. He moved room to room, sweeping each section for survivors but came up empty.

A sound footsteps? He froze, flattened against the wall, and raised his weapon. Finger on the trigger, he held his breath until silence reassured him. No one walked through his crosshairs.

He stepped back into the aisle and moved cautiously toward the front of the plane. At the base of the ladder to the upper deck, he stopped and checked his clip. Enough rounds, for now.

He slung the rifle across his back and climbed. At the top, he slowly poked his head up, scanning the dim space. To the right, legs. Someone was there. Likely a terrorist.

Harvey gripped his rifle tighter and crept forward.

His instinct was dead on.

A sudden bump into an armrest gave him away. Boris, crouched nearby, peeked out. Harvey reacted instantly, firing several rounds. Boris ducked behind a divider and returned fire.

The exchange was short but violent. When the shots ceased, Boris unleashed a few wild suppressive rounds and bolted. Before retreating, he lit the gauze on a homemade Molotov cocktail and hurled it down the aisle.

It smashed into a seat near Harvey, erupting in flames.

Boris fired again, then vanished behind a forward divider, racing toward the hostage compartment.

Chasing the hijacker, Harvey advanced cautiously through the rear cabins, rifle at the ready. His eyes locked onto the open lavatory door, flapping slightly in the plane's turbulence.

He raised the nose of his rifle and swept it across the lavatory's interior, firing a controlled three-round burst. The bullets ripped through the thin surfaces but the hijacker wasn't there.

Harvey moved to the next lavatory and repeated the process. Empty again.

He hefted the rifle, weighing it in his hands, then checked the clip just a few rounds left. He slapped it back into place and switched from automatic to single-shot mode.

"They don't pay me enough for this," he muttered.

Harvey leaned back against a window pane and closed his eyes for a moment. When he opened them again, the world was a wash of color and distortion. No shapes, only shifting blurs.

His vision slowly adjusted, each blink sharpening the haze. Shadows on the walls dissolved, and the outlines of seatbacks came into focus. It felt like surfacing from underwater muted, disoriented, breathless.

Then something caught his eye.

He reached up and opened a window shade that was halfway down. There, streaking across the sky a squadron of United States fighter jets.

Harvey exhaled, shoulders slumping as he released a deep, grateful breath.

CHAPTER TWENTY-SEVEN

(HERO'S WELCOME)

THE ANTONOV-225 WAS NOW completely surrounded by jets bearing the emblem of the United States military. Its massive silhouette loomed like a dark monolith against the star-dusted night sky. The aircraft's powerful engines hummed a deep, steady rhythm a low bassline in the otherwise silent expanse.

Then, a new sound pierced the quiet a higher-pitched whine, rising in intensity as seven fighter jets slid into formation. Their navigation lights blinked in a silent, precise ballet two jets flanking each side of the transport. The sleek, angular forms of the fighters stood in stark contrast to the bulky cargo plane.

"Alright, ladies and gentlemen, hold your formation,"

Teddy commanded, tipping his wings left and right as a signal that everything was proceeding as planned.

The squadron held formation, awaiting further instructions should a threat arise. Suddenly, Mriya was no longer a sitting duck.

Inside the Antonov, Boris kept running. The upper cabin had become a narrow gauntlet. He charged down the aisle, heart pounding, breath ragged. The overhead bins loomed overhead like the walls of a claustrophobic tunnel, and the pounding footsteps behind him blurred into a distant thrum as he gained ground.

His eyes darted side to side as he sprinted until finally, he reached the hostage holding area.

"Boss," he gasped, folding forward, hands braced on his knees as he fought to catch his breath.

Petrov and Sasha stared at him, waiting for the report.

"He's coming."

Petrov didn't need to ask who.

"Guns up," he ordered sharply.

They raised their weapons and aimed down the corridor. "Anything that moves fire."

Any hostage who whimpered was met with the same threat of violence.

Sasha and Boris tightened their grips on their rifles, eyes locked on the shadows.

Petrov scanned the hostages like a bouncer at a nightclub, his gaze sweeping over them until it landed on one.

"You. Come here," he said, pointing at Kassandra.

Frightened and on edge, Kassandra made her way to the lead hijacker. She knew she could have refused, but the man meant business. She had already seen him kill once and she wasn't willing to be the second.

Petrov yanked her closer. She screamed in panic. He pressed a pistol to her temple and told her to be quiet. She obeyed.

Vira clung to another hostage. Both turned away as Petrov raised his weapon to Kassandra. Vira struggled to stay composed, but tears streamed down her face, her expression twisted in anguish as she wrestled with her conscience.

"You! Why do you look at me like that?"

Petrov pointed the muzzle at Vira just briefly, but enough to make clear the question was meant for her.

"Do you think I'm a monster?"

Frantically, Vira shook her head. "No."

"When someone borrows your property and refuses to return it, what do you do?"

Vira wasn't sure if it was a real question or a rhetorical one. She kept her eyes on Petrov. Her lips trembled, but no words came.

"You take it back by force."

Petrov grinned, amused that he'd answered his own question.

Suddenly, Vira found her voice.

"The man you shot earlier … did he deserve to die?"

"Yes. Absolutely."

Petrov didn't hesitate. His reply was cold and dark.

In the cockpit, the pilots were still doing their best to keep the plane on course to Belarus. Yulian glanced at the instrument panel and noticed strange blips on the radar. He leaned in for a closer look, then craned his neck toward the cockpit window.

At first, all he saw was the inky blackness of the sky, pierced by faint, distant stars. Then something else. Not a star. Something faster.

He leaned in further, squinting against the dim glow of the instrument panel. One shape appeared. Then another. And another. Sleek, dark forms emerged from the shadows, closing in.

Fighter jets, he realized.

His eyes darted back to the instrument cluster, watching the synchronized dance of blinking lights. The silent arrival of the jets was a stark, unnerving contrast to what had once been a solitary flight.

"Goddamn it. The Americans are here. We're not going to make it."

Webb seized the moment.

"You're damn right. Now untie me so I can stop them from blowing us all up."

His plea was cut off by a loud, "SHUT UP."

Pavlyuk grabbed his handheld radio and brought it to his lips.

"Boss, we have a problem."

Webb felt a surge of disgust hearing him call the terrorist "Boss."

Petrov shoved Kassandra back toward the other hostages and barked at Sasha, "Shoot anybody that moves."

Sasha gripped her weapon tighter and swept it over the terrified group.

Petrov bolted for the front of the plane, a desperate blur of motion. His boots pounded a frantic rhythm on the worn carpet. A sudden lurch of the aircraft threw him into a seatback, but he recovered quickly.

He hurdled over several lifeless bodies that had lain there for nearly an hour, eyes fixed on the cockpit door. The metallic scent of ozone thickened as he closed in.

Petrov moved from section to section of the plane sweeping the area for potential threat. He was a man fighting the clock and reaching Russian airspace in one piece could mean everything. Petrov stopped and hid when he thought he heard something or someone. After afew moments of silence, he resume the sprint towards the front of the plane.

Petrov burst into the crew area and saw nothing but a television still broadcasting the news. He ran for another three minutes until he reached the forward control area. He saw the busted cockpit door and ran for it. When he entered, his eyes landed on the dead Americans and hostages, sprawled in a pool of blood.

"Boss … look."

Yulian pointed at the radar.

Petrov stepped in, the implication of the unwelcome guests tying a hard knot in his gut. Fear crept in, but he forced himself to project calm because right now, confidence was everything. No one knew if they would live or die.

"How many?"

"We counted seven," Pavlyuk replied.

Petrov swallowed hard. His mind raced for solutions.

A big problem one shaped like the United States military.

He leaned over the pilots, his broad frame crowding the tight space.

"How much time do we have?"

"About an hour," Yulian said.

"Okay. Stay the course. They won't shoot us down."

Petrov sounded almost confident. His hand gripped the armrest as every dip and lurch felt like gravity and the universe betraying him, a terrifying reminder of while he held the gun, something far more powerful was in control.

The plane jolted through a patch of turbulence. The shake was violent enough for everyone to think they'd taken a hit. Petrov squeezed his eyes shut, but fear was a physical force prying them open again. His face, usually a mask of calm authority, twisted with panic and anxiety.

"Boris."

No response from the radio.

"Boris, come in."

Silence. He shouted again, then stormed out of the cockpit with a resounding thud that seemed to rattle the entire plane.

Yulian glanced out the window again and froze. The jets were much closer now. He could almost make out the pilot's helmet.

The fighter jets held pace with the cargo aircraft.

Lieutenant Abby Smith adjusted her microphone.

"You want me to ... what?!"

She asked, incredulous.

"You heard the order loud and clear. Now make your presence felt," came the reply. Teddy Bear, his voice crackling over comms.

"Roger that, sir."

In perfect sync, Abby and Jamison tipped the wings of their F-15 Eagles, flaring out wide before swooping back into formation alongside the cargo plane one on the left, the other on the right of the Mriya.

"It's showtime, ladies," Teddy Bear said from the highest point in the formation.

On his command, both jets tilted, revealing their weapon systems to the pilots of the Mriya, a clear show of force then leveled out again. It was a statement that said, I can destroy you at any minute.

"225, change course to 020. This is a direct order."

Captain Teddy's voice echoed through the cargo plane's cockpit.

"Change course now, or you will be shot down."

Pavlyuk and Yulian exchanged a tense glance, paralyzed by uncertainty. They did nothing. The aircraft remained on course.

The two pilots sat motionless. Panic flickered in their eyes but so did grit and defiance.

The hijackers weren't convinced. They didn't believe the United States champions of morality on the world stage would really commit mass murder over international waters.

Webb coughed.

"If I were you," he muttered painfully from the floor, "I'd do what they say." Coughing.

But no one paid him any mind. The man had been reduced to nothing.

The President and her advisors were still poring over satellite images from high above the Black Sea. The Situation Room felt quieter now since several military personnel and advisors had left to tend to other matters, leaving the core team of nine or ten behind.

Markle slipped off her suit jacket and hung it over the back of her chair.

"Are they buying it?" she asked softly.

General Pope met her gaze. He bit his bottom lip and slowly shook his head. The motion was slight almost imperceptible but it carried weight. The message was clear: the terrorists were prepared to go all the way.

"Do we have Moscow on the line?" the President asked.

"Not yet. We're still working on it," General Pope replied.

He turned and glanced at his aide, who was feverishly working the phone lines.

"Something seems off," Markle said.

"Why haven't they made any demands? Isn't that what terrorists do?"

It was rhetorical she wasn't expecting an answer. But the General gave her one anyway.

"Maybe they've already got what they wanted. They've got Zelensky's family … and the plane they always wanted."

A line on the spider phone began to blink.

"Go ahead, patch it through," the President said, her voice carrying a note of eager urgency.

A White House advisor scanned the LED display and spoke up.

"That's Colonel Kramer from the Pentagon."

"Colonel, you there?" Markle asked, leaning forward.

The Colonel's voice came through the speakerphone.

"I was just thinking"

"No, Kramer," the President cut in sharply. "We're not shooting down that plane."

Just then, White House Press Secretary Kelli Dunn entered the room.

"We have Zelensky on the other line."

"Patch him through," Markle ordered.

"The switchboard is doing that now," Dunn replied.

Within minutes, the phone flashed again. General Pope pressed the speaker button.

"President Zelensky, this is General Pope. You're on a secure line."

"Thank you, General. Thank you for your leadership, Madame President."

"You're welcome. Mr. President, what is your situation?" Markle asked.

"My family is in danger, Madame President. They've most certainly been captured and taken hostage by now. We cannot allow that plane to cross into Russian airspace."

"My intention is not to escalate the situation. We're working very diligently to remain diplomatic." Markled informed him.

"I met your pilots briefly, and if they are anything like I assumed, I believe they're fighting to regain control of that plane," Zelensky replied, his voice crackling through static on the line.

Markle felt a surge of pride hearing another world leader speak so highly of her troops. She began to respond with gratitude but was suddenly cut off.

A burst of static overwhelmed the speaker, sharp and immediate, completely drowning her voice. The room fell silent for several seconds, faces frozen in a tableau of confusion.

Aides scrambled to restore the connection, working feverishly with mitigated solutions but to no avail.

"General, what else do we know about this Major? Our mystery man," she asked.

The last part was unnecessary, but Pope wasn't going to correct the President.

"Major Arnott and Captain Webb were tapped by General Higby, Wing Commander at Travis. They come highly recommended. Harvey is prior enlisted PJ and graduated top of his class at the Air Force Academy. He's done two combat tours Djibouti and Liberia."

An image of Harvey in PJ training flashed onto the screen. Pope continued.

"Pararescue Jumpers are among our elite combat forces. They're nicknamed Guardian Angels for a reason. So if Higby recommends him, then he's the real deal."

An aide waved toward the table of decision-makers.

"We have him back."

General Pope pressed the button on the speakerphone.

"Sir, are you there?"

After a few seconds of silence, Pope muttered, "We've lost him."

CHAPTER TWENTY-EIGHT

(A BLAST FROM THE PAST)

WITH HIS BACK AGAINST the wall, weapon at the ready, Harvey scanned left, then right. Left would take him toward the rear of the plane where he hoped to find the hostages. Right would lead him to the cockpit.

He flipped a mental coin.

Hostages first.

He moved left.

With precision and stealth, he crept toward the back of the aircraft and spotted a ladder descending through a hatch. Swinging the nose of his rifle over it, he swept in a slow circular motion. No sign of Boris. No sign of the other hijackers.

Harvey closed the hatch and sealed it cutting off anyone below.

He scanned the surrounding area with the barrel of his weapon, alert to the silence. "Quiet" could mean one of two things, either the coast was clear, or someone knew he was here.

Lurking. Waiting.

Always assume the latter.

He held his breath and moved forward, committing every detail of the room to memory. It was empty, but not untouched. Personal effects littered the floor—laptops, cell phones, tablets. Chaos in the wake of panic.

A pocketknife lay open on the floor.

Still scanning the room, he crouched, scooped it up, folded the blade, and stuffed it into a side pocket. Then he checked his MP5, sliding out the magazine. Only a few rounds left. He slapped it back in and switched off automatic.

Harvey had learned to feel rooms.

You could sense it whether someone was watching. An itch in the air. A weight on your back.

This room? Dead. No life. Just him.

He trusted his gut and exhaled slowly, preparing to move on. But distant voices yanked his mind into go-mode.

He pushed forward.

Each step was urgent but calculated. Then his boot struck something firm, slightly elastic. He paused. Looked down.

A hand.

He crouched again, eyes scanning the body.

Open eyes. Blood pooled beneath the skull.

"Oh shit," he muttered.

It was a Ukrainian agent someone he'd met briefly in Kyiv at the plane hangar.

Things really were as bad as they seemed.

For a brief moment, he worried about the innocent lives on the plane Pavlyuk, his daughter, and his colleague Webb. The thought of Webb being injured or worse turned his stomach. He hadn't realized just how much he cared about his friend. Well, I guess hell has frozen over after all, he thought.

Harvey glanced at his watch, 0135 hours. He gave his rifle a quick service check, removed the magazine, and slapped a fresh one into place. The bandage around his bicep was soaked through with blood. No time to waste. He pushed forward toward the noise.

He halted outside the rear cabin area. The tense murmurs drifting through the wall told him hostages were being held just around the corner. Harvey pressed himself flat against the bulkhead. His heart pounded like a war drum. So many lives depended on him staying hidden, staying silent.

He peeked inside and took silent inventory. Threats. Movement. Angles.

Boris was scrolling through photos on a phone that belongs to Kassandra. From the smirk curling across his face, Harvey knew exactly which album he'd found. The private one. Boris's eyes flicked back and forth between the images and Kassandra. With a little imagination, he was undressing her over and over again. Each glance a calculated, predatory scan.

To Boris, she wasn't just a hostage. She was a fantasy. He objectified her curves, the way her blouse hugged her shoulders, the fall of her hair. His gaze reduced her to a collection of aesthetic fragments.

Then Harvey clocked the woman with the Uzi.

For a moment, the murmurs dulled into a heavy hum. A jolt, sharp and sudden, shot through him. It's her, he thought. The woman from Club Heaven. The mystery woman whose silhouette haunted his memory.

But how?

A wave of memories vivid and raw crashed over him. He ducked back behind the bulkhead, breathing hard.

Inside, Boris rose and ambled toward Kassandra. He let go of the MP5, letting it swing loosely at his waist, tethered by the sling across his shoulder.

"You. Come with me."

He grabbed Kassandra by the arm and yanked her to her feet. The other hostages reacted instinctively, but the sight of two raised guns pushed them back into their seats. Sasha shot him a disapproving look, sensing what he was about to do, but Boris was determined to play his game while the boss was away.

Kassandra dug her heels into the carpet, her body going limp, a deadweight against Boris's pull. Every muscle in her body tensed, resisting his grip. His fingers dug into the flesh of her biceps as she twisted and writhed in pain, trying to break free.

"Hey."

Boris turned. A gun was trained on his head. It was the American he realized. Harvey was standing in the entryway. He had a clear shot. Boris's hand was just inches from the MP5.

Harvey squeezed the trigger as Boris reached for his weapon.

The man's head exploded across Kassandra's blouse.

She screamed as both she and Boris dropped to the floor. The cell phone he'd been holding clattered beside them, the screen flashing a bikini photo. Boris's head landed in her lap. She looked down and screamed again.

Her cries were instantly drowned by the violent chatter of an Uzi.

Harvey dove just in time, evading a burst of bullets from Sasha. Lying prone, he looked up and saw a flurry of bullet holes stitched across the spot he'd just been standing.

Too close, he thought.

Chaos erupted. Hostages screamed, scrambling in all directions.

To avoid hitting a civilian, Harvey dropped his rifle and drew his sidearm. Muzzle first, he rounded the corner, pistol raised and eyes searching for threats. When he stepped into the room, he saw her tactics. Sasha was already positioned behind a human shield. She had a hostage in front of her, the Uzi pressed to the woman's head.

In a slow, crouched walk, Harvey advanced into the room. Hostages flanked him on either side. He glanced quickly around, never lowering his weapon.

Then, their eyes met.

In that instant, it clicked. She was there that night with the attacker. She was most certainly used as the decoy that night, the way her eyes taunted him that night. Was she supposed to lure him into a room where they would've finished the job together? Maybe Fedir had saved his life by showing up.

His brain churned through the implications, spitting out static analysis. Focus.

He shook his head, trying to clear the thoughts. The hostage at gunpoint whimpered, sobbing, pleading for her life.

"You. Drop it. Or she dies."

Sasha pressed the barrel of her weapon hard into the hostage's neck, issuing her ultimatum.

Harvey kept his pistol trained in her direction, but he didn't have a clean shot. Sasha wasn't about to make it easy.

"Do it now, or I'll shoot!" she barked.

"Put down your gun," Harvey shot back, his voice steady.

He tried to reassure the hostage, telling her to be brave, that everything would be okay. Sasha sounded mildly surprised by Harvey's composure.

"All your friends are dead. It's over. Time to give it up," Harvey said.

"Put down your gun. Last chance," he warned.

Sasha didn't flinch. Harvey could tell this wasn't her first standoff. She'd done this before. More than once.

"You some kind of hero or something?" She sneered.

"No," Harvey replied, "but I'm a decent shot."

A sudden sound from behind made Sasha turn her head just for a split second.

The hostage seized the moment and bit down hard on Sasha's hand.

Startled, Sasha spun, but it was already too late. In a swift, fluid motion, Harvey fired two quick shots into her torso. The bullets struck her midsection, and she staggered backward, as if punched in the gut. She looked down, saw the blood, surprised.

She tried to lift her weapon again.

Harvey shot her once more.

Her right leg gave out, and she collapsed sideways, hitting the wall before sliding down to the floor. The gun slipped from her hand, clattering across the floor with a metallic clang that echoed in the stunned silence.

Harvey rushed in, kicked the weapon away. But it was over, she was already dead.

He turned to the hostages, who were huddled together, terror still etched on their faces. Kneeling beside them, he pulled out a pocket knife he'd found earlier and began cutting through the zip ties binding their wrists.

His calm, efficient demeanor stood in stark contrast to the punishment he'd just unleashed.

"It's over now," he said quietly. One of the hostages tried to tend to his wound, but he waved her away.

He looked around the room, then raised his voice.

"Listen up. We need to get out of this room and head downstairs to safety. Everyone on your feet, single file. We should be long gone before the rest of them get back."

The hostages began rising quickly, urgency replacing paralysis.

"But what about the plane who's …" someone began.

One of the hostages tried to speak, but Harvey cut them off before they could finish.

"Don't worry about that. Right now, I need to get you all to safety."

One of the hostages bent down, picked up Sasha's gun, weighed it in his hands, then took up a post by the exit. He waved the others forward.

The group emerged from their holding area and moved swiftly toward a nearby stairway.

Harvey turned to Kassandra. "Take them down to the lowest level and get to your father's plane in the cargo bay."

Kassandra nodded, a spark of purpose lighting in her eyes. "Got it."

She led the hostages down the stairs, her stride confident.

Meanwhile, Harvey ran in the opposite direction toward the center of the aircraft. Midway down the corridor, he spotted an open hatch. Without hesitation, he dropped into it, descending to a level just beneath the top cabin. Then he took off again, sprinting toward the front of the plane.

The White House was under immense pressure. News had broken that a plane tied to U.S. interests was under attack allegedly by Russian operatives.

CNN was the first to report the story, broadcasting live from Ramstein Air Base with no restraint on detail. The moment the Antonov-225 reappeared on the world stage, people all over began googling the name to understand what made it so important.

In the West Wing, the pressure mounted. Inside the James S. Brady Press Briefing Room, the White House Press Secretary was about to face a swarm of questions.

"People … please. Quiet, please!"

Kelli's voice rang out, sharper than she intended but she had a job to do.

"I have a prepared statement. The White House confirms that the situation over the Black Sea is real. We have fighter pilots trailing the Antonov to ensure her safety and the safety of all onboard. The cargo plane was, in fact, hijacked and is currently under the control of foreign nationals."

Reporters erupted.

"Where is it heading?"

"Who are these foreign nationals?"

"Are they Russian?"

The Press Secretary was being peppered with questions as murmurs turned into shouts.

"Please…!" Kelli called above the noise.

"For security reasons, I cannot comment any further than I already have except to say that the President is doing everything within her power to resolve the situation."

"Where is the PRESIDENT?" one last voice boomed across the room.

Before she could answer, Kelli was swiftly ushered away by a man who had been standing just feet from the podium. The press was left behind, stewing in frustration.

Kelli and her escort moved quickly, weaving through corridor after corridor of the West Wing, doing their best to avoid anyone holding a microphone.

They trotted past hallways steeped in neoclassical elegance and historical gravity, lined with portraits of past presidents and first ladies. A silent gallery of American legacy. The walls, painted in soft neutral hues creamy whites and pale yellows allowed the vibrant art and rich mahogany furniture to stand out. The polished floors, sometimes softened by ornate Persian rugs, echoed with the hurried steps of dignitaries and staff.

Along the way, they nodded at marines and soldiers stationed at key junctions. The architecture boasted intricate crown moldings and carved archways, symbols of power and permanence.

After nearly ten minutes, they reached the ground floor. The Situation Room awaited.

Her escort remained outside as Kelli stepped through the door.

Inside, tension crackled in the air.

The President stood at the head of the table, facing a speakerphone. A male voice crackled from it, cool and deliberate.

"I understand your predicament, Madame President," said the voice. "But if you don't instruct your men to fall back, I'm afraid they'll soon be violating Russian airspace. Remember you have a treaty with NATO."

Nikolai Petrov let his words hang heavy in the air.

The President met the silence head-on.

"What are your demands?"

Markle broke the silence.

"Madame President, please don't insult me. All my demands have been met."

She fired back with another question. "What about the hostages?"

Petrov didn't miss a beat. "The way I see it, you have two choices. Shoot the plane out of the sky and everyone dies. Or allow us safe passage to Russia, where we'll all be … comfortable."

Markle shook her head in frustration, though her expression remained composed. It didn't matter everyone in the room was looking to her, waiting for direction.

"Do you get my point?" Petrov asked.

Though his face wasn't visible, the contempt in his tone painted a clear picture. The room could almost feel his smirk.

Markle said nothing.

"Goodbye, Madame President. It was nice chatting with you."

The line went dead.

"He's right," said General Pope, staring at the tablet in his hands.

"I've got satellite imagery showing the plane entering Russian airspace in approximately thirty-seven minutes."

"Do you think anyone's been killed onboard?" she asked, the question laced with reluctant dread.

"I wouldn't put it past the Russians, ma'am," Pope replied.

Markle leaned back in her chair, a finger pressed to her lips, lost in thought. The thought of shooting down the plane did cross her mind but she quickly did away with it.

Kelli remained at the back of the room. She knew better than to disturb the President when she was this deep in contemplation.

"Put every base in the region on the highest alert," Markle finally ordered.

CHAPTER TWENTY-NINE

(DENOUEMENT)

PETROV STOOD AT THE rear of the cockpit communication area, glaring at the phone he had just used minutes ago. He snatched the receiver and yanked it off its base, severing the cord. The frayed end, still connected to the system, dangled in the air.

"No more talking."

His voice was low and menacing. His face was expressionless, his eyes cold as ice. He glanced down at the Americans lying facedown, their hands bound behind their backs, with undisguised contempt. Seeing almighty America groveling at his feet filled Petrov with a twisted sense of righteousness. He felt like a god with a superpower in his grip.

He checked his watch: 0230 hours.

"Gentlemen," he said to Yulian and Pavlyuk. "Set your watches. In thirty minutes, we'll be home free."

Yulian and Pavlyuk already knew the plan, but hearing it aloud ignited a spark of excitement. They high-fived. Pavlyuk turned instinctively to look at Webb after the gesture like flipping him off without lifting a finger.

"Please direct my daughter to the cockpit. I would like to see her immediately."

Petrov stiffened. This was the first he'd heard of it. No one neither Pavlyuk nor anyone else had mentioned a daughter.

His face tightened. "Come again?"

"My daughter, Vira, is on the plane. I told her to rest in the crew lounge."

Petrov had passed through the lounge earlier and hadn't seen anyone.

"I'll check. What's her name?" he asked.

"Vira," Pavlyuk replied, reaching into his breast pocket and pulling out a worn photo. "There."

Petrov studied the picture. Recognition hit instantly that she was among the hostages seated in the rear cabin.

"Sorry I didn't inform you. It was a last-minute decision."

A big one, Petrov thought. And a stupid one for a pilot. He kept the revelation to himself. No point alerting the father just yet.

"I'll find her."

Casting one last sneer at the American captives, Petrov stormed out of the cockpit. Once out of earshot, he raised his radio to his lips.

"Drago. Viktor."

He moved quickly through the upper-level cabin, heading toward the back of the plane. He called again.

"Drago!" No response."Svengei." Silence. "Boris, come in." He waited. Nothing.

An icy knot tightened in Petrov's gut as he stared at his radio, waiting for a response. The static hiss, once a comforting backdrop to his team's chatter, now felt like a cruel taunt. He pressed the transmit button again, his thumb raw from repetition, as he came upon an open hatch.

He dropped into a defensive stance just behind it.

Drawing his Walther pistol, he quickly examined the steel frame. Smooth. Cold. Efficient. He pressed the eject button, and the magazine popped out into his palm. Less than half-full. He let it drop to the floor and replaced it with a fresh one from his pants pocket.

He glanced down the hatch. Nothing. Slid it shut and kept moving now with serious urgency in his step. He still had half a football field to cover.

Unknowingly, Petrov and Harvey passed one another. Petrov trotting through the upper level toward the back of the plane, while Harvey sprinted beneath him, racing for the cockpit on a lower level.

Petrov cycled through call signs as he ran.

"Boris! Sasha! Do you copy?"

Mid-stride, he switched radio channels. Then switched back. A futile gesture, driven by mounting dread.

Ahead, a hatch laid open midway through the upper deck. Harvey froze. Scanned the area. Silent. Empty. Carefully, he climbed out and returned to the upper level.

Near the base of the hatch, he spotted a magazine emblazoned with Walther PPD. More than half the rounds were gone.

A bad guy was here.

Harvey went to and peered out a nearby window. U.S. fighter jets were still in tow but time was bleeding away.

Harvey kept his pistol low and tight as he dashed toward the cockpit.

Moving quickly, each passing second deepened Petrov's dread. Sweat streamed from his face as he raced toward the rear cabin. Every breath was heavier than the last. The cocky look he'd worn when leaving the cockpit was gone, replaced by raw panic, reinforced each time he vaulted over a corpse.

His hands, once steady and sure, now trembled as he lowered the radio. The crushing silence from his team weighed heavy.

He reached the rear cabin.

The first thing he noticed: bullet holes stitched along the entrance where Sasha had missed.

He kicked open the door to the hostage room. Empty except for one of his men, face-down and dead in the center of the room. And Sasha, his girlfriend, slumped against the far wall. Also dead. Eyes wide. Staring into his soul.

Petrov let out a guttural war cry. Sound traveling through the fuselage.

He dropped to his knees beside her, pulled her into his arms, and cradled her limp body. He stroked her blood-matted hair, whispering curses at the perpetrator. But beneath the grief, something else boiled.

Vengeance.

Someone had beaten him at his own game. Now he wanted blood.

Harvey kept sprinting toward the cockpit when something outside caught his eye through a raised window shade. He skidded to a halt and pressed his face to the tiny pane.

Through the glass, he saw fighter jets veer into a wide arc, peeling away from the aircraft.

He knew exactly what that meant.

The fighters were pulling back either to engage a threat or, more likely, because Washington had ordered them to abort the mission.

It was the latter.

President Markle had been watching the Antonov close in on Russian airspace less than fifteen minutes out. With no resolution in sight, she was forced to issue the recall. If U.S. fighters crossed into Russian territory, it would be seen as an act of aggression. And it's always hard to rally allies when you're the one who fires the first shot.

Russia would be within its rights to defend itself by any means necessary.

And with re-election looming, President Markle didn't want a war dominating her campaign.

Harvey watched all seven fighters bank hard, splitting left and right, disappearing into the distance. A grim realization settled in:

America had backed off.

They were on their own now. In God's hands.

Still, Harvey calculated fast. There was a chance to turn this around. He'd made it this far, dodging death at every turn. He wasn't quitting now.

"Give up now or give up the ghost later." A saying his father had drilled into him as a teenager. It had stuck. Never give up.

In the cockpit, Yulian and Pavlyuk had seen the same retreating jets. It filled them with glee.

"Ha ha. Fuck you … stupid Americans," Yulian sneered.

Pavlyuk flashed a wicked grin at his partner in crime.

Meanwhile, Harvey crept closer to the cockpit, eyes sharp for movement. The plane felt too quiet. Too dead.

As he approached, voices grew louder, two men speaking Russian, back and forth. He couldn't yet identify who was in charge, but he knew one thing: pick them off one by one, and he'd eventually find out.

Bodies littered the path. Lifeless. He stepped over them without hesitation. No time for sympathy.

The burn in his arm, from a bullet graze an hour earlier, still stung. But it wasn't enough to stop him. Not now.

He needed to find Webb. Potluck. Potluck's daughter. And together maybe they could still take this plane back.

Time was running out.

The cockpit door was in sight. Harvey slowed, stepping cautiously around the shattered entrance. He didn't want to spook whoever was inside.

The engines hummed loud behind him.

"Hey," Harvey said softly.

Yulian turned his head slightly to the right and was met with a THWACK! One moment, his world was a whirlwind of jubilant anticipation; the next, it spun into a dizzying blur. The unexpected blow struck the side of his skull with a sickening thud, a brutal punctuation to what had felt like a victory lap in his mind.

Pavlyuk jumped in his seat at the sound of Yulian being pistol-whipped. For a split second, time seemed to slow. He watched as vibrant crimson spilled from Yulian's head, the man's body slumping sideways against the paneling.

"Oh good, you're back," Pavlyuk said to Harvey. "Don't worry. Everything's going to be fine."

Harvey holstered his pistol, grabbed Yulian by both armpits, and yanked him out of the pilot's seat. He dropped him in the center of the floor, then looked at Pavlyuk and nodded toward the others.

"You. Take this. Cut them loose."

Harvey handed Pavlyuk a pocketknife just as Webb and the others screamed.

"Nooooo! He's got a gun!" "He's with them!"

Harvey froze, momentarily stunned, trying to process the outburst as Pavlyuk reached for the knife. That's when he saw it: a glint of metal between Pavlyuk's legs. A handgun. His mind raced why would a hostage be armed, seated beside his supposed captor, and not use the weapon?

The answer hit him like a gut punch. Pavlyuk wasn't who he claimed to be. Either he'd been turned, or he was never on their side to begin with.

A heavy silence settled over the cockpit, broken only by the rhythmic hum of the turbo engines. Both men froze. Their eyes locked unblinking, searching for the slightest flinch, any cue to move first. A bead of sweat trickled down Pavlyuk's temple.

Harvey's instincts took over. He dropped the knife, drew his pistol in a fluid motion, and leveled it at Pavlyuk.

Pavlyuk was already going for his own weapon, tracking it left toward Harvey but it was too late. Harvey had the drop.

He squeezed the trigger twice.

Two rounds slammed into Pavlyuk's right shoulder, stopping him cold. Blood splattered across the fine Corinthian leather seat. One bullet punched clean through, exiting into the cockpit wall. A sudden hiss of pressurized air whispered through the breach.

"Oh shit!" Pavlyuk screamed as his gun clattered to the floor.

In the chaos, he'd nudged the flight stick.

The plane pitched into a nose dive and shook violently.

Captain Webb shouted to his friend

"Hey asshole, cut me loose!"

Harvey's heart lifted when he heard the voice of his old friend again.

Quickly, he rushed over to Webb and sliced through the zip-tie binding his wrists. As soon as his hands were free, Webb grabbed the blade, cut through the restraint around his legs, and lunged toward the pilot controls.

Pavlyuk was still alive barely but completely incapacitated. He offered no resistance as Webb grabbed him and hurled him to the floor. Pavlyuk writhed in pain, clutching his bullet-torn shoulder. Webb delivered a punishing kick to his abdomen for good measure before jumping into the seat.

Together, Harvey and Webb gripped the controls, making frantic adjustments to steady the aircraft.

The plane twisted and tilted downward a full-blown nightmare. They were bleeding altitude fast. The altimeter read 19,000 feet and dropping. Alarms blared in the cockpit, warning the pilots to slow down and reverse the descent or risk catastrophe. A red warning light pulsed on the instrument panel as audible warnings sounded. ALERT, ALERT. DANGER, DANGER!

With a series of sharp corrections and recalibrations, the plane began to level off then slowly, steadily started to climb but shook violently. A very familiar sceen for both men. At last, it inched back up toward 25,000 feet … 26,000 feet.

Harvey's eyes locked onto the radar screen.

"We're five minutes out from Russian airspace," he said tightly.

At approximately 27,000 feet, the aircraft banked left, adjusting its course to remain clear of hostile skies.

Meanwhile, at the very back of the aircraft, Petrov was descending the narrow staircase, raging. Fury twisted his features, but beneath the anger was something deeper: fear.

He suddenly stopped.

Something shifted beneath his feet.

At first, it was subtle, just a gentle tilt, easily mistaken for a pocket of turbulence. He steadied himself against the wall, but the sensation deepened. The floor tilted further. His world began to rotate, slowly but deliberately.

The aircraft felt eerily graceful as it banked through the turn. Vibrations thrummed up through the soles of his shoes, rising with intensity.

Petrov glanced at his watch.

Less than four minutes until the plane crossed into Russian airspace.

This turn wasn't scheduled but here it was, turning away from Russian controlled airspace. Something had gone wrong.

Then it hit him, there was still another pilot on board roaming free. One he hadn't accounted for in all the mayhem.

"No, no, no," he muttered, voice rising into a cry of frustration.

Petrov raced back up the stairs and, with every ounce of strength, sprinted toward the front of the plane. The aircraft was still banking in the turn, and he staggered as he bumped into seatbacks along the aisle but he didn't stop.

He was alone.

Pulling out his radio, he barked into it:

"Yulian!"

No response.

Only the sound of ragged breathing came through. Harvey, listening from the cockpit, guessed that Petrov was closing in.

Then, a new voice crackled over the comm.

"Peter, come in!"

Silence.

"Peter!"

Still nothing. Growing more desperate, Petrov tried one last time this time, using the man's last name.

"PAVLYUK!"

Webb glanced back at Pavlyuk, who lay motionless on the floor, hands and feet zip-tied.

"Hey, Potluck. Your boss is calling. You gonna answer?"

The question was rhetorical and Pavlyuk knew it. He simply lowered his head in shame.

He'd backed the wrong horse in the fight.

CHAPTER THIRTY

(A FIGHT TO THE END)

THE SUN HAD ALREADY set along the Potomac, streaking the sky with shades of deep red and fading pink. The lights of the White House bathed its iconic columns in a glow befitting the most powerful residence on Earth.

Deep below, in the Situation Room, the day hadn't quite ended. While a few staffers had gone home, the core team remained, locked in discussion over the next steps.

Kelli was taking notes as the President gave instructions on how to spin the story for the press when General Pope suddenly pointed to the radar screen on the wall.

"Look!" he shouted.

The room fell silent.

On the screen, a single dot the Antonov was completing a full turn, veering away from Russian territory.

"Impossible," muttered the White House advisor. "What's happening?"

"He did it. The son of a bitch actually did it."

The general was too elated to censor himself. The tension he'd carried in his gut for nearly twenty-four hours finally began to ease. Realizing his slip, he offered a quick apology.

But Markle waved it off. "Don't worry about it."

"Ma'am," said General Pope, regaining composure, "I strongly believe our boys have retaken the plane."

"Get them on the phone. Let's confirm it."

Meanwhile, a fresh news story broke across the CNN feed. This one had nothing to do with the Antonov, but it was no less urgent.

"The territorial dispute between Russia and Ukraine has taken another turn," the anchor began.

"CNN can now confirm that just a few hours ago, Russian tanks and aerial drones positioned on the outskirts of Kharkiv launched multiple strikes deep into Ukrainian territory. Along the riverbanks near Kherson, satellite images show Russian forces advancing into occupied zones.

"World leaders are set to meet in Brussels next month for a NATO summit, and this will no doubt dominate the agenda."

The reporter signed off with, "Back to you in the studio."

Markle turned to her aides, eyes searching for any sign they'd reestablished communication with the aircraft. They simply shook their heads no.

"General," she said quietly.

Pope already knew what was coming. He lived for moments like this.

"Get our boys back in the fight. This time, the mission is simple protect that plane at all costs. If fired upon, our fighters are authorized to engage. Destroy anything that gets in the way."

"I'm on it, ma'am," Pope replied.

Petrov was barely halfway through the cabin when his wrist alarm began to beep. Enraged, he tore off the watch and hurled it across the aisle.

The path ahead was chaos a tunnel littered with papers, shoes, clothing, and the occasional body. He stumbled forward, dodging swinging overhead bins left ajar during the turbulence. His gaze locked on the glowing "Fasten Seatbelt" sign above the crew rest area.

The roar of the engines faded beneath the pounding in his ears.

Inside the cockpit, Harvey knew an unwanted visitor was on his way.

He switched on autopilot, unbuckled, and released the yoke. Rifle in hand, he slipped out of the cockpit, parting the curtain that separated the crew rest area from the main cabin.

PRRRRRRRP!

A burst of automatic gunfire ripped through the silence. Harvey's volley sent Petrov diving for cover, bullets slicing through the air inches from his head.

Harvey took shelter, careful not to hit anything structural. His rifle stayed trained on Petrov's last known position.

"Who are you some kind of hero?" Petrov shouted.

"Show me your head and find out," Harvey snapped back.

Both men rearmed quickly, tension thick between them. Petrov flipped his selector to full auto and waited.

Harvey fired blindly into the bulkhead.

Petrov answered with a hail of his own rounds.

He crept along the side wall, shoulder scraping metal. His heart thudded in sync with the staccato rhythm of gunfire. Peeking around the edge, he caught the flash of muzzle fire, bullets ricocheted off metal with a bone-rattling clang.

Then silence.

From the cockpit, Webb's voice cut through the lull.

"Harvey! We've got a problem!"

Webb sounded frantic and he had every reason to be. Things had just gone from good to bad in an instant. On his radar, three red dots suddenly appeared out of thin air. Positioned behind the plane, there was no doubt: enemy aircraft. He was right. Three Russian MiGs were jockeying for position, rapidly gaining ground and closing in on the Antonov.

"Oh no. That's not good,"

Webb muttered aloud. Around him, the others clutched their seats, hoping for the best. Webb hated the thought that raced through his mind: We're sitting ducks, about to get our goose fried.

Suddenly, a buzzer blared from his display. A red button flashed on the screen, Missile Lock. Webb let out a gut-wrenching yell, and Harvey knew instantly that something had gone terribly wrong. He needed to get back to the cockpit. The plane tilted hard, forcing Harvey and Petrov off their feet. They fought to brace themselves against the seatbacks, then the plane leveled off again. Whatever Webb was trying to do it wasn't working. Webb needs help, Harvey thought.

With one last desperate effort, Harvey stood, weapon at the ready. He laid down suppression fire, but after five or six rounds CLICK. CLICK. the rifle went silent. Out of ammo. Bad move, he thought.

As expected, Petrov rose from cover, stepped into the aisle, and leveled his weapon at Harvey, an evil grin spreading across his face. Harvey dropped his rifle and raised his hands.

In the cockpit, Webb was fighting the machine, but it was no use. He made one last desperate call:

"Mayday! Mayday! We've got MiGs on our tail!"

If they were going to die here, he wanted his voice recorded on the black box. He wanted the U.S. military to know exactly who was responsible so they could come back and kick some ass.

The plane shook violently as it tore through rough air. Webb struggled to regain control, overcompensating as the Antonov rocked from side to side. He glanced at the radar. For a brief moment, the dots had vanished. He swallowed hard. When the lump in his throat finally dropped, the dots reappeared closer than ever. The Antonov was locked in their sights. Webb said a silent prayer.

The MiGs shifted formation. Two fell back, and the lead jet surged forward in an arrowhead position. The Russians had chosen their shooter. The lead pilot flipped on his targeting computer and locked onto the Antonov. He throttled down, lining up the kill shot that would end Mriya and her occupantsfor good.

In the cockpit, more warning lights flared. The one Webb feared most read: MISSILE LOCKED. The voice repeated, "MISSILE LOCK." Defeated, he exhaled, closed his eyes, and accepted his fate.

Elsewhere in the cabin, Harvey faced the same end. Petrov had him dead to rights and was preparing to pull the trigger.

Suddenly, two bright, burning streaks came ZOOMING toward the Antonov from the front of the plane. They were AIM-120 AMRAAMs advanced medium-range air-to-air missiles fired from the belly of an F-22 Raptor. At first, the missiles appeared to be locked on the Antonov. But at the last moment, they curved sharply around the cargo plane, redirecting toward the lead MiG, a mile behind the Antonov.

The Russian pilot, moments from death, never saw it coming. The stealth fighter had screamed into the zone at 9 Gs, far too fast to detect. Webb opened his eyes too late and only caught the tail end as the two missiles screamed past. Long, blazing, and terrifyingly fast.

Seconds later, BOOM!

The night sky exploded behinded the Antonov as the lead MiG erupted into a fireball. The shockwave from the blast rattled the Antonov violently, slamming both Harvey and Petrov into the wall. Petrov lost his grip on his weapon as bodies flew, colliding with seats and bulkheads. Both men groaned in pain, each waiting for the other to make the next move.

Petrov rose to his knees, crawling toward his gun when the plane tilted again, and the weapon slid toward Harvey. They locked eyes. It was closer to Harvey.

Both lunged. Harvey reached it first but before he could gain full control, Petrov launched himself like a battering ram, crashing into Harvey. The gun slipped from his grasp as the two hit the floor in a tangle of limbs.

The two men traded blows after blows on the floor, both man screaming in pain. Petrov zeroing on Harvey's bloody bicep, gave it a direct punch. Harvey writhed but never stopped fighting.

Harvey found an opening and clamped both hands around Petrov's throat. Petrov kicked and thrashed, snarling in Russian. But Harvey held on tighter and tighter until Petrov's neck gave a sickening crack. His body went limp.

Meanwhile, the remaining MiGs peeled off in a scissors maneuver, breaking in opposite directions. Webb looked out ahead and saw lights approaching fast.

What the hell? he thought.

Seconds later, the lights resolved into fighter jets, unmistakable against the dark. Painted boldly on their fuselages: USA. He could make out a couple of F-15 Strike Eagles, some F-16s, and another Raptor.

"Hell yes!" Webb shouted, pumping his fist.

Help had arrived and they weren't screwing around. The squadron executed a wide arc and swung into position behind the AN-225, ready to escort it to safety.

In the lead, satisfied with his kill, Captain Teddy Bear keyed the mic and addressed his team.

"Okay, ladies and gents, it's time to earn that paycheck. We've got two on the loose. Someone get on them."

"Roger that," said Hollywood.

"Roger that," echoed Whiskey-One.

The two F-15 pilots shot after the fleeing MiGs at breakneck speed, banking hard toward their targets. The Russian jets instantly realized they were being hunted the F-15s now pinging clearly on their radar.

The MiG on the right of the formation saw an Eagle closing in fast. The guttural roar of the engines vibrated through the air as her finger curled around the trigger.

Hollywood fired. The 20mm M61A1 Vulcan Gatling gun roared to life, spitting out a fiery stream of lead that tore through the sky missing the MiG by inches. It banked sharply, trying to escape, but didn't get far.

On Hollywood's heads-up display, a box locked onto her target. She selected an AIM-9 Sidewinder and fired. The missile detached cleanly and chased down the MiG with deadly precision.

It connected. The MiG exploded into a fireball.

"Target neutralized," said Abby.

The remaining MiG scanned the sky, searching for the Americans only to witness its wingman blown out of the sky in a burst of flames. The pilot checked his systems; for now, he was intact.

He rolled the aircraft and dove toward sea level. Whiskey-One gave chase, matching speed with the MiG as it leveled out again. The Russian pilot twisted to look over both shoulders and spotted the F-15 closing in.

The American fired. Another Sidewinder launched, tail glowing hot, arcing through the air in pursuit. The MiG dropped altitude, skimming just above the Black Sea's surface. It twisted, turned, and executed a barrel roll, trying to shake the missile.

The Sidewinder dove low but couldn't match the MiG's sudden rise. It veered downward and exploded in the water.

The MiG pilot keyed his radio to report the situation but he was alone with a dogfighter right behind him. Desperate, he turned toward the coast and pushed the afterburner to full throttle. The F-15 shadowed him effortlessly, matching every move.

Lieutenant Jamison heard the captain's voice in her headset. He'd been monitoring the engagement while the others escorted the Antonov.

"C'mon, Whiskey-One. Stop screwing around. End this thing already so we can rejoin formation."

The F-15 repositioned itself directly behind the MiG. The Russian broke into another evasive maneuver but it was too late. Whiskey-One had already fired.

The missile struck the MiG's engine dead-on. The explosion shredded the fuselage. Flames erupted from the jet's body as the pilot fought to keep it airborne. As fire consumed the cockpit, he yanked the emergency canopy handle and ejected.

"Target neutralized," Jamison said over comms.

"Bring it in. Rejoin formation."

Within minutes, Jamison was back in formation, flying beside the Antonov like a patrol unit escorting a funeral procession down a boulevard.

Captain Teddy Bear held a higher position in the formation, scanning the horizon for threats. The coast was clear.

He ran through a series of comms adjustments. First, he patched through to German air traffic control.

"This is U.S. air escort. AN-225 is under our control battered but stable. We're en route to Ramstein Air Base."

"Roger that. Copy," came the response.

Teddy Bear was instructed to direct the plane on course zero-four-one point six for immediate landing.

Teddy Bear got on the horn with the White House. To his surprise, the Situation Room was now buzzing with decision-makers, all locked in on the satellite radar feed showing the AN-225 surrounded by American fighter jets. Eyes were glued to tactical screens. Ears were tuned in to the radio chatter. The President needed reassurance that the situation was under control.

"Madam President, AN-225 took some indirect hits, but no structural damage. She'll make it."

After hanging up with the Situation Room, Teddy Bear radioed the Antonov directly.

"Two-Two-Five … we're going to arc a flat one to the right. Got it?"

"Got it," Harvey replied.

"Alpha One, is that you?"

"Roger that, sir. This is Alpha One. How's it looking up there?"

"You took some hits but you're good."

"And the MiGs?" Harvey asked.

"What MiGs?" Teddy Bear replied, dry sarcasm in his voice.

Harvey grinned. Webb beamed and gave him a high-five. In the back of the cockpit area, Pavlyuk was tied up and curled on the floor, silently watching it all unfold.

"We've got your back, Two-Two-Five. Maintain full throttle," said Teddy Bear.

Suddenly, a familiar buzz echoed through his headset. He glanced at his tactical computer new contacts. A couple of blips had just bloomed on radar.

"Uh-oh. Looks like we've got trouble," Teddy Bear said over comms.

"Well … go get 'em, goddamnit," came the reply.

Teddy Bear scanned his Radar Warning Receiver (RWR) and spotted four bogeys unknowns, fast-moving, and closing in. They were too far to pose an immediate threat but were gaining ground fast. And the orders were clear: engage all threats shoot first, ask questions later.

He keyed his mic and called to his team. He selected pilots who hadn't yet seen action and still carried a full payload.

"Rocky, Moneybag you take the two on the left."

Then he radioed the Navy and Marine pilots.

"Tomcat, Hornet you're on the right. It's four-on-four, boys. Show them who rules the skies."

Without a moment's hesitation, the Navy pilot broke formation in his F-14 Tomcat, followed by the Marine pilot in his F/A-18 Hornet. Not to be outdone, the two Air Force jets peeled away: Lieutenant Grant Seymour in his Raptor, and Captain Christian Fingerle flying an F-16.

Teddy Bear stayed behind with the escort group.

"Godspeed, boys. Rocky you've got lead on this one."

"Roger that," said Christian.

The four pilots made wide arcs and reversed direction. Moneybag, piloting the most advanced aircraft in the fight, pinpointed the bogies' locations from miles away well before anyone else.

With a price tag of about $530 million, the F-22 Raptor stealth fighter remains unmatched. Dubbed the most lethal fighter ever built, its speed exceeds 1,500 miles per hour. Moneybag went supersonic and closed in before the MiG-29s even knew he was there.

Using the Raptor's stealth features and thrust vectoring, he stayed invisible until it was time to strike. When he had a clean line of sight on the MiG at the far left, he selected an AIM-120 missile and released it from the weapons bay.

The MiG turned sharply, firing off maximum flares but the AIM-120 didn't flinch. It stayed locked. On impact, the MiG exploded, lighting up the sky and exposing the other three jets nearby.

"MiG down. Moneybag One."

Moneybag pulled hard on the stick, and the Raptor climbed vertically trading speed for altitude, exiting the kill zone, and leaving room for his teammates to engage.

Down below, the Hornet pilot scanned his Radar Warning Receiver (RWR). A blip appeared a MiG-29 had locked on.

"I'm being painted! MiG-29!" the Marine shouted over the radio.

Both pilots had each other in their sights and closed in at crushing speeds.

"Me too!" the Navy officer in the Tomcat called out.

The Hornet and Tomcat pilots selected Sidewinders, but the enemy had a plan. The MiGs dove low, skimming the terrain to reduce lock-on accuracy.

Meanwhile, the last MiG broke formation and peeled off alone, heading east. Rocky, in his F-16, spotted the move and gave chase.

The Tomcat's radar lit up with a fuzzy contact then it split into two. The F-14 locked onto one target. The Hornet locked onto the other.

The planes twisted and turned in a brutal aerial dance, each pilot jockeying for position. With every sharp turn, the Marine and Navy officers grunted into their oxygen masks forcing blood into their heads to avoid blacking out. The dogfight was intense, physical, and exhausting.

Extreme G-forces flattened them into their seats.

Suddenly, both MiG pilots saw LOCK warnings flashing in their cockpits. They banked hard. Instantly, the warnings vanished.

The Marine lifted his finger off the weapons release trigger as the targets disappeared from his HUD.

"I've lost him where is he?" the naval officer asked.

"On your six coming in hot," the Marine replied.

The naval officer yanked the stick hard, and the Tomcat executed a jaw-dropping turn. The MiG screamed past.

The Americans were growing frustrated. This thing should've been down to one MiG by now, the Marine thought.

Suddenly, the enemy jets reappeared on radar twelve nautical miles out. They must've shut down their radar and GPS. That's why we lost them, the Marine reasoned.

They locked on again then the MiGs vanished a second time.

"What?! What's happening?" the naval officer shouted into his mic. These bogies were really starting to get on his nerves.

"Lost it again," said the Marine. He was having the same issue.

Elsewhere, the F-16 was toying with the lone MiG. Meanwhile, the Tomcat and Hornet pressed their chase across the sky until their radar screens lit up with multiple detections ahead.

A sudden spike.

They'd detected a battery of S-125 NEVA surface-to-air missile systems.

"It's a trap. What do we do?"

The enemy had lured them into a kill zone. In the darkness, there was no way to visually detect the hardware on the ground.

The pilots made a bold decision: continue the pursuit. They feared that if they turned back, the Antonov's escort could come under attack again. The RWRs clicked with increasing urgency, enemy radar was locking on faster and more frequently.

This was the plan all along.

As the Americans focused on the surface threat, the MiGs looped around and launched a surprise approach this time, head-on.

Fifteen miles.

The MiGs were coming in for the kill.

The Americans pulled their aircraft up sharply, jettisoning external fuel tanks and banking hard wings slicing vapor trails through the sky. They turned to face the incoming threat.

At just seven miles out, both the Tomcat and Hornet registered MiG-29s on their RWRs. Each pilot locked onto a separate target.

"Aiming away," the Hornet pilot announced.

He released a Sidewinder. The missile dropped into the night air, tail flaring, and tore through the sky slamming directly into the MiG's nose.

BOOM!

The MiG exploded into a fireball, plunging into the Black Sea.

At the same time, the Tomcat opened fire with its M61 Vulcan 20mm cannon. A torrent of rounds ripped through the air, punching straight through the MiG's canopy.

It was a direct hit.

But the MiG was still coming hurtling toward the naval officer like a wrecking ball. He caught a flash in his view and slammed the stick forward, barely avoiding a collision. The enemy jet screamed past too close for comfort.

He looked back and saw the MiG engulfed in flames, spiraling downward into the deep, dark sea.

The remaining MiG was doing a good job evading the F-16, but the American fighter stayed close, relentless. The Russian pilot had one goal in mind: cross into Belarusian airspace and lose the tail. Surely, he thought, the American won't risk crossing into Russian ally territory for a kill.

The MiG pilot glanced over his shoulder and didn't see the F-16. A wave of relief surged through him. At just 1,000 feet, he pulled into a dive.

He thought he was in the clear.

But what he didn't know was that the American had anticipated the move. While the MiG was busy pulling evasive stunts to avoid a missile, the F-16 had surged ahead, cutting a new angle of approach. Rocky had turned north flying perpendicular to the MiG's flight path.

Because of the angle, the MiG didn't detect him until it was too late. They crossed at close proximity.

The Russian pilot realized, he could've taken me out. He knew now: the American was toying with him.

The F-16 turned northeast and got back on the MiG's tail. Rocky selected the contact on his radar and locked in. Inside the cockpit, the Russian pilot heard the LOCK alert scream to life. He pulled hard into a steep climb but it was useless. The lock was solid.

Rocky hovered his finger over the weapon release.

The MiG broke left. Rocky inverted and yanked hard on the stick, cutting into the MiG's circle. Ten Gs crushed him into his seat. His Raptor groaned, pushed to its limits. The MiG roared past in front of him. Rocky pulled left and stayed with it.

He had the advantage.

Onboard were AIM-120 AMRAAM long-range guided missiles.

The MiG dove, trying to trade altitude for speed. The Russian's teeth rattled as the jet went nose-down, plummeting toward the darkness below.

Rocky followed diving straight toward the Black Sea.

The German-American pilot gritted his teeth. A born dogfighter, he felt the vibrations shaking his helmet as he closed the gap. He pulled hard, blood draining from his head, muscles straining against the Gs.

He kept the MiG in his sights.

The Russian pulled up into a wide looping climb. Rocky followed, both jets racing in vertical circles like two Hot Wheels spinning in a child's bedroom racetrack.

Ten Gs. His body screamed. But Rocky powered through.

Through the crushing force, he saw the MiG's flares burst, blazing through the night. He led his aim just ahead of the MiG and fired.

The missile screamed after its target, tracking the heat, chasing the vapor trail and slammed straight into the MiG's tailpipe.

KABOOM!!

The MiG exploded into a fireball then a thousand flaming fragments rained down into the Black Sea.

Rocky gasped for breath. He pulled up, dove low to the deck, skimming the water.

He glanced at his watch.

0315 hours.

One last look at the burning wreckage, then he lit his afterburners blasting westward into the dark.

CHAPTER THIRTY-ONE

(THE SECOND COMING)

HARVEY GAZED INTO THE night sky, inky black, streaked with greying clouds. The horizon was beginning to pale; dawn crept slowly over the edge of the world. The Antonov-225 was surrounded by a halo of American fighter jets, escorting her safely back to Ramstein Air Force Base.

The last check-in with Air Traffic Control had been fifteen minutes ago, and the beast still had clearance to land. As Master Sergeant Elliot had put it:

"Sir, you are priority one. We've been waiting all night for your safe return."

The words had moved Harvey. He felt the weight of every syllable.

Outside the cockpit, the world was a swirling vortex of rain and storm. Inside, a fragile hope flickered. Major Harvey Arnott gripped the controls, knuckles white. He exchanged a glance with his co-pilot, Captain Webb. A quiet kind of bromance had grown between them over the past twenty-four hours, though neither man was ready to admit it.

The cargo plane battered and bruised by fate, shuddered violently with every gust, each tremor a reminder of the peril they'd faced.

Three decks below, freed hostages huddled in the cramped private jet parked inside the Antonov's belly. Their faces were pale, silent, etched with fear and prayer. Kassandra clutches her mother's hand, eyes fixed on the ceiling, counting each second. Nearby sat Vira still unaware that her father had been captured, and would soon face justice for his role in the hostile takeover of the AN-225. He had spared her the truth of his plans. For that, she was lucky even if she didn't know it yet.

As the Antonov approached the runway with visibility still low, the massive aircraft descended through sheets of cold, German rain. One final message crackled through the pilots' headsets, the voice a mix of calm professionalism and suppressed urgency:

"You're clear for immediate landing. Godspeed Two-Two-Five. Welcome back."

Webb looked once more at his wingman. Harvey's jaw was clenched, his eyes locked forward. Every fiber of his being focused on this moment. He had carried the weight of every soul aboard.

Webb called out altitude and speed, voice steady despite the tremble in his hands.

The wind howled like a banshee, threatening to rip the wings from the fuselage. The engines roared above Ramstein Air Base as the aircraft dropped sharply. A collective gasp rose from the passengers below. Kassandra buried her face in her mother's side.

Below them, the network of taxiways and hangars came into view, a testament to the scale of the American global footprint. The white runway markings flickered into sight, barely visible through the downpour. The landing gear extended with a whining groan, followed by the flaps and slats unfurling from the wings.

Harvey adjusted the controls, fighting the drag and the punishing crosswinds. The runway lights shimmered like distant stars through the storm. This wasn't just another landing, it was a dance with the elements.

The skies above the base still roared with fighter jets searching for a place to park.

And then THUD.

A bone-jarring impact echoed through the plane as the landing gear struck tarmac. A wave of relief washed over everyone so deep, it felt like pain.

The Antonov skidded, tires shrieking in protest, hydroplaning on the waterlogged runway. For a moment, it looked like the aircraft might veer off.

But with a surge of adrenaline and years of flight experience, Harvey and Webb wrestled the beast into a hard, controlled stop.

The reverse thrusters roared. The biggest bird in the sky came to a halt.

The final whine of the engines was deafening.

Crew members on the ground approached in full protective gear. Emergency vehicles stood by. The rear cargo bay began to open, slowly, with a mechanical whirr.

Passengers disembarked into waiting arms, blankets, and hot coffee.

Harvey and Webb were greeted by Elliot, Boyd, and Colonel Bailey all waiting on the tarmac. Their faces a mixture of awe and immense relief.

The two pilots snapped to attention and saluted. Bailey returned the gesture.

"Major. Captain," the Colonel said, his voice thick with emotion. "That was damn impressive. Brave. Your country's proud of you."

Harvey managed a tired smile. He stifled it into a quiet, "Thank you, sir" revealing no trace of the pain in his bleeding left arm.

Though his heart pounded with the aftershocks of fate, he turned to look at the Antonov. It now sat still, battered, soaked. A behemoth at rest.

Just a machine.

But today it had come alive.

Not far from where they stood, the First Lady, her daughter, and her daughter's best friend were being ushered into a waiting black SUV. The vehicle pulled away moments later, disappearing toward an undisclosed location.

Another black SUV pulled up, and its door swung open. Four men in crisp blue suits stepped out, adjusting their jackets as they moved. There was no mistaking them, they were FBI. Badges swung from lanyards around their necks, catching the lights.

They approached the plane just as Pavlyuk was being led out by security forces. Without ceremony, he was handed over to the agents.

Harvey wasn't sure if this moment technically qualified as irony, but it felt close. In the end, Peter Pavlyuk's obsession with flying matched only by his obsession with greed had led to his downfall. That he had backed the wrong side was simply more proof of his recklessness and poor judgment catching up with him.

He'd fooled many to gain the level of security clearance granted by the U.S. government. But back home, not everyone had been so easily misled. Most didn't know the Department of Defense had recently initiated a covert probe into Pavlyuk's questionable financial activities. The man had been buying up half the city blocks in his hometown, living like a king.

While no hard proof had surfaced of Russian compensation, DOD intelligence believed it was only a matter of time. In men like Pavlyuk, hubris was always the fatal flaw.

They knew where he was going when he boarded the C-5 with the Americans. They just hadn't known if or when he'd return. Now, his destination was anybody's guess.

The agents paid no attention to his injuries. One stepped forward.

"We're placing you in custody under suspicion of violating the Terrorism Act."

"Pardon me?" Pavlyuk blinked.

"Turn around, sir," another said, grabbing his shoulder and spinning him to face Harvey and Webb.

As the cuffs tightened around his wrists, his expression went blank.

"You were careless with your money," said one agent. Then, after a beat: "Even more careless with your loyalty."

With one agent gripping each of his thick biceps, they frog-marched him toward a waiting SUV.

Harvey felt the ground tremble beneath him. A deep rumble announced the arrival of three topless military jeeps rolling in from the rear of the tarmac. He turned as they came to a stop.

Two people sat in each vehicle, still in their G-suits, fresh off the job.

"Smith? Is that you?" Harvey called out.

From the lead jeep's passenger side, a woman leapt down her fighter pilot gear unmistakable. It was her. Even bundled in military gear, there was no hiding that California surfer-girl figure.

Harvey stepped toward her, and she ran the rest of the way crashing into his arms, all military decorum forgotten.

They held each other for a long moment, then eased back just enough to meet each other's eyes. Her lips hovered inches from his.

She barely noticed Webb watching from nearby.

"We'll leave you two to it," Colonel Bailey said with a wink. "Sounds like you've got some catching up to do."

He, Boyd, Elliot, and Webb turned and walked toward the Antonov for a closer look at the beast that had brought them all here.

"I love you, Abby," Harvey said.

"What took you so long to say that?"

"Stupidity, I think."

She smiled and rested her head on his chest. Jamison, Teddy Bear, Fingerle, Grant, and the naval officer stood nearby, watching the embrace with quiet approval. No one had any complaints.

"So, I still can't wrap my head around the fact that Potluck was ever a spy. He ate and drank with us."

Harvey said nothing. He was still processing everything that had gone down but he couldn't deny it made him sick to his stomach that the enemy had been right under his nose the whole time.

She whispered, "You were very brave today," and gave his stomach a light tap.

It would be a few days before Harvey truly grasped how well-crafted the gambit had been. Moscow had gone to extraordinary lengths for a damn airplane. It reminded him of one of those movies where a robber goes to prison, only to get out years later to reclaim his buried treasure.

Except this robber came with missiles.

They're gone, he thought. All those people who died on that plane ... they're gone. The thought looped in his mind like a haunting refrain. The open waters and skies where the enemy had chosen to challenge the United States had become an unmistakable graveyard.

"Did they really think they could take on our most advanced technology with MiGs?" he asked his new fiancée.

"Let's hope they learned their lesson. My guess is, Moscow will think twice about retaliating," Abby replied.

But Abby didn't want to talk about war right now. She just wanted to be with her man. Any moment now, she could be called back to the USS Midway, parked somewhere in the middle of the ocean.

"You think what the President said will make a difference?" he asked.

Abby cleared her throat and launched into her best impression of President Maurene Markle:

"Hey Russia, you've had your fun with Crimea, Estonia, Georgia, and Moldova. Don't push your luck with Ukraine."

Harvey laughed. The accent was spot-on, she sounded just like the real thing.

"That won't scare him. The man's ex-KGB."

"Probably not. But he's no idiot either. He's going to have to make a choice."

Harvey took her hand in his.

"Enough of this talk. What are your plans for thanksgiving?"

Before she could answer, Harvey got ding on his cell phone, He pulled it out and saw an email alert from his grandfather. He tapped the screen and the email opened to new page. It read: Hey, I've been watching the news, We have a lot to discuss. Call me.